NEARCUS
VERSUS
THE
GODS

Robert Bartron

ISBN: 1466238237
ISBN-13: 978-1466238232

To

Angelina, Eliana and Hateya,

three sisters who helped their uncle

Novels by Robert Bartron

Crew Eleven

---

*The Autobiography of
Terry Ryan, A Shooter*
(with Pat Bartron)

Nearcus Versus the Gods

To Steal a Million

To Murder a Ghost

A Blind Man's Walk

Wylie Finds His Special Place
(Children's story)

All Titles are available at mcavepublishing.com or Amazon.com

ACKNOWLEDGMENTS

The author wishes to thank his wife and life's partner for the past four decades for her forbearance and understanding in his often times eccentric interests and projects.

CHAPTER 1

His teeth hurt. That might be understandable for others, but not for the twelve-year old son of a mastic gum farmer. For in the thirteenth year of the reign of Emperor Nero, mastic gum was the primary means of dental hygiene. With all the wonderful advances the Romans had brought to the world by 67 AD, nothing had replaced mastic gum as the best way to clean teeth and kill germs in the mouth. It gave mint fresh breath and was used to treat heartburn, indigestion, and stomach ache. Throughout the Roman Empire, healers prescribed mastic gum or a distilled version of it in liquid form for lung complaints to include colds, coughs, sneezes and congestion. In fact, many Greek cooks even used it as a spice to give a hint of vanilla flavor to their favorite dishes. But its primary use was by healthy citizens to keep a clean mouth every day.

And the only place in the entire world where the Pistacia Lentiscus tree that produces mastic sap grew was in the southern part of the Greek island of Chios. This is where young Nearcus lived with his widowed father and little sister. His father, Aegospotami, was one of the largest farmers of the mastic gum producing trees. Like his grandfathers and father before him, Aegospotami took great pride in the preventative and healing powers of the sap from his trees. He felt that by growing trees that provided so much good the gods would favor him and his family. If he learned that his only son, the heir to the family farm and business, had bad teeth it would devastate him. He would think that the gods had turned against him. Nearcus could easily imagine the lecture he would get if his father knew about his tooth ache. Aegospotami would wave his arms and raise his voice in an emotional tirade. In his mind Nearcus heard his distraught father cry out, "Nearcus! You are my son! You cannot have bad teeth! You could ruin our business! How can a toothless man sell mastic gum? No one will believe it works? What have you done son? You have ruined us! What have you done to make the gods angry at me?"

Of course, Nearcus was not becoming toothless. He had one tooth in the back of his mouth that was growing in at an odd angle. It hurt now but once his molar has fully grown-in the pain will go away. But he still knew better than to show tooth pain in front of his father. Nearcus loved and admired his father very much, but Aegospotami was very emotional. It was better to just chew more mastic gum and suffer in silence than let his father know.

Besides, currently it was easy for Nearcus to avoid his father these days. For the first time since he was old enough to walk, Nearcus has not been helping his father in the orchards. Since last summer he has spent his days in training to earn a spot on the Chios team going to the upcoming Isthmian Games. At dawn each morning Nearcus has eaten two raw eggs and a handful of whole grains then started trotting along a well traveled road that leads north from the farm. By the time the sun is fully above the eastern horizon, he has covered nearly half of the five miles between his home and the training grounds. Southern Chios is mostly flat and excellent farm land, but a ridge of mountains rising to above 4,000 feet covers the spine of this small isle. So the run from his farm to his training ground is slightly uphill the entire way. The first weeks that Nearcus covered the route were quite hard for him. He had to stop many times to catch his breath and slow his rapidly beating heart. Now he found it easy and just a "good stretch of the legs." With winter's cooler weather having given way to the early spring he fully enjoyed the dawn run. The green fields dotted with the many wild tulips that were just starting to open their faces that early in the morning provided a beautifully calm and relaxing scene. During these hours just after dawn he had the road to himself and it gave him the opportunity to think about how the gods have treated him. He wondered why he had been so blessed by not being born a slave or a woman and having a successful father and by being given such strong athletic skills. He also thought about what he would do if he had the chance to leave this little island and then he thought about what was planned for his training that day and then about the chores waiting for him when he returned home. He just thought a lot, not even bothered by the rapid pace he was running.

Just outside the village of Vavili the island's experienced athletes and their slaves had set up a camp to prepare the men and youth who were seeking to qualify for the Games. In just four days the qualification trials were scheduled. Only the best two athletes in each event would be selected to travel to Corinth to represent Chios.

Nearcus wanted very much to travel to Corinth. His father had made the voyage across the Aegean Sea several times on business, but Nearcus has never been off Chios. At twelve years old he figured it was finally time for him to see more of the outside world. The chance to travel was much more important to him then any glory or honors that might come should he somehow win at Corinth. Just to qualify for the Games was his goal. It was his chance to see what lay beyond the shores of Chios. It was his chance to visit the Temple of Apollo and to see the shrines of Aphrodite and Demeter. Nearcus has dreamed of seeing important sites ever since his father had taken him to visit the "Teacher's Rock" in Vrontados, the birthplace of Homer on the north end of Chios. Nearcus was thrilled to touch the very stone where the great poet had once sat. But the sights of Corinth would be so much more grand and impressive! He just had to qualify for the trip to the Games!

When his father had seen Nearcus easily defeat the local boys in playful wrestling tussles near the orchards, the idea had come to Aegospotami that perhaps his son might have the talent to compete in the Isthmian Games. So for the past months Nearcus trained six days a week. His training had been in three parts and at the end of each phase he could have been eliminated from the classes.

The first part was physical conditioning. Each competitor had been required to run great distances to build stamina and to carry heavy stones to build strength. After nearly two months of nothing but day long training sessions the most physically fit were allowed to pass to the next phase of training. Nearcus was big for his age, standing nearly six-foot tall with a solid build for a youth that was the result of years of working in the mastic orchards carrying heavy buckets and tools while helping his father. The strength training had been easier for Nearcus than for other boys, but the long distance running that built stamina had been a struggle for him. At the end of the first phase of training half the boys were sent home, but Nearcus was selected to move onto the next step.

In the second phase the athletes were finally taught the specific skills needed in their individual events. Those who were to compete in the foot races were taught how to start quickly and then to pace themselves to finish strongly. Those who were in horse riding events were introduced to the care of horses, riding and racing. Wrestlers and boxers were taught the rules of the bouts and the different punches and grappling holds. Poets and musicians went to classes on how better to construct their compositions.

Nearcus was competing in an event that required the most instruction to master well. It was the most difficult and most glorious of all the events. It was always the event that drew the loudest cheers and most interest from the spectators. Nearcus was in training to compete in the pankration. Besides being the most glorious, it was also the most brutal and physically challenging of all the contests. It was a fight with another athlete where there were no rules like in boxing or wrestling. Punching, kicking, choking, punishing joint locks, and grappling were all allowed. The only prohibitions were gouging of the eyes and biting. To be competitive in pankration an athlete must be in great physical condition. Superb stamina, superior strength, and most of all, a natural ability to use balance and intelligence to defeat your opponent were all absolutely necessary to be successful. Plus you needed extraordinary courage. The athlete must be able to absorb great pain without being deterred from his plan to defeat the other contestant.

In this second phase of his training Nearcus was assigned a personal paedotribae who would act as his coach in charge of his physical education. His paedotribae was a Thessalonian slave named Marcus. A man in his early thirties, he was unusual because he had not been born into slavery. He had been drafted into the service of his local city regiment when he was only seventeen years old. Two years later the city revolted against Rome rule, but was quickly defeated. Marcus was captured and made a slave. Now he belonged to a wealthy merchant who lived nearby and provided slaves to the training camp to help build the best team to represent Chios.

Marcus taught Nearcus the basic holds and kicks and punch combinations that every pankration competitor must master. It had been grueling and painful work but Nearcus impressed Marcus with his dedication and toughness. Even when he suffered training injuries like a dislocated finger, a broken nose and a twisted ankle, Nearcus would show up every day and complete the full training schedule for that day, ignoring the intense pain he often felt. Marcus thought Nearcus wanted to win so badly that he did this to ensure he would be victorious at the Isthmian Games. In reality,

Nearcus was not interested in gaining the champion's wreath; his real goal was to qualify for the team so he could earn a trip off of Chios and see famed Corinth.

After months of mastering the basics, phase three of the training program began. Now that the athletes were in superb physical condition and understood the basics of their event it was time to teach them how to win. It was time to learn the strategy of each event and the techniques on how to gain maximum advantage over your opponent. It is not enough to run fast to win races. You must know when to lead, when to follow, when to coast and when to sprint during a race if you are going to win. In this phase the athletes competed against each other and their coaches in practice competitions almost on a daily basis.

Of all the events held at the games, a strategic plan on how to defeat each opponent was most important in the pankration. There were no weight divisions as in wrestling or boxing, so an opponent could be larger or smaller than you. This required a specific plan for each specific challenger to determine what holds, kicks, punches, blocks and choking techniques would be most effective. And this plan must be flexible enough to adjust it as the bout advanced in case your initial strategy was not working. These personal combat skills could only be mastered by intense training and practice, practice, and more practice.

Now after ten months of daily, tiring and brutal training the qualification trials were only four days away. There were three permanent Pan-Hellenic Games training camps on Chios. Each year either the Olympic, Pythian, Nemean, or Isthmian Games were held. So each year the best athletes in each training camp were sent to qualification trials to determine which two individuals would represent Chios in each event at that year's games. This year the trials were held at Nearcus's training camp. He was very glad because this meant his father and little sister, Apollina, could attend.

Both were so very proud of Nearcus for completing all three phases of training.

It had been hard for Aegospotami to work the orchards the past seasons without Nearcus, but the extra work load seemed light to him when he thought about how well Nearcus was doing. On the day of the qualification trials Aegospotami would declare a business holiday and let his three slaves have the day off while Apollina accompanied him to the qualification trials festival. The family business would be put away for one day to celebrate what his son had accomplished.

Marcus thought that Nearcus's training had been building perfectly to peak on the day of the qualification trials. Nearcus was in great physical condition, had mastered most of the basic techniques of the sport, and was currently injury free. But Marcus thought Nearcus was truly ready because of his intelligence, natural balance and, of course, courage. Marcus was sure that Nearcus only would need basic techniques to beat most opponents because the boy seemed to instinctively know what his opponent was about to do. And this anticipation coupled with his quick mind meant that Nearcus could make a plan to counter the opponent's attack and strike back where the opportunity existed. Yes, Marcus looked forward to enjoying a good day at the trials watching his student be victorious. It would bring great honor to Marcus to have a successful student and the slave was in a great mood when he called Nearcus to his side and told him to take a seat.

"Today, young Nearcus, you will not be fighting. For the next three days I want you to run only ten miles then walk another five. You are ready for the competition and there is nothing you can learn in the next couple of days that will prepare you more," Marcus said. "Be sure to stretch your muscles before and after you run. Spend the days preparing your mind. Your body and knowledge are as strong as they can be for these trials. Now you must focus on the contests.

Think of nothing except the challenges you will face. Anticipate what you will see and then nothing can surprise you."

"Yes, Paedotribae," Nearcus answered, just as he has done for months. What his trainer says is always what he does. By being a good and obedient student, Nearcus hoped to earn his chance to get off this island. But neither the teacher nor the student could anticipate what was about to change their plans and put success out of reach.

CHAPTER 2

The qualification trials would not start until late in the morning. Aegospotami rose early that day and went to his small home shrine just behind the rear entrance to their large home. The shrine was a separate structure of three sides made of block stone with a wooden roof. In it Aegospotami had idols of the six gods he prayed to almost on a daily basis.

He was raised to understand the relationship between gods and himself. He had a contract with the gods. This agreement promised that if he served them, then they would provide services to him. His duty was prayer and sacrifice and the performance of required rituals. The gods' duty was to respond with protection, prosperity and guidance.

Aegospotami had taken a long time to determine which of the dozens of Greek and Roman gods he should include in his shrine. Of course he would include Apollo, or as his grandfather had called him, Zeus, because he was the god of healing and prophecy. Apollo's son was the god Asclepius and Aegospotami also must have a shrine to him because he was the god of healing. A producer of mastic gum had to worship the primary health gods. But the tree farmer also knew he must worship the gods that control the harvest and agriculture. So he had idols of the goddesses Demeter and Rhea. But a mastic gum farmer was also a businessman, so he also worshiped Herakles the god of victory and commercial enterprise and Hermes the god of merchants.

These idols were not cheap. He had traveled to the village of Myrmighi where the best gods are made and paid dearly for each of his idols. It was part of his responsibilities in worshipping them to invest in the best idols he could find and afford. His grandfather had built the stone shrine room many years ago, but as Aegospotami's business grew he knew he must invest in improving the home of the gods. So he replaced the thatched roof with a solid wood structure and purchased new idols to honor these important gods.

This morning he stood in front of the idols and placed an offering of fine wine and fresh bread in the middle of the shrine. He looked intently at each idol and prayed to them in turn. He started with Demeter and said to her, "Great goddess I ask for your protection of my orchards while I must be away today in support of my son." Then he stared at the idol of Rhea and repeated the same prayer. He turned to Hermes and asked the god to watch over his business while he was away.

Next he turned his vision to Asclepius and almost whispered, "Loving and kind Asclepius please give my son good health and strength this day, and heal him of all injuries he might sustain. I offer you this sacrifice as a payment for his protection in the games today." Then he pushed the wine and bread towards the idol.

Turning next to Apollo, Aegospotami raised his voice and pleaded, "Oh powerful master of all gods who has the gift of prophecy, I pray that you will look into the future and bend it so that my son can be victorious. I lift up my petition that you will reward his hard work with success. Bless us your faithful servants."

Aegospotami saved his most reverent prayer for Herakles. He again whispered and this time begged for victory, "Mighty Herakles I plead with you to give Nearcus your strength and your power. Great god Herakles you have blessed me with business success but what I desire more than anything this day is for the honor of being the father of a great champion. Give my son victory!"

Aegospotami then turned and rapidly walked back into the house. He had done his duty by the gods and now it was their duty to do their part of the agreement. With great confidence he packed bread, wine, dried meat and four fresh eggs into his traveling sack. It would make a good lunch for his family later that day. He then took another bag and went to the room where he kept his business books and opened a basket in the corner. From it he drew out handfuls of his best mastic gum. The sap from each tree in the orchards was slightly different and dried into varying qualities of gum. Being a good businessman, he made it a practice of keeping some of the gum from the best trees as samples to give to potential new customers. He was going to the qualification trials to watch his son compete, but great crowds from around the region and from over the whole of Chios would be there. A good father can also be a good businessman so he planned on using his best samples to identify new customers. The trip could be quite profitable as well as a family victory.

It had been hard for Nearcus to sleep last night. He believed his coach and he knew he was primed and ready to compete in the trials so he was confident about how well he would do. It was not nervousness that kept him from sleep. It was his tooth. Throughout the night, the pain had grown more intense and constant. Nearcus's face felt like he had failed to block a kick to the jaw when he was fighting. Only, unlike a blow to the head, this pain did not go away after a short period. The whole left side of his jaw was a large mass of dull, throbbing, terrible pain. When his father had come to awaken him for the big day, Nearcus was already sitting on the edge of his bed and trying to smile confidently. Aegospotami did not notice that the left side of Nearcus's face did not move with the smile.

As the family sat down for their traditionally small breakfast, Apollina noticed the swelling on the side of Nearcus's face. When Aegospotami turned to reach for the bread, she pointed to the swelling and started to say something when Nearcus gently grabbed her hand and lowered it before Apollina could utter a word. Nearcus held his finger to his lips and winked at his eight-year-old sister. Apollina gave him a confused look but did as she was directed and remained quiet. That morning Nearcus ate his breakfast by only chewing with the right side of his mouth.

One of the slaves put the family's biggest donkey in harness and prepared the two-wheel cart used for transporting mastic gum to market. Then he brought it to the front of the house. Aegospotami, Apollina and Nearcus boarded the small wagon and started the one hour trip to the site of the qualification trials. As his father guided the donkey along the narrow dirt road, Nearcus looked behind them in an attempt to hide his swollen jaw.

Nearcus hoped his pain might lessen as the trip progressed but it only grew worse. In fact, the pain became so intense he began to grow dizzy and tears formed in his eyes. But he never cried out or even moaned. Nearcus had just completed ten months of being trained on how to endure and mask pain. A pankratiast must never let his opponent know when he has been hurt. The pain in his tooth however, was unlike any he had experienced while fighting. In a bout the pain from the blows would subside after a few minutes. By contrast, for the past twelve hours his tooth pain has remained and grown and grown. It was almost too much to bear.

Upon arrival at the trials, Nearcus was unable to smile or say goodbye to his family. He just slipped off the back of the cart and trotted to where he was to meet Marcus. Aegospotami and Apollina overlooked Nearcus's rudeness because he was normally a very polite and obedient boy and they figured he was just very nervous about the contest.

Marcus could tell immediately that there was something very wrong with Nearcus. Not wanting to let the other pankratiasts know that there was a weakness in his athlete's fighting ability, Marcus quickly took Nearcus by the hand and led him to a private spot behind the preparation tent.

"What is wrong, young Nearcus?" he asked.

When Nearcus tried to answer he discovered it was too painful even to open his mouth to form words. He just cradled his left jaw in the palm of his hand. Knowing that his student could tolerate much pain, Marcus could tell by the tears in his eyes that the boy was suffering greatly. Regardless of how much it was going to hurt, the slave had to look inside the athlete's mouth. As gently as he could, Marcus slipped his fingers between Nearcus's teeth and spread the mouth open. The pain was so violent that Nearcus could feel his knees wobble and then his vision grow bleary; then things began to grow dim, and then dark.

Marcus had to remove his hands quickly from the boy's mouth in order to catch Nearcus as he fainted. Carefully Marcus lowered the limp body of his student to the grass. What he had seen in Nearcus's mouth told him that all the months of hard training and great effort were wasted. The entire left side of Nearcus's lower jar was red and swollen and puss was oozing from the impacted molar. Marcus felt the head and face of Nearcus. He was very hot. Nearcus had a high fever caused by the infection in his mouth and it was only going to grow worse until that tooth was cut out.

As Marcus shook his head with the disappointment he felt for this hard-working young man, Nearcus woke up. While unconscious he received the only relief from the pain he had known since yesterday. For just a quick second upon awakening, he felt no pain. But then his jaw immediately began to have a fiery throbbing that raced over his entire face and then throughout his whole body. Nearcus began to shake from the fever. Marcus saw the pain, disappointment and fear in the boy's eyes.

Marcus drew close to his student's ear and whispered, "Nearcus, you prepared well and were ready to make your goal. But I am afraid this is not your year. We must get you to a physician to have him fix your tooth. Next year you can fight to be chosen to go to the Pythian Games."

Nearcus lay there and forced his brain to concentrate on the situation. He forced his thoughts to ignore the pain and to focus on his goal. He did not work this hard, for this long, and suffer as much as he did to go to the *Pythian* Games. The Pythian Games were held in the little city of Delhi and that was not what he had labored so fiercely to see. He worked hard to see famous Corinth, the largest city in Greece. He was determined not to let the gods take from him his goal of going to the Isthmian Games.

Nearcus learned something about himself while lying on his back on the grass behind the preparation tent. He learned that he could control his fears and his ambition and his pain. Marcus fell back to the grass as Nearcus pushed him aside and quickly stood. Rising to his full six-feet, Nearcus stiffened his back and without looking at his teacher he marched around the corner and entered the preparation tent. Marcus was speechless and amazed. He scrambled to his feet and followed young Nearcus.

Nearcus went to the corner assigned for the pankratiasts and removed all his clothes. He dipped his hands into the large barrel of olive oil and rubbed it all over his body. Marcus silently joined the determined athlete and dipped his hands in the oil as well. He smeared it over Nearcus's back. Once glistening with the oil, Nearcus chose the largest robe from those laid out for the competitors. It was a chilly spring morning and he would wear the robe until his first bout.

Marcus looked into his student's eyes. He could see the tears still there, but there was something more. There was a mature determination to be the master over his pain and the drive to finish what he had started and prepared to do.

The opening formalities of the competition took only fifteen minutes to welcome the hundreds of spectators and to explain how the different events would be contested. As this was being done, three members of the local ruling council passed through the audience looking for married women. As the athletes always completed completely naked, married women were not allowed to attend any competition except the music and poetry readings. Any married woman caught watching the athletes compete would receive harsh punishment. But on Chios, a very traditional and conservative community, none were found.

Nearcus was oblivious to the proceedings. All his strength was funneled into ignoring the intense pain in his jaw. His fever was growing and his forehead was covered in sweat even before he started his warm-up drills.

Together with Marcus and eleven other pankratiasts and their trainers, Nearcus waited his turn to determine who his first bout would be against. When it was Nearcus's turn to draw a bean-sized lot from the silver urn, Marcus went forward with him. Marcus tried to hide the fact that he was holding Nearcus to keep the athlete from falling.

Smiling to the officials, Marcus whispered to them so the crowd could not hear, "It is first competition. The young lad is quite nervous." Upon hearing this, the officials laughed and nodded.

Nearcus mumbled his required prayer and pledge to Apollo and then Marcus lifted the boy's right hand and placed it in the urn. Nearcus grasped a lot and pulled the square tile out. It had the letter Beta written on it. Marcus helped his student to return to the line of pankratiasts. After all twelve athletes had drawn a lot the head official called out for them to announce what they had drawn. There had been six pairs of letters in the urn and the two who drew the same letter would fight in the first round. This same process would be repeated until five rounds had been completed. The two pankratiasts with the most wins would then be selected to represent Chios at the Isthmian Games.

When Nearcus and Marcus saw who their first opponent would be they were disappointed. Only one other competitor in the Boys Division had the same large size as Nearcus and that was the first challenger Nearcus had drawn. They looked evenly matched so it promised to be a long fight. There were no rounds or timed periods in pankration bouts. The competitors would start and not finish until one had either submitted or been knocked unconscious, or in the very rare bout, been killed. It was a brutal sport.

Marcus had intended to discuss strategy with his student before each bout. However, it was obvious to him that Nearcus could not concentrate on anything but the pain. Marcus knew that Nearcus would have to fight purely on instinct and hope for the best. While they waited for the Alpha bout to be completed, the coach and student silently sat in the corner of the preparation tent. Normally Nearcus would be running and stretching and grappling with his coach to warm up for the bout, but not on this important morning. Nearcus could do nothing except remain still, consumed by the pain and fever. Marcus could do nothing except sit by his student and offer silent support.

Marcus finally spoke, "Nearcus, I know I cannot talk you out of competing. Of course, that is no one's decision but yours alone. But I do ask you to re-evaluate your decision after every bout. There is no disgrace in submitting or withdrawing if your jaw makes it impossible for you to win today. There will be other days, other competitions where your talent will be seen."

Nearcus looked into Marcus's eyes. He saw true concern and caring in this slave. From what he saw in his eyes, Nearcus now was sure that this slave cared more for his athlete than he did about winning. That was so unusual in this brutal sport. But what Nearcus saw actually made him even more determined to fight so as not to let down his mentor.

Soon the Alpha bout was complete and it was time for the Beta pair to start. Nearcus rose slowly from his seat on the grassy floor of the tent. He carefully removed his robe and handed it to Marcus. The cool spring air hit his nude body and the fever immediately gave way to chills. Spots floated across his vision as he made his way to the pankration field. Nearcus was surprised by how his jaw pain began to subside the closer he got to the official standing in the middle of the competition field. The surge of pre-contest adrenaline forced his focus to move from his pain to his opponent. Standing in front of him was a young man who physically matched Nearcus in almost every way. Both were tall with tone muscles and short cropped hair. But Nearcus could tell that his opponent had been in training and competing much longer. The opponent had more scars on his shins from blows that had ripped the skin. He had a deformed right ear from having it kicked and pulled in fights. And there was one other obvious difference. Nearcus was only twelve years old and not close to being ready to shave. His opponent was hairy and had stubble from a heavy beard. Nearcus thought he must be at least sixteen.

All these considerations about his opponent were made in a matter of a second. There was no time to dwell on what his opponent may or may not have done in the past to arrive at this fight. Nearcus had a job to do and hopefully to do quickly before his adrenaline left him and the fever made him weak.

The referee stood in the middle of the competition patch holding a long staff in one hand. The two contestants approached him and placed their right hands on the staff. As soon as both had touched it, the official immediately drew the staff away and stepped to the side. The bout had begun. Nearcus lunged at the legs of his opponent. The quickness of his attack caught the visitor off guard and resulted in his takedown. Nearcus was much faster and more aggressive. Before the other boy could react, Nearcus's speed and innate balance enabled him to secure his opponent's left arm in a perfect arm lock. As they both lay on their backs, Nearcus pulled his opponent's hand tightly into his own chest and he dug one heel in the other boy's side and his other heel he jammed into his neck. With his opponent successfully immobilized, Nearcus kept a tight grip on the opponent's wrist with his left hand and then he made a fist with his right hand and began to pummel the face and ears of his opponent. There was no escape for the older boy. Try as he might to free himself from Nearcus's tight arm lock he could not escape the blows being rained down on his head. After absorbing two minutes of intense beating on his face and ear, the opponent had enough and gave the submit signal to the official. Nearcus had won his first bout in record time.

The speed and ability he had shown were praised by the entire hometown crowd with wild cheers and applause. His talent was also noted by the other pankration opponents who began to pray to the gods that they did not draw Nearcus as a competitor in the next rounds.

As the official raised Nearcus's arm in victory, Marcus rushed to his pankratiast's side. Rather than a big smile, Marcus's expression was one of deep concern. He knew that Nearcus's strength had come from the rush of combat and now that the combat was over he wanted to be there to catch his student when he came down off the adrenaline high.

The slave knew his business, because he reached Nearcus just as the young man's knees started to buckle and he slumped into the slave's arms. Marcus always remained close by his students because he knew that odd things happen in pankration and he must protect his charge from dying for the sport. Foremost in his mind was the fabled story of Arrhichion. Centuries before in the Olympic Games, Arrhichion had been in the grip of a choke hold when he flailed about and in desperation broke the ankle of his opponent. The pain of the injury caused the opponent to submit. But when the official tried to raise Arrhichion's arm it was discovered that he had died from the choke hold. Arrhichion won the bout but lost his life. Marcus was not going to let that happen to Nearcus.

Marcus placed the robe on Nearcus's shoulders and helped the young athlete back to the preparation tent. Once there he had him lay on one of the tall wooden tables. Marcus began to rub Nearcus's shoulders and back.

"That was impressive, Nearcus," said Marcus. "We can only hope that the next round will be as successful...and quick."

"I got lucky," Nearcus mumbled through clinched teeth.

"You probably received some divine help."

"Yeah, I guess."

Aegospotami and Apollina had almost missed his son's first bout. He was engaged in giving a sales demonstration to a potential new client from the northern region of Chios when he heard the stewards running through the crowd announcing the pankration Beta bout. Apollina pleaded with her father to hurry to the event, but since these contests can last an hour or more, Aegospotami felt they did not have to hurry; so he took another five minutes to continue his discussion on how his mastic gum was the best grown. When they finally arrived at the competition field he had managed to push himself and his daughter to the front of the spectators just as the official jerked the starting staff away. If they had taken five more minutes in arriving they would have missed seeing Nearcus compete.

After the surprisingly fast victory, Aegospotami and Apollina jumped very high and screamed with joy! Nothing like that had been seen in years at the qualification trials. Although Aegospotami had seen many athletes compete in pankration bouts, he had never seen his son fight. Granted, he felt he might be biased, but Aegospotami was sure he had never seen a better pankratiast. He had never seen one so swift and agile. His chest expanded in great pride. Right then, all the extra work he had done during the past ten months because Nearcus was away training was worth every drop of sweat. He was confident that his son would win the top qualification spot for the Isthmian Games. Aegospotami started to plan for the trip across the Aegean Sea he knew they would be taking together very soon.

Nearcus was lying quite still in the preparation tent corner when the last bout of the first round was completed. The pain in his jaw had only grown worse in the past two hours. He sweated profusely from the fever and then he shook with severe chills and then the fever would return. This cycle continued throughout the morning. Marcus had rigged a couple of spare robes to resemble a small lean-to facing the tent wall in the corner. This was to keep the other opponents from learning just how ill and weak Nearcus truly was. When word came that the lot drawing for the second round was about to take place, Marcus looked into the lean-to and whispered to Nearcus that it was time.

Together, the athlete and his devoted trainer joined the other competitors in a straight line all facing the official with the urn. But this time there were only eleven of them. One pankratiast had suffered a broken shin and had withdrawn. The bone had broken so severely that it protruded three inches out of the skin. The injured athlete's family only hoped that he would be able to walk again in the future, let alone ever compete again. Upon hearing this news, Nearcus had two thoughts. First he thought that maybe having an infected tooth might not be so bad compared to being permanently crippled. Second, he gave a silent prayer to Apollo asking that he would draw the lot that would not match any other in this round. That would give him an automatic victory without having to fight. Nearcus was not sure how long he would be able to keep fighting at these trials and anything that could help him survive to the last round would be good.

Once again when it was Nearcus's turn, Marcus assisted him to the urn. Once again he drew the Beta lot. When the last lot had been drawn the athletes revealed their letters. Nearcus had his eyes shut as each competitor shouted out in turn what letter he had drawn. When the second from last opponent shouted out "Beta," Nearcus's hopes left him quickly. He would have to fight this round.

News of his technique to earn a quick victory had spread throughout the trials. Nearcus was sure it would not work a second time. As he took his starting position on the field, he devised a different strategy to determine early on what his opponent was expecting. Across the field, Nearcus saw his opponent, a short boy thirteen years old. Although he was nearly a foot shorter than Nearcus, the other boy weighed the same. He was stocky with a protruding stomach and muscular arms and legs. Nearcus immediately noticed that the boy's stomach did not seem to be very hard. He decided that would be his primary target. Nearcus would keep his distance and stay away from the challenger's blows and lunges while he used his height and leg reach to kick that stomach over and over. Once he had slowed the challenger to where Nearcus's speed would be a great advantage, then he could maneuver to acquire a choke hold and bring his opponent to submission. But first he felt he wanted to strike fear and confusion in the other boy's heart.

The two opponents quickly approached the official and reached him at the same time. Nearcus held out his right hand as if he was going to touch the staff simultaneously with his challenger. But an inch before he touched it, Nearcus hesitated and stopped his hand. His smaller challenger touched the staff and then jumped back in anticipation of another rapid charge and take down attempt by Nearcus. The stocky boy looked uncoordinated in this unusual move and Nearcus would have smiled except his tooth hurt too much.

Nearcus now placed his right hand on the staff and left it there. The challenger approached the staff again very warily. Finally, he slapped the staff with his little finger and immediately both the official and challenger quickly jumped back. Nearcus just stood there, frozen in position with his right hand still raised. The crowd howled with laughter at the sight of the pudgy boy jumping back and this embarrassed the challenger. His tactical move to avoid a quick takedown by Nearcus made him look like a coward who was afraid of his opponent.

So he charged Nearcus to regain his honor. In this bout the adrenaline was not sufficient to completely stop the intense pain in Nearcus's jaw and the very high fever had him unsteady on his feet. But his mind was able to focus in spite of the pain. As the stocky boy charged him like a small pony with his head down, Nearcus held his ground and at the last second raised his left foot to strike the on rushing challenger at the base of the rib cage, hitting him right on the solar plexus.

Nearcus did not have to use much force in his kick. He just held his heel out there and the challenger ran into it at full speed. The blow drove all the air from the stocky boy's lungs. He fell to his knees and then tumbled face down on the grass. Quickly he started to rise because he knew he was in a very vulnerable position. But Nearcus was quicker. As soon as the challenger got to his knees, Nearcus was on him from behind. His right forearm pressed against the challenger's neck and having gained this advantage Nearcus knew he was in position to achieve another quick victory. The challenger tried to rise to his feet, but Nearcus cinched the choke hold tighter and then wrapped his legs around the stomach of his opponent. He squeezed with his legs and pulled his arm tighter with all his might. Nearcus wanted to finish this right now.

But the challenger was a fighter. He grabbed at Nearcus's forearm to loosen the hold if possible and reached with his other hand for the face of his opponent. Nearcus moved his face to the other side of the stocky boy's head. The challenger switched hands and reached for Nearcus's face again. He found Nearcus's eyes and desperately tried to hurt him. Suddenly a sharp slap caused great pain on the back of the challenger's hand. The official had used his staff to stop the challenger from gouging Nearcus's eyes which was a violation of one of the two rules. However, no further involvement was necessary by the official. The loss of air from the kick to the solar plexus coupled with the choke hold that grew tighter and tighter with every movement of his head like a snake coiled about its prey, was sufficient to bring the challenger to unconsciousness.

When Nearcus felt the stocky boy's body go limp, he released him and slid backwards. His opponent gently rolled to the ground. In a matter of seconds the young man awoke from his short sleep. He jumped to his feet and turned to start the fight again but the official stepped between the two pankratiasts. The official grabbed Nearcus's arm and raised it in victory. Once again Nearcus had defeated his opponent in a very short time. Once again the crowd was cheering and clapping. Once again Aegospotami's chest puffed out as he loudly let everyone around him know that Nearcus was his son. Once again Marcus rushed to his athlete and put the robe on Nearcus and supported him as they quickly returned to the preparation tent. Only this time, Nearcus was overcome by the fever and pain. Marcus had to carry him the last few steps to the lean-to in the corner. Nearcus had passed out, but Marcus did not try to awaken him. It would be at least another two hours before Nearcus had to fight again. And while he was unconscious he could not feel the pain and perhaps he could get a little rest.

The shaking of his whole body from severe chills awoke Nearcus an hour later. Not knowing how long he had been unconscious, Nearcus started to stir and look for Marcus. But he did not have to move far because the slave was just outside the lean-to.

"So the mighty and swift warrior is awake now," Marcus said with a smile.

Nearcus could only whimper in a mumble because his jaw had swollen to where he could barely move it. However he forced out a question, "When do I fight again?"

Marcus was amazed at the focus of his young pankratiast. Nearcus did not wonder how long he had been out or about the status of his infected tooth. All he wanted to know was how the trials were proceeding and when he had to return to the fight. Marcus was impressed that winning was the only thing on Nearcus's mind.

"There are two more bouts then we start the next round," Marcus responded. Then he asked, "Are you hungry yet?"

Nearcus thought of the pain it would cause to chew on any food. Yes, he felt hungry but the cost in terms of pain to eat was more than he thought he could bear. So he decided it was better just to go hungry. He knew he needed to replenish his strength, but he was at the greatest level of pain he could bear. Adding to it by chewing would be more than he could take. So he shook his head to indicate he did not want to eat.

"You need food to fight and to combat your sickness," Marcus said. But Nearcus just pointed to his jaw and shook his head more vigorously. Marcus nodded that he understood why his athlete was refusing food. Then Marcus said, "I will make you something you can drink that will help you feel better."

Then he left the preparation tent. Nearcus shut his eyes and tried to think of the sights and excitement that were in Corinth. He tried to convince himself that the pain would be worth the reward. He tried to think of anything except his impacted tooth and the fever that had returned.

Marcus returned with a wooden cup filled with two raw eggs mixed with honey. "Here, drink this," he said as he helped Nearcus sit up and take the cup. Nearcus had tears running down his cheeks as he swallowed the grog Marcus had mixed. The food felt good when it reached his stomach, but the pain of even moving his jaw slightly to part his lips was so intense it caused him to cry. But once the cup was drained he felt better when he laid back down. Marcus was smiling because he knew the energy from the drink would help his athlete regain some of the strength that had been drained by cycles of chills and fever.

Sooner than he expected, Nearcus found himself on the line waiting to draw his lot for the third round. This time he drew the letter Epsilon. As he was listening to the others call out their letters Nearcus felt a new energy come over his body. The food and rest had helped him greatly. In fact, he was anxious to fight again. He remembered that while in a contest his pain had not been present. He wanted to do anything that would lessen the intense throbbing that encompassed the entirety of the left side of his face.

His opponent for the third round was a fourteen year old boy named Theophrastus from his own training camp. In fact, Marcus was the slave of Theophratus's father. Marcus was assigned to train pankratiasts for many months of each year because Theophratus's father thought it brought honor to his household to support the athletes this way. Theophrastus was very friendly and all those in the camp called him Theo. He lived in the nearest village and he was always the first at camp in the morning and the last to leave at the end of the day. He worked very hard but his skill level made him just an average pankratiast. His pleasant personality and willingness to help others made him a very popular athlete. Nearcus had regularly defeated Theo in practice bouts, but once in a great while Theo would win. Knowing the skills and techniques of your opponent was normally a real advantage in pankration. But Nearcus knew that Theo was so familiar with his style that it would be a very long match to beat his camp friend. A very long bout would be nearly impossible for Nearcus to finish in his current pain and sickness.

It was mid-afternoon when Nearcus and Theo stood on opposite sides of the pankration field. Both approached the official's staff at a quick walk. Both wanted to engage and hopefully end the bout quickly. Unknown to Nearcus his opponent was near exhaustion. While Nearcus had scored two remarkably fast victories, Theo had fought for hours already that day. He had won the first bout in less than an hour, but his second bout went on for more than an hour and eventually Theo had to submit. Now Theo faced a challenger he knew could beat him so he approached the staff with fatigue and resigned to another loss. Nearcus approached the staff with his focus uncharacteristically scattered. He had no plan on how to beat Theo. He was going to react to what he saw and hope his concentration would return as they proceeded.

Once the official jerked the staff away, Theo immediately charged for Nearcus's legs. But Nearcus easily side stepped the clumsy attempt and twisted around to fall on Theo's back. Then Theo used a wrestler's technique that Nearcus had not seen his opponent use previously. Theo got to his hands and knees and then simultaneously stepped his left foot forward and slipped his right hand beneath Nearcus's shoulder as he quickly twisted to his right to reverse their positions. As soon as Theo was behind Nearcus he slid his forearm up the chest to his friend's neck in order to apply a choke hold. With this sudden turn of events the crowd became a wall of noise shouting, "Theo! Theo! Theo!" Most of the crowd were local and those from Theo's village outnumbered all others.

This thunderous support empowered tired Theo and suddenly his fatigue was forgotten. He thought, "Wow! Nearcus made such a bad mistake! That is not like him. Maybe I can win! Maybe this time I will score the quick victory!"

As Theo maneuvered his forearm to gain pressure against his opponent's throat, Nearcus regained his focus and was berating himself for letting Theo gain the advantage so easily. Without any conscious effort but rather in a natural response to his opponent's pressure on his back, Nearcus shifted his own weight from one knee to the other. Once he had the rocking motion of Theo started it was just a matter of seconds before Nearcus collapsed one knee under him, using Theo's own momentum to slide him off his back. With both fighters lying on their sides, Nearcus no longer needed his arms for support. This freed one hand to pull on Theo's choking arm and another hand to punch him in the thigh. On the third punch to the thigh, Theo's leg went into a spasm which momentarily caused him to loosen his choke hold. Using his great speed and agility Nearcus twisted free of Theo.

The bout progressed with each fighter engaging the other and then backing off. Things had started to favor Nearcus when Theo regained the upper hand quite by accident. As the two pankratiasts pushed apart from each other Theo flailed his arm in a defensive maneuver. It landed squarely on Nearcus's left jaw. The blow caused the impacted tooth to burst through the top of the gum. Blood and puss gushed from the wound. The pain shook all of Nearcus. A hot flash raced from his jaw to his toes. Out of his mouth poured thick gobs of puss mixed with blood. The sight of this horrific wound caused momentary remorse in Theo for so severely hurting his friend. Theo unconsciously slid backward, fear and sadness filling his eyes.

Nearcus was filled with pain and anger. He was not mad at Theo but at the pain. But Nearcus had to strike out against the pain somehow. Before him stood the boy who had caused his face to be on fire and his body to tremble. With no control over his anger, Nearcus lunged for Theo who was in shock at the sight of his friend's face. Nearcus smashed his fist into Theo's throat and then rapidly kicked him repeatedly on the knees and thigh. Theo fell to the ground and Nearcus jumped on top of him, both fists pummeling his friend. Almost immediately Theo gave the submission sign. He could have continued the fight but his concern for his friend outweighed his need to win a pankratiast bout. By submitting he knew Nearcus could receive immediate medial attention for his mouth.

Upon seeing Theo submit the official ran to the fighters where he pulled Nearcus off of his opponent. Nearcus had stopped thinking when he lunged at Theo and so it took great effort to pull him from the tremendous rage that he was expressing against his pain. Soon Marcus was there and helped the official gain control of Nearcus. And it was just in time because the crowd was mad that Nearcus continued to beat a local athlete who had already submitted. The angry local citizenry had started to approach the athletes to grab Nearcus, but Marcus arrived in time to stop the beating before the crowd could get involved.

After the official raised Nearcus's hand, Marcus put a robe on the victor and quickly led him away to the preparation tent. There he was surprised to see Aegospotami waiting for his son. When he had seen the bloody mess explode out of his son's mouth, he had immediately moved towards the preparation tent. He had left Apollina outside the entrance to the tent while he waited for the injured Nearcus to return. Marcus was glad to see Aegospotami there. Together they helped Nearcus to the lean-to in the corner. After lying Nearcus down, the father turned to Marcus.

"What is the matter with him" he asked.

Not caring what Nearcus's wishes might be, Marcus thought it best to give the father the whole truth and said, "He has an infected tooth and with it fever and chills. The blow to his jaw must have ruptured the swelling."

Aegospotami looked at his son who laid there shaking in great pain and thought about the bouts he had seen Nearcus fight not knowing the terrible torture he was experiencing in those victories. The father felt pride in his brave son and shame in himself for not noticing the boy's suffering. A tear formed in his eye and he bent down and put his face close to Nearcus's. Then he whispered, "Oh my dear Nearcus. You are so brave and yet so foolish. Let me look in your mouth. I might be able to help your pain."

Nearcus let tears run down his cheeks. His father was not mad at him for having a bad tooth. No, his father loved him and wanted him to be free from pain. Nearcus knew that he had misjudged his father and misunderstood what was important to him.

Nearcus knew the pain was so intense that it could not get any worse by opening his mouth. When he did so, Aegospotami could immediately see the problem. A man in his profession was knowledgeable about teeth and gums and mouth diseases. He whispered to his son, "It is bad Nearcus, but I can make you feel better."

Aegospotami reached into his bag of samples and rummaged around until he found a small roll of canvas. He untied the cord around the canvas and rolled it out. Inside were a small jar of clove oil and three instruments: a sharp pick, a very sharp narrow knife and a pair of iron pliers. The mastic gum farmer and merchant made a habit of always carrying these dental tools with him whenever he left home. On more than one occasion he found that by helping those with toothaches he could create a customer for life, for no one who suffers from a bad tooth ever wants to experience that pain again. Payment for his assistance was always in the form of a new sales order for mastic gum from the patient and then more business from the patient's family and friends usually followed.

Nearcus never knew his father had experience in helping to fix teeth pain. He always assumed he only sold gum to prevent tooth decay. His father tore a corner from a nearby robe and poured the clove oil on it. Then he pressed the cloth against the infected gums. In just seconds the pain in Nearcus's jaw grew less. Nearcus opened his eyes and stared at his father. The pain was still there but it was much less than before. Nearcus thought about the miserable hours he had spent in great pain when all he had to do was trust his father and go to him. Nearcus felt foolish and also great love for his father.

After five minutes the pain was even less. Now Aegospotami looked straight into Nearcus's eyes and solemnly said, "Son, this next part is going to hurt a lot but it has to be done. I will be as quick as I can but you must be still and let me do my work. You can scream if you must, but you must try to be still." Then he looked at Marcus and said, "Sit on his legs and hold his arms by his side."

Marcus straddled Nearcus and did as he was directed. Then Aegospotami lifted his head and spoke a prayer, "Oh caring Asclepius, god of healing, help me in my work."

Nearcus felt the pain return in giant waves as his father pulled open his mouth to its widest. Next he started to cry when his father took the narrow knife and slit the gums around the molar that was protruding slightly through the puss and blood. After cutting enough to expose the molar sufficiently to allow a good grip with the pliers, Aegospotami removed the knife and set it down. He paused before the next part and looked into his son's eyes. Aegospotami thought once again about Nearcus's courage and how the boy had yet to scream. But this next part of the procedure causes grown men to cry like children.

Aegospotami grabbed the pliers and looked at Marcus and nodded. Marcus nodded in reply and pressed harder on Nearcus's arms. The father reached into his son's mouth and expertly clamped his tool on the exposed molar. He twisted left then right then rocked it back and forth while gently pulling out. Nearcus's eyes grew very wide and tears streamed from them. Then they rolled into the top of his head and he went limp. Aegospotami gave a momentary thought that the pain and infection might have killed his son. But that thought passed quickly as he felt Nearcus's rhythmic breath exhaling slowly from his mouth. Wanting to finish the extraction before his son became conscious again, Aegospotami worked faster and rougher. In two minutes he had worked the tooth sufficiently to allow the roots to be pulled free. With one last great jerk the molar popped loose and out it came from the boy's mouth still clamped in Aegospotami's pliers.

The next step was to stop the profuse bleeding out of the hole where the tooth had been. Aegospotami put the clove oil soaked cloth on the gum and pressed with great pressure. A minute later Nearcus opened his eyes which were full of confusion, fear and shock. He saw his father's smiling face. Upon making eye contact with his son, Aegospotami said, "That tooth will never bother you again. Now the healing can start. I want you to bite down on this rag very hard to stop the bleeding. I will tell you when you can let go."

It hurt tremendously, but Nearcus was a good son and did as his father directed. After a few minutes his father took another square of cloth, folded it and then poured clove oil over it. He told Nearcus to open his mouth and he replaced the original cloth with the fresh one. Over the next quarter hour he repeated this process three more times. When he pulled the last one out there was only a little blood on it. So Aegospotami soaked a clean cloth in the last of his clove oil and placed it on the open wound. Minutes later Nearcus could feel the lessening of the pain in his jaw. But the chills had returned. He shook uncontrollably. His father felt his head with the back of his hand and nodded knowingly. Now that the tooth that had been poisoning him was removed, he knew Nearcus would be able to beat the fever and chills in another day or two. Aegospotami told Nearcus this and then left the tent to tell Apollina what had happened.

Marcus got Nearcus's clothes and brought them to the boy. Nearcus looked at them and asked through clinched teeth, "What are these for?"

"To get dressed for the ride home so you can return to your bed and get well," the slave answered.

"But I am not done yet. I will finish the trials."

Marcus was not sure how to feel about this decision. Nearcus had already proven his skill and talent and courage as probably the best pankratiast at the trials and there was no need to put his long-term health at risk to prove anything more. But he also was very proud that this young man had a warrior's heart and never considered giving up.

After moments contemplating the situation, Marcus set the clothes down and said simply, "As you wish."

When Aegospotami returned and heard Nearcus's decision he too decided to let the boy determine his future.

At the next lot drawing something good finally happened for Nearcus on this day. He drew the odd lot and was given an automatic victory by forfeiture. Now he had been credited with four victories with only one round to go. A victory in the last round would earn him a spot on the Chios team that would travel to Corinth next week. Just one more victory was all that stood between Nearcus and his goal.

The luck of the draw for the final round resulted in Nearcus having to face one of the only other two competitors who had not been defeated in the trials. The other undefeated pankratiast had competed earlier in this round and been victorious. All other competitors had at least one defeat on this day. The last two remaining undefeated athletes were Nearcus and Dioxippus from the northern Chios training camp. The winner of their bout would end the day with no losses and be chosen as the second member of the island's pankration team for the Isthmian Games. The situation was very clear to Nearcus; defeat Dioxippus and his goal to reach Corinth would be achieved. He had to win.

Beating his opponent was not going to be easy. Dioxippus was four years older than Nearcus and fifteen pounds heavier. The northern Chiosian was experienced and extremely strong. And he had the advantage of not running a high fever and suffering from a massive, bloody hole in his jaw. It would take all the skill and stamina that Nearcus had left to beat Dioxippus.

Before leaving the preparation tent, as Marcus oiled Nearcus's back he whispered instructions to his athlete, "I have seen Dioxippus fight before. He nearly qualified for the Olympic Games last year. He is very experienced and very mean, but you are quicker and smarter. Keep your distance and choose your kicking attacks wisely. Keep him at a distance until he makes an error, then pounce on it and don't let-up until he has no choice but to submit. Remember that he can take a lot of punishment and you will need a perfect hold to make him submit, so don't close him until you see the chance for that perfect hold."

Nearcus listened intently to his coach. He nodded that he understood his instructions and then they made the slow walk to the field. Once on the edge of the field, Marcus removed the robe. Nearcus felt the late afternoon breeze sweep across his naked body. It was a cool breeze and he started to shiver immediately. His vision grew dim and he tasted the blood swirling around his tongue and then he felt it run down his throat. Looking at Dioxippus across the field, Nearcus sized up his opponent and he concluded that on his best day it would be extremely difficult to win. But then Nearcus remembered the weeks and months of training to reach his singular goal; now only Dioxippus stood between him and reaching that goal.

As Nearcus walked to the official he wobbled and could not maintain a straight line. Some in the crowd thought that he was frightened of Dioxippus, but Aegospotami knew his son was near fainting from the fever and the pain. Inside, the concerned father felt the urge to run onto the field and pull his son from the competition to get him to a sick bed before he was permanently injured. However, Aegospotami knew

---

that he could not fight Nearcus's battles and that this was an important step to his son growing into a man.

When both right hands touched the staff and the official jerked it away, Nearcus immediately stepped back very quickly. Dioxippus did the same. Both circled to their left for a few steps then the older boy gave a forward faint which caused Nearcus to back away a couple more steps. After three minutes of the fighters maneuvering in this manner the crowd began to jeer for them to engage. But neither of the fighters could hear the crowd noise. Nearcus and Dioxippus only concentrated on the moves of their opponent. They knew that just one mistake could cost them the victory and the honor of going to Corinth.

Then Dioxippus thought he saw Nearcus lose his balance as the younger boy's knees wobbled with the fever and chills. That was the opportunity Dioxippus sought. As quickly as he could he closed the distance to Nearcus and lunged at him for a take-down. But when Nearcus swiftly moved to avoid the lunge, Dioxippus grabbed only air and quickly began to realize how unusually fast his opponent truly was. He had never faced someone as quick as Nearcus before. Once again the pankratiasts circled looking for an opponent's mistake.

The first to grow frustrated by this inactivity was Dioxippus. He had learned that Nearcus was fast and now he wanted to see if he could deliver a hard punch. Dioxippus advanced on Nearcus to within striking distance, offering the younger boy the chance to hit him. But Nearcus did not strike with his fists. He moved to his left a half step then flicked out a swift kick to Dioxippus's right knee. This started the contact of the bout in earnest.

For the next quarter-hour the two pankratiasts exchanged a short series of kicks and blows and then spread apart to seek a good opening in their opponent's defense. Dioxippus's tactic was to maneuver closer to Nearcus to where he could grab the younger boy and use his greater strength to beat on him. Nearcus delivered sharp, well aimed kicks that landed on Dioxippus's legs and head and then he would retreat to a safe range. This cycle of exchanging blows then separating continued as the crowd cheered the action then jeered the separation. Although this was proving an effective strategy by Nearcus and resulted in Dioxippus becoming more and more frustrated, it had a great weakness because of the younger boy's physical problems this day. Normally this strategy would be effective in lengthening the bout for an extended period. Eventually the larger athlete would wear down and grow fatigued. Once this had happened, then Nearcus could use his superior stamina and quickness to maneuver to where he could get a choke hold from behind or obtain some other hold to successfully immobilize his opponent and get him to submit. But on this day, Nearcus had no stamina left. His sickness had drained all his energy and the only competitor growing tired now was Nearcus.

Aegospotami and Apollina could see that Nearcus was growing faint. A true fan of pankration, Aegospotami admired the technique his son was using to defeat the larger opponent. Yet he knew that Nearcus was too weak to keep it up for the hour or more it usually took to be effective. From what Aegospotami saw he was sure it was only a matter of time before Dioxippus would be able to grab Nearcus and then his son would be defeated.

Ten minutes later, Nearcus landed a powerful front kick to the left side of Dioxippus's head as the larger opponent passed him in an ineffective lunge. Nearcus thought the blow strong enough that he might have dazed Dioxippus and sensed that he might have the advantage he sought. Nearcus spun around quickly and jumped on Dioxippus's back. The strong boy did not lose his feet even with Nearcus on his back. Adrenaline surged through Nearcus's exhausted body as he could feel victory approaching. He worked his right forearm around to the front of Dioxippus's neck. With his left hand he grabbed his own right wrist and started to squeeze with all his might. With the help of the gods, Nearcus just knew that in a few seconds Dioxippus would go unconscious and Nearcus would have the win and a trip to Corinth. But something strange was happening in his body that Nearcus had never experienced before. Although he squeezed with all his might, his muscles were not responding to what his brain was willing. Then dark circles formed on the edges of Nearcus's vision. Slowly the blackness grew inward and as it did, Nearcus tried to apply more pressure to his choke hold. He was confused and becoming frightened. He thought, "Why isn't my body responding? I have this match won. I have the perfect position and the perfect hold. Why can't I get my arms to cinch it tighter?"

Everyone in the crowd was screaming! Once again they were amazed at the agility and talent of Nearcus. His head kick and quick application of a winning choke hold from the rear were things of athletic beauty. They all knew that Dioxippus had been defeated. Dioxippus knew it too. He struggled to free himself, but he knew that whenever he had an opponent in such a choke hold victory was assured.

The darkness in Nearcus's vision had grown to where only a pin-hole of light remained in the middle of it. Then that hole closed and Nearcus went limp, falling off Dioxippus's back. His body hit the ground with a loud thump. Dioxippus did not know what had happened. The official did not know what had happened. The crowd did not know what had happened. But Aegospotami and Marcus knew what had happened. They both rushed to Nearcus as quickly as they could.

Aegospotami shouted to the official as he ran, "It is over! It is over! Nearcus is done! It is finished!"

Dioxippus stood over the unconscious Nearcus and looked for any movement. He was about to pounce on him when he heard Aegospotami shouting. Dioxippus hesitated and looked at the official. The official went to Dioxippus and raised the victor's arm. As Dioxippus's arm was going up, Marcus was the first to reach Nearcus. He lifted Nearcus's eyelids to check his eyes, but there was no life in them. The slave put his head on Nearcus's chest and listened for a heart beat. It took a few moments, but eventually Marcus could hear the young boy's heart slowly beating. Aegospotami arrived and Marcus looked up at him and said, "He is alive but there is only a faint spirit in him. "

Dioxippus stood over the two men tending to the boy and he was filled with anger and embarrassment. Dioxippus knew in his heart that Nearcus was faking. He did not know why the boy did it, but Dioxippus was sure Nearcus had let him win only after he showed the entire crowd that he could defeat Dioxippus. As he stood there, Dioxippus grew more angry because all attention was on Nearcus when he knew everyone should be celebrating his victory. A hatred for Nearcus grew in Dioxippus's heart. The older pankratiast felt his face turn red as he looked up at the crowd. He was humiliated by what Nearcus had done.

Marcus wrapped the robe around Nearcus's limp body and together with Aegospotami they quickly carried the boy to the preparation tent. They put Nearcus's body on a rub down table, and then Marcus rushed to retrieve a cup of water. Aegospotami could see that Nearcus was not breathing correctly. He opened his son's mouth to see why he was not taking in normal breaths. The father was frightened by what he saw. Quickly he turned Nearcus on his side and used his fingers to spread his son's lips apart. Aegospotami reached into Nearcus's mouth and scooped out blood and blood clots that had assembled there. A small stream gushed from the mouth as if a dam had broken. Once the mouth was empty, Aegospotami gave a hard slap to the middle of Nearcus's back. When there was no reaction, he repeated the slap. This time Nearcus coughed and then drew a large breath and his body jerked on the table. Next his eyes opened and were full of confusion as if he had just been unexpectedly awakened from a deep sleep.

When Marcus returned with the water he saw a giant smile of relief and tears of joy on Aegospotami's face. Nearcus rolled over onto his back and immediately his body began to quiver from exhaustion. Marcus forced the water into Nearcus's mouth. Then he ran to his satchel and grabbed his jar of honey. He knew that his athlete needed energy now to overcome the total exhaustion he had just experienced.

Nearcus, still confused, looked up at his father and mumbled, "I did win, right? I'm going to Corinth, right?"

Aegospotami gently stroked his only son's brow as he slowly shook his head and said, "Your will and spirit never gave up, but your body did. The gods stopped you from winning this year. Maybe the gods will let you win next year's trials."

CHAPTER 3

Apollina had made it her job to care for her big brother. When the trio boarded the cart to return from the trials the sun was setting and the early spring night had become quite cool. Apollina had cradled Nearcus's head in her lap the entire bumpy ride back to the farm. She had made sure that he was covered well and softly sang to him as they bounced along. Her father and brother had not said a word the entire trip home. After Nearcus was placed in his own bed, Apollina had tended to his needs throughout the night. As Nearcus slept that night, Apollina sat next to him and listened to his breathing. If he had started to struggle again to draw breath she was ready to run to alert her father. But that had not happened and eventually Apollina had fallen asleep in the chair next to her brother's bed.

Over the next four days Nearcus stayed in bed. His sister brought him broth and soft foods and changed his blankets when they had become soaked with his fever induced sweat. Those two days and nights had been miserable for the young athlete; fever then chills then fever then fitful sleep then awakened again with chills. But on the morning of the fifth day he had awakened with strength he had forgotten he had once possessed. The fever had left, his jaw only hurt a little and his appetite had returned. For the first time since he passed out on the back of Dioxippus, Nearcus sat up by himself in bed. Soon he was able to swing his legs over the edge of the bed and, eventually, to stand. He walked out to the eating table under the shade tree near the gods' shrine and sat on the small bench. He sat with the sun directly beating down on him and there he enjoyed the heat on his face.

With the fever gone, he felt like a new man. However, when he began to feel better physically, disappointment over his failure at the trials swept over him. Then the sun no longer felt good. Nothing could feel good to Nearcus when he contemplated how closely he had come to his goal only to fail. Nearcus looked over at the shrine and a frown covered his face. He and his father had prayed for strength and victory and had done all that the gods had demanded of him. He was angry that the gods had not met their part of the agreement. He was sure they had just toyed with him; they had enjoyed teasing him and having sport with him. He stared at the idols inside the shrine and before long his frustration grew to an all consuming bitterness. Then he tasted the blood that was still slowly trickling from the hole where his tooth had been. Nearcus spit the blood out in the direction of the shrine. He mumbled to himself, "Some help you were. Don't count on me worshipping you ever again."

Aegospotami approached Nearcus from behind, but he was too late to hear his son spew the bitter words towards the idols. The father was in a good mood. He was overjoyed at seeing his son out of bed.

"Nearcus! The gods be praised! You are out of bed! I am so happy" he cheered.

"Yes father, my body is feeling better but my spirit is still beaten."

Aegospotami's smile quickly vanished from his face. His son had fought magnificently and everyone at the trials knew that he was the best pankratiast there. The gods had robbed his son of what he had earned and Aegospotami's heart felt the same bitterness that consumed Nearcus. Yet, being much older and wiser than his young son, he also knew that the games come and go, but your health you must nurture always. Still, the father could not think of anything to say to help ease the pain in Nearcus's spirit. So he went over and placed his hand on his son's shoulder and just stood there.

Finally Aegospotami said, "I am glad you are able to get out of bed now. That fever was bad and I had worried over you."

Nearcus heard his father's words and knew that he meant well, but his disappointment was so intense that all he could do was nod in response. It would take more time for the pain of failing to leave the young athlete. Nearcus easily accepted the pain of the rotten tooth and the infection and the extraction and the pain from blows received on the competition field, but the pain of failure was much harder to suffer. And in his mind, Nearcus was sure he had failed. He started to think about all the exciting things he had planned to see and experience in Corinth but then he immediately forced such thoughts from his brain. He would force himself not to think of what he lost. He would force himself to concentrate on the duties of the day. He would get a large breakfast then report to his father to help in the orchards. Nearcus planned to forget his disappointment through hard work along side the three family slaves. He was sure that hard physical labor would leave him too exhausted to dream of Corinth.

That afternoon, Nearcus felt weak and exhausted two hours before the workday was to end. His father saw that the young man was totally spent and not wanting him to suffer a repeat of what happened when Nearcus was on Dioxippus's back, Aegospotami directed his son to quit work and return to the house. It was nearly a half-mile to the house and half way there Nearcus decided to rest under a tree in the orchard. As he sat under the tree he closed his eyes and rested his head against the trunk. A moment later he heard a rustling along the orchard pathway. He raised his head and looked around but he saw no one, so he shut his eyes again and smiled at how the wind had fooled him. But then he heard it again and opened his eyes again. This time it was louder and he was sure someone was there. Nearcus called out, "Who is there? Show yourself and state your business."

But no one answered. Nearcus kept his eyes opened and scanned the trees around him. He saw nothing. Then he heard a voice that seemed to echo in the far distance. The voice said, "In Corinth you will be chosen." Nearcus jumped to his feet, his fatigue suddenly had left him. He quickly jerked his head from side to side and up and down as he turned around looking for the source of the voice. There was no one there. Nearcus called out loudly, "I cannot be chosen for I am not going to Corinth!" There was no answer. So Nearcus called out again, "Who are you? Where are you? What will I be chosen for?" Again there was no answer. Nearcus was frightened and started to walk quickly for home. After a few steps he started to jog towards home and then he broke into a full run. The entire way there he scanned the orchards and sky for the source of the voice.

Upon reaching home he saw Apollina sweeping the front stone stoop. She saw that he was frightened and near exhaustion and so she ran to meet him.

"What is wrong dear brother?" she asked with concern.

"Have you seen anyone in the orchards today?" Nearcus said with great urgency.

Apollina answered, "Only you and father and the slaves this morning."

"No, I mean in just the last couple of minutes."

Apollina showed her confusion on her face and shook her head. Then she said, "Tell me brother, what is bothering you?"

"I must lie down again. I think the fever is returning and making me faint. I am hearing things that are not there." Nearcus pushed his way by his little sister and went straight to his bed without washing his feet or hands. He collapsed on the bed and tried to sleep because he was sure sleep would clear his confused mind.

Sleep and clarity did not come to Nearcus that afternoon. So later he got up and ate dinner with his family. After the evening meal, Aegospotami sipped his wine and looked at Nearcus. He noted to himself how pale the boy was.

Aegospotami said, "Son, your sister told me you were upset when you reached home this afternoon. What was bothering you?"

The care his father had given him at the trials had made Nearcus see his father in a new light. Now he felt he could share his concerns with his father, so he replied, "On the way home I stopped and rested under a tree. While there I must have fallen asleep and dreamed that I heard a voice. When I awoke I thought it had been real and it frightened me, so I ran home."

Aegospotami looked into his son's eyes and slowly nodded. After a moment he said, "You are still very weak from the sickness. Perhaps I should not have let you work so hard in the orchards so early. Sleep well tonight. Tomorrow I will have you do chores around the house until you recover more of your strength."

Nearcus replied, "As you think best, father."

That night though, Nearcus did not sleep well. It took him a long time to finally fall asleep because in his heart he knew that he had not dreamt that voice. For hours he had tossed and turned as he wondered what it meant. What did "In Corinth you will be chosen," mean? The more he pondered the events and the words the more confused Nearcus became. When sleep finally did come, it was not restful but rather it was full of even more confusing dreams.

The next day, Aegospotami took the family slaves and left to work at the far side of the main orchard. Apollina kept busy drawing water from the well to fill the cistern near the house and washing linen, and doing sewing repairs to her father's and brother's field clothes. A hundred yards from the house, Nearcus used an axe to chop into firewood a tree that had fallen in the nearer, older orchard. With each blow he tried to smash thoughts from his mind. He concentrated on his wood chopping to keep from thinking about the voice and to help him forget that if he had only had a little more strength left he would be leaving tomorrow for the boat to take him to the Isthmian Games. But try as he did, that mystery and disappointment still flooded his mind.

About mid-morning Nearcus looked up and in the distance saw two men approaching the house. He sunk his axe into the tree and returned to the house to greet the visitors. He arrived at the same time the men reached the front stoop. They called into the house for someone to come out. Nearcus rounded the corner of the house and greeted them, "Good day travelers. How may we help you on our journey?"

"Nearcus! Have you already forgotten me?" said Theo with a big smile.

As Nearcus drew closer and heard the visitor speak he recognized his friend from the training camp. "Theo! You have come to visit! Come sit with me and I will have my sister prepare us something to eat."

Theo turned to the man with him and said, "Nearcus, this is my father, Leonidas. We have come with great news!"

"Greetings Theophrastus's father. Our home is honored to have you here. Please come and sit in the shade and rest," Nearcus said as he led the visitors to the dining table behind the house. Once they were seated, Nearcus said, "I can send my sister to the far orchard to retrieve my father if you desire."

"First we must speak to you, young Nearcus," said Leonidas. "I watched you compete at the trials and was very impressed with your talent and skill. Everyone there impressed. I can honestly say that you are the best young pankratiast I have ever seen and I am sure I can find many,

many others who will agree with me. However, I must ask, what caused you to let Dioxippus win at the end?"

Nearcus was not ready for that question. He was hesitant to let anyone know the cause of his weakness because he was afraid it might hurt his father's business. He decided to leave out any explanation about his teeth and answered, "I had come down with a fever that morning and it had drained me of my stamina and strength."

"See! I told you father there was a reason he lost!" exclaimed Theo. He wanted to ask his friend why so much blood poured from his mouth when Theo had hit it, but Theo was just relieved that his blow had not been the cause of Nearcus's loss.

"I see," responded Leonidas. "I thought there must have been a reason because you had the bout won until you let Dioxippus go. Well, I have come here today as a representative of the Chios athletic commission. Hopefully we have good news for you if your father agrees. Perhaps now it is time to ask your father to join us."

Nearcus was really confused. What could this news be? He wanted to know the news right now, but it was obvious that Leonidas felt it was necessary only to speak of it when Aegospolami was there. So, Nearcus sent Apollina to retrieve his father and he told her to hurry!

CHAPTER 4

Nearly an hour passed and Apollina and Aegospotami had not returned yet. Nearcus had set before the guests bread and goat cheese and the trio had discussed the mastic gum business as they ate the refreshments. Nearcus was dying to know what the athletic commission wanted to discuss with his father, but it would have been impolite to ask a guest in your home about his reason for being there. Proper manners forced Nearcus to keep his questions to himself.

Nearcus heard the heavy footsteps of his father before he saw him. Aegospotami was breathing heavily when he approached the table under the shade tree. He was very dirty, his tunic covered in dust and dirt smudges and dried mud ran up the length of his arms and legs. On his face was a look of curiosity mixed with irritation at being pulled away from his day's work even before the lunch hour had arrived. But on Chios a visitation by guests required very formal hospitality and actions. Aegospotami replaced his scowl with a forced smile as he approached the table.

"Greetings traveler! How may we help you on your journey?" Aegospotami said in a loud voice, giving Leonidas and Theo the proper welcome to his farm. Then he turned to Apollina who had been trailing her father and spoke to her, "Daughter, bring a wash basin so that I may clean the dirt from my body and sit with our guests. And then bring some of our finest nectar to share." Apollina quickly entered the house to comply with her father's wishes.

Leonidas smiled broadly and replied, "Dear Aegospotami, thank you for your welcome. I apologize for taking you from your important work, but I feel I come with glad news."

Nearcus and Theo stood upon Aegospotami's arrival and stepped away from the table. It was not the place of boys to be part of an adult conversation unless a question was directed to them. So they kept quiet and listened. Nearcus wanted to shout out very loudly, "Stop all the polite greetings and tell us the news!" But he kept quiet and stood very still next to Theo.

After Aegospotami washed his hands, arms and face he motioned for Leonidas to sit down again. The two men took seats across the table and sipped their wooden cups full of peach nectar. Finally, Leonidas spoke.

"This is good nectar Aegospotami, and we appreciate your wonderful hospitality. I would like to state our business now, if you care to hear?"

Aegospotami nodded, giving permission for his guest to continue. Nearcus's eyes grew wide as he said to himself, "Yes! Tell us! Tell us! The waiting is killing me!"

Leonidas continued, "Our dear island and community nearly met with a terrible dishonor and much disgrace, which but for the grace of the gods would have stained us for all time. This morning all the Chios athletes who qualified for the Isthmian Games gathered at my house to spend this night. Tomorrow morning they will depart for the port of Limenas where they are to board a ship bound for Corinth. As my guests were arriving from across our island a messenger came to me with very shocking news."

Leonidas paused to take a sip of nectar and Nearcus thought he did this just to torture him. Racing through Nearcus's head was the thought, "Why can't he just get to the point? Tell us, what is the news?"

Leonidas put down his cup and wiped his mouth with the back of his hand and then continued, "The messenger reported that an imposter was present in my home already. As you know the two youth division pankratiasts chosen to represent our island were Dioxippus and Eirenaios. I was shocked when the messenger from the east country told me that Eirenaios had entered the trials illegally. Eirenaios had presented himself as a free man who spoke Greek in accordance with the games' strict rules. Yes, he does speak a little Greek but today I learned he is a slave of Isokrates, the grain merchant in Thymiana. It was reported to me that last year Isokrates had seen the young man fight while on a trip to Ephesus and purchased him to place him in training. Isokrates presented him to his village as an adopted son, but really he is a slave."

"But why? Why would Isokrates do such a thing?" Aegospotami, a man of great virtue who would never consider such a deceit, asked innocently.

"He was greedy for glory. He wanted his household to be known as that which produced a great champion."

"Why did he not just free his slave and actually adopt him as a son? Then Eirenaios would be eligible to participate in the games?" Nearcus said, forgetting his place was to be silent. He really wanted to know the answer to this question so it just popped out of his mouth before he knew he had spoken.

Leonidas turned to Nearcus and said, "I guess because a free son can choose not to fight and a slave cannot."

All four of them nodded in agreement. After a short pause, Leonidas continued, "If he had been allowed to compete at Corinth the shame of the deception would have stained our island for eternity as the home of cheaters and liars. My business, your business Aegospotami, would have been hurt terribly."

Again, all four nodded. As Aegospotami gave more thought to the danger he felt a shiver run down his spine. Then he said what was obvious to him, "So you come to ask if Nearcus can go to the Isthmian Games in place of this slave?"

When Nearcus heard these words come from his father his heart jumped in excitement. His thoughts raced, "Can this be true? Will I get to go after all? Is it possible that my dream will come true?" When Nearcus saw Leonidas nod in agreement and a giant smile come on Theo's face his excitement grew even more.

Aegospotami turned to face his son. When Nearcus saw the pained look on his father's face his excitement and hope transformed into disappointment. He could tell by what he saw in Aegospotami's eyes that what was about to happen would break his heart.

"He would have to leave with you now to go to the games?" Aegospotami asked.

Again, Leonidas nodded his head and then added, "Yes, we would have to depart within the hour."

"I want my son to go. Every man should visit Corinth once before he dies. And to go as a competitor to the games and to see the festival and the celebrations at the temples is a chance of a life time. But I cannot send my twelve-year old son to such a place alone. And I cannot leave my business and my orchards without days of prior planning. We are in the middle of the spring pruning and repairing the irrigation systems."

Nearcus felt his heart fall. Again he was so close to his dream and again it was just out of his reach. But he could not disagree with his father. It is impossible to leave the orchards and business unattended for many weeks without proper preparation. The entire income for the year could be lost if the trees were not attended to properly in the spring.

Nearcus thought of the ax he had left sitting in the tree. He wanted to just go back there and start chopping again. He wanted to get alone again where he could take out his anger and frustration on the dead tree. He wanted to slam that ax blade into it over and over again as hard as he was able.

There was silence as both men and boys stared at the table. After a few moments, Theo timidly asked a question in a soft voice, "Father, what if Marcus went with Nearcus?"

Aegospotami looked up quickly and Nearcus saw a brightness in his eyes. His father's sad face now had a grin on it.

"Marcus is a good man, a trustworthy man," said Aegospotami, "And he took excellent care of my son at the trials when Nearcus needed much attention. But, Leonidas, you should not be made to lose the services of your slave for such a period. You will need him in your house."

"Marcus *is* a good man and even a better slave and I do depend on him. But my house will suffer more if our dear island is shamed. For if only one youth pankratiast participant attends from Chios there will be questions and the shameful reason why there is not two will surely be discovered. And then we all suffer. Better my household do without Marcus for a few weeks than the whole island suffer."

Aegospotami stood and went into his house. He returned with a gold coin in his hand. He laid the coin on the table and said, "Will this be sufficient to pay for my son and Marcus to travel to the games?"

Leonidas looked at the gold aureus and knew it was more than a roman soldier earned in a month. He picked up the coin and looked Aegospotami in the eyes and said, "You are too generous, Aegospotami. This is far too much. I would be happy to donate the services of my slave to bring honor to our Chios. And with your son representing our island I am confident great honor will come to us, for your son has the makings of a true champion."

"I am grateful for your assistance and kind words. I trust my precious son to your hands," Aegospotami replied and then he turned to Nearcus and said, "Come son, we must get you packed now."

CHAPTER 5

The Roman merchant ship was a wide vessel called a ponto. It was 65 feet long and nearly half as wide as it was long. It had one main mast that carried a large square sail held aloft by a giant wooden boom and another smaller square sail was rigged on the large bow sprint. At the stern was a high wood carving of a swan's head that faced aft and reached ten feet above the deck. Aft of the main mast was a cabin built on the main deck. Behind the cabin was an elevated deck where the helmsman stood. At this steering station there was a beam that connected to the two large oars, one situated on each side of the stern. By moving this beam the helmsman could twist the oars which would turn the ship. The ponto carried nearly 250 tons of cargo in its large hold and over 100 passengers on its main deck and in the cabin. The ship was sailed by a crew of sixty experienced and tough seamen. They knew the ship and they knew the sea, but theirs was a clumsy, poor handling vessel and it could only sail with the wind behind it. So if the winds were not right, the ship would not be able to reach its destination as planned.

When Nearcus started down the hill on the road leading to the port city of Limenas he had looked out over the large bay. His eyes had fallen on the ponto and he just knew that of all the ships in the harbor it would be this squatty merchant that would be his passport to reach Corinth.

Leonidas led the Chios team through the port city to the very dock where the ponto was moored. Nearcus was excited and wanted to tell others how he had picked this vessel from the top of the hill. But Nearcus remained silent and stood at the back of the line of athletes and coaches preparing to board the ship. He did not know the others and he was younger than them. There were twenty-six athletes on the men's team along with four coaches and twelve horses that had to be loaded. The youth team consisted of twelve athletes and three coaches. Normally there were only two coaches for the young men, but Marcus was coming to chaperone as well as train Nearcus. The other boys were all fifteen or sixteen years old and did not require escorts. It was the last time they could compete in the youth division because after turning seventeen they were considered men. For a few of them, this was not their first trip off Chios. Nearcus was not the smallest but he definitely was the youngest and he knew it. He kept silent around the others and tried to stay out of everyone's way while he absorbed all the new sights and sounds around him.

As the loading progressed, Leonidas came to Nearcus, pulled him aside and said, "It will be a two day trip to Corinth if the winds are favorable. It is too early in the season to worry about pirates or big storms so I expect you will enjoy the trip. Just trust Marcus to look after you and enjoy yourself. I know you will make your father and all Chios proud. Have a great experience and remember to trust in the gods for your safety and victory."

Nearcus thought it nice that Leonidas would take the time to say farewell to him personally. Yet in spite of the encouraging words, Nearcus grew concerned when he heard Leonidas mention pirates and storms. Nearcus had not even considered those possibilities! He began to think that maybe this trip could be more than just the chance to see Corinth; maybe the journey had dangers he had not realized.

It took several hours for the horses, their feed and all the athletes to be boarded. Then another couple of hours for the rest of the cargo of dates, olive oil and mastic gum to be loaded. Marcus had found a spot on the port edge of the main deck away from the cargo hold hatches and sail rigging where he placed both Nearcus's and his bags. He and Nearcus lay on their bags on the deck away from the deck activity and enjoyed the bright sun. Nearcus had not slept well last night at Leonidas's house because he was too excited for the journey to begin. Now, despite all the shouting by the sailors and the loud squeaking of the hoists lowering the cargo into the holds, Nearcus easily drifted off to sleep under the hot sun.

It was the smell of fish cooking that finally awakened the napping athlete. Raising his head above the bags he was using as a pillow, Nearcus saw Marcus squatted by a small fire flickering in a large metal bowl. Above the flames were two small fish speared on the ends of sharp wooden skewers.

Nearcus sat up and said, "Marcus, is that your lunch already?"

"It is our lunch, Nearcus," the slave responded. "And you have slept well for it is far past lunch time. I believe we will be leaving very soon. It looks like everything is finally loaded."

"I am ready to leave Chios so I say let's go!" Nearcus said as he moved to a position next to Marcus. The slave tested the fish with his hand and being satisfied that it is done enough, he offered a skewer to Nearcus. "Thank you, Marcus. I am also ready to eat—I am hungry!"

"I have brought enough food for us to last three days and water enough for four days if we are careful on how we use it," Marcus said as he ate his fish and took a sip of water from the jug by his side. "If the winds are with us, we should be in Corinth by the time our food and water are gone. But you never know, so we should plan on the worst happening."

Nearcus was impressed by the foresight and care of this slave. Obviously he was more than just a knowledgeable pankration coach. He was also an intelligent and trustworthy companion. Nearcus was glad Marcus was here to guide him.

The tide was running out to sea when the ponto took in its mooring lines and raised the sail. With the wind coming from the northeast it was an easy task for the captain to steer the ship to the open sea. Before long Nearcus lost sight of the land. He was amazed at how quickly the ship seemed to glide through the water. He estimated that the ship with its tons of cargo and people was actually traveling faster than a man could walk! This was exciting to a young boy from a farm on a small Greek island.

Then something happened that Nearcus did not expect and did not like. His stomach started to roll like the ship's hull. He felt queasy and his head started to ache. He realized that to him the rolling motion of the ship was not natural. Nearcus's body seemed to be fighting the constant motion and this was making him very fatigued as well as nauseous. He was about to lay down on his bags when Marcus approached with news.

"Come, Nearcus," he said. "All passengers must assemble before the captain to hear the voyage rules."

All Nearcus wanted to do was to lie down and feel the sea breeze on his face, and to stay near the ship's railing so he could vomit over the side and into the water if he needed. But he did as he was told and accompanied Marcus to where the passengers had gathered in a group. In the middle of the crowd was a short, bald man with a loud voice. Even though Marcus and Nearcus were standing on the outer rim of the crowd, they could easily hear the captain's voice over the wind and creaking sail rigging.

"Look here! You are all just another load of cargo to us. So find your spot out of our way and stay there. Sailing is always a complicated and dangerous enterprise and it is even more so in the early season which we are in now. I won't tolerate you getting in the way of the crew and you will be heaved overboard if you become a nuisance," the captain shouted with complete sincerity. Some of the passengers grumbled that having paid their fare they did not want to be berated like this. But Nearcus took his cue from Marcus who just stood there, his head held high and his eyes focused on the direction of the captain's voice. Nearcus did the same and accepted the directions quietly. In fact, it would please Nearcus very much just to return to his out-of-the-way nest right now and lie down until they reached Corinth. Nearcus was feeling very ill; he was not a good sailor.

Night came quickly and Marcus prepared the evening meal, but Nearcus did not want to eat. He still felt like he was going to vomit the fish they had eaten for lunch. Marcus knew that Nearcus must eat whether he felt like he wanted to or not. So for dinner, Marcus had put a handful of ground oats into a cup of boiling water. Soon the oats had expanded into a thick mush. Marcus insisted that his young athlete eat the entire bowl of this heavy oatmeal. As he always did when Marcus told him to run or exercise, Nearcus followed his coach's direction. Nearcus ate the entire bowl of mush. Before long Nearcus's stomach began to feel better. The sticky, bland mush settled in his stomach and eased the queasy feeling. Nearcus could raise his head without being dizzy and could stand without feeling the need to hang over the rail to vomit. Nearcus began to think that by morning he might be able to enjoy this sea voyage.

The next morning, just as the sun started to peek over the eastern horizon, Nearcus and Marcus watched the crew start their workday. The sailors drew sea water with buckets and then, starting at the bow, scrubbed the entire main deck using stiff bristled brooms. They sang a rhyme over and over as they worked in unison. Nearcus saw that the singing kept their sweeping in a straight line and it kept the crew coordinated and unified in this tedious daily housekeeping chore.

After the ship was cleaned, then little fires started to glow in many cooking pots along the deck. The sailors squatted around the fires and drew their breakfast from a pot of mush, plopping the food into their individual cups. In their other hand each had a piece of hard, flat bread. Many would dip the bread in the mush to soften it before they ate a piece. Nearcus noticed that there was not much being said around the cook fires. It seemed that each man was lost in his own thoughts or he had not completely awakened yet despite the heavy labor before breakfast.

Since the sailors seemed occupied with the morning meal, Nearcus thought it was a good time to walk about and explore this craft. He started by going aft to where the helmsman stood. The skill it took to maneuver the ship impressed the young boy, but the gruff sneer he received from the sailor on watch made Nearcus step back. Without saying a word he turned and retreated toward the front of the deck cabin. As he passed the portholes on the side of the cabin, Nearcus heard the voices of the other youth athletes. He thought it would be good to go inside and visit with them. Since he had joined the team very late, Nearcus had not had the opportunity to get to know his fellow competitors.

As he came to the next porthole he heard something that made him change his mind.

"You do what you like, Dioxippus," said a deep voice, "That kid can fall off the ship and be lost at sea for all I care. But you had better be careful that the captain doesn't find out. He might not like losing a paying customer."

"I know you don't care," said a voice that Nearcus recognized as belonging to Dioxippus, "But you were not the one embarrassed in front of the entire crowd at the trials. Nobody can show me such disrespect and get away with it."

"Do as you feel you must, but remember that it is between you and him. The rest of us have no part in it," said the first voice. Others mumbled their agreement to the statement.

Dioxippus then demanded, "Just stay out of my way."

Upon hearing this, Nearcus quickly moved up the port side of the deck and returned to his bags. As he flopped down, Marcus noticed that something was bothering the young man and asked, "Something the matter, Nearcus?"

Nearcus just shook his head and kept his chin low. The joy in the new day which had such promise just minutes ago was now gone. It was replaced with doubt and worry. Nearcus sat looking out over the passing sea, watching the horizon gently bob up and down while he thought about what he had heard. He remembered that Marcus had told him that Dioxippus was very mean. He remembered, too, that Marcus also said that Nearcus was smarter. He pondered many questions, "If I am so smart, how come I cannot think of what to do? Should I tell Marcus? What if it is just big talk? If I tell Marcus and he talks to Dioxippus then I will be thought of as a baby who cannot take care of himself. I am a pankratiast who represents the island of Chios. It would not do to have the reputation of being a baby." Although he gave it much thought, Nearcus could not decide on the right course to take. For now, he decided he would just stay away from the deck edge. Nearcus thought, "If Dioxippus was to try and push me into the water, I will be sure there is enough room to fight him before he gets me over the side."

The winds remained fair throughout the day. The crew seemed in good spirits because the crossing was going smoothly. The ship made good time and the crew began making plans on how to spend the bonuses they would get if the vessel arrived early to Corinth. But just when all was going smoothly, in the afternoon the wind shifted from directly astern to coming from the north. This pushed the vessel farther south than desired and slowed its speed. Suddenly, the high morale of the crew turned into bitter curses and blasphemous rages against Poseidon and Amphitrite and Triton and all the other gods associated with the sea. After the crew had wailed against the gods, they next started to complain about the passengers. One young, but rather large sailor started to tell others of the crew near him that he had seen one of the passengers praying to a god who hated the sea and seamen. The sailors stopped their work and gathered around this loud troublemaker and asked him what he had seen. Seeing the group form, Nearcus was curious about what was happening. He got up and walked across the deck to be near them and then he bent to a knee pretending to readjust the strap on his sandal. He stayed in this position, unnoticed behind a pile of date-filled bags strapped to the deck, and listened to the conversation.

"I saw that slave over there bowing his head before he ate and say prayers to the god Jesus. Have you ever heard of this god? It was right after he prayed at the mid-day meal that the wind shifted. He has caused us to lose our bonus money!" the young sailor said as he pointed across the cargo hatches towards Marcus.

Nearcus looked at Marcus with a new, questioning thought concerning the slave, "Was Marcus the cause of the bad luck?" He had noticed Marcus praying before, but Nearcus had never thought to ask which of the gods he was beseeching.

As he had these thoughts, another three members of the crew gathered around the large, loud sailor. Some started to agree with him and suggest that it was Marcus's fault that the journey had started to experience troubles.

Just then, the chief mate, a much older and experienced sailor, approached the sailors and shouted, "Look mates, if you don't have enough to do, then I can find something for you to do. Now break it up."

"But Chief, this is important," said the young sailor, "That slave prayed a curse on us to his god and now the wind has shifted."

The chief shook his head and gave a sly smile as he answered, "The wind doesn't need a god to tell it how to move, especially not a god of a slave. Why would a slave want to spend more time at sea? Get to work shipmate before the captain hears you saying such nonsense. The captain is a very suspicious and superstitious man. If he hears you then all of us will suffer from his fears. Just keep quiet and your mind on your work."

The chief went forward to check the rigging on the foresail and the group of sailors watched him leave. As soon as the chief was out of earshot, the young sailor said to the others, "The chief doesn't know as much as he thinks he does. That slave is free from his master as long as we are at sea. If we get pushed off course and land somewhere deserted, then maybe the slave thinks he can escape. I just know that slave and his god are costing us all a lot of money and something should be done about it." All the other sailors nodded.

Nearcus waited until the group of sailors had disbursed before he stood and walked back to where Marcus was watching their bags. He carefully watched the slave. His trust in Marcus's loyalty was not as strong as it was before he heard the sailors talking. Nearcus had begun to doubt just who he could trust. A teammate was planning on throwing him overboard and his chaperone could be trying to use this trip to escape. Nearcus was very confused and he felt very alone and, although he did not want to admit it to himself, he also felt frightened. His wonderful dream trip was becoming a real nightmare. As he pondered his situation another scary thought crossed his mind. That voice had said, "In Corinth you will be chosen." Chosen for what? Nearcus thought, "Maybe I was chosen to die on this voyage to Corinth?"

The sun was starting to quickly fall into the western horizon when Marcus started the dinner cooking fire in the metal pot. Nearcus sat watching the slave work while being sure to keep a position where he could see anyone approaching their location. Throughout the day he had seen a few of the youth team on deck, but Dioxippus and others must have stayed in the cabin because Nearcus had not noticed them all day. But as it began to grow dark, Nearcus knew that Dioxippus might try to sneak up on him and he felt that it was possible that the crew might move against Marcus during the night as well. The pressure on twelve-year old Nearcus was very great and he wanted help from someone somewhere.

As Marcus continued to prepare the meal, Nearcus finally said what was on his mind, "Marcus what god do you pray to before we eat?"

"The great Jehovah and his son, Jesus the Nazarene," Marcus answered simply and honestly.

"Who are they? I do not know those gods. Are they the gods of slaves?"

"Jehovah is the god of everything, young Nearcus," Marcus said in a gentle fatherly voice.

Nearcus was not very interested in the great Jehovah, but he was concerned about the future of his chaperone. So the young athlete asked, "Can Jehovah make Poseidon or Triton angry?"

Marcus was confused by these questions and wanted to know what prompted them. "Why do you ask, Nearcus?"

Nearcus took the plate of boiled beans being handed to him by the slave and took two spoon scoops before he answered, "I am worried. I heard some of the crew blaming you and your Jesus for the change in the wind."

Marcus did something that Nearcus did not expect. He smiled. He shook his head and then smiled even more. Soon the smile grew into a soft chuckle. Nearcus looked at the slave and thought that maybe the slave did not understand how dangerous it was to have the crew mad at him. All Nearcus could do was sit there in surprise and watch Marcus chuckle.

Finally, the slave noticed the concern on Nearcus's face and stopped laughing. He said, "Oh young Nearcus, you are concerned for me! Thank you, but you needn't fear. Jehovah and his son control all and if the wind shifts it is their doing and if the crew thinks I can tell Jehovah or his son what to do and they want to cast me into the sea, then Jehovah and his son will control that as well."

"I do not understand, Marcus. Please answer me plainly. Did you tell your gods to change the wind and delay our arrival on land?"

Marcus made eye contact with the young man and said, "I only pray for our safety and I give thanks for our food and water and lives."

"Then we should tell the crew so they do not try to harm you."

Again, Marcus was smiling at Nearcus as he responded, "The crew are blinded to the truth and will not be convinced by anything I say. My fate is only in the hands of Jehovah and Jesus. Now eat your dinner and fear not. Your fate is in their hands as well."

Nearcus was even more confused now. But something in the way that Marcus told him to "fear not" made the young athlete feel better. But regardless of what the slave said, Nearcus knew that he was not going to get any sleep that night. He would be awake throughout the dark and on alert for Dioxippus and the crew.

CHAPTER 6

By the time the ship's watch changed in the middle of the night the weather had grown more severe. The wind continued to come from the north and it had increased in strength. The calm seas of the afternoon had grown rough as the night progressed. With each passing hour the tempest in the Aegean Sea grew worse. Soon the choppy waves began to crest and the foam from the wave tops blew across the flat deck of the ship. The hull pitched violently up and down as it rolled from side to side. Marcus had tied a rope to the port railing and given one end to Nearcus and he held the other end. The young man wrapped the rope around one wrist and tightly held onto it with both hands. All Nearcus wanted now was for the ship to stop throwing him back and forth. All he wanted was to get off this ship and get back on dry land.

The storm had arrived rapidly and it smothered the sailboat with a thick blanket of clouds that hid the stars. Now the night was totally black and Nearcus wanted not only to be on dry land but in the sunshine. Everything was more frightening in the dark. He wanted light again. And he did not want to feel alone in the dark anymore.

"Marcus? Are you alright?" Nearcus said in a loud voice to be heard over the noise of the sea slamming against the ship and the sail rigging slapping in the wind. There was no answer coming from the darkness around him. He cried out louder, "Marcus? Are you there?"

Nearcus felt his heart jump when a hand touched his shoulder. Then he heard Marcus's voice, "I am here, Nearcus. Fear not, we are safe."

"But the storm, Marcus! The gods are angry at us! We may perish!" Nearcus did not want to sound so frightened, but he could not help it. And it made him a little angry that this slave did not understand the true danger.

"We will not perish. God had has told me that we will see Corinth."

Nearcus was confused by what Marcus said, but he wanted to believe that the storm would pass and that he would be safe. The young man was about to ask the slave how the god told him that, but he was interrupted by shouts coming out of the darkness. There were heavy steps on the deck and the sound of men scurrying about the ship. Nearcus tried to peer through the heavy, salty mist and blackness to see what was being done. But he could not make out what exactly was taking place. He asked himself, "Were the crew coming to throw Marcus overboard to appease Poseidon and the other sea gods? Should I fight to defend the slave? Or is the crew right?"

The next voice Nearcus heard loud and clear over the din of the storm and the shouts of other men eased his fear a little. He heard the chief mate yell, "Standby your main halyard and both sheets and prepare to lower away!"

Out of the night came the voices of many men replying to the chief. Then the chief shouted a warning, "All hands stand clear of the mainsail boom. Now lower away!"

Nearcus heard a loud, slow squeal as the ropes holding the mainsail aloft started to slide through their guides. Then the squeal grew higher as the speed of the long, thick pole that held the top of the mainsail started to accelerate as it was lowered. A frightened, panicky voice from one of the crewmen was heard over the noise of the storm and the rigging, "There she goes! Look out!"

Suddenly Nearcus was hit by a flying body. Nearcus's first thought was that Dioxippus was using the storm to attack him. However, he quickly realized that it was Marcus who had grabbed him and threw him to the deck, the slave's body landing on top of the athlete. The surprise attack coming from the dark knocked the wind from Nearcus's lungs. He was stunned and gasping for breath when a tremendous crash shook the entire ship. The sound of splintering wood and the cries of panicked men filled the dark night. Nearcus's breathing problems were made worse by the sudden weight and smothering effect of a heavy wet canvas covering both Marcus and him. Nearcus coughed and gasped for air. Marcus put his palms on the rolling deck and pressed his arms upward to remove weight from Nearcus's chest. This helped the young man to fill his lungs. In short order the coughing and gasping stopped and Nearcus could breathe again.

The deck continued to roll and pitch and now it had taken on a slant to the left. This alarmed the two travelers pinned on the deck below the fallen mainsail. They fought hard to free themselves from the heavy wet canvas because they both were afraid that the ship might slide under the water while they were trapped in this mess of sail and ropes. Just as real panic started to build in Nearcus he heard a voice in the dark that helped him control his emotions. Once again it was the voice of the chief mate shouting over the noise of the storm and the crew's confusion.

In a clear and unconcerned tone, the chief bellowed, "Alright you lousy seamen. That was a real disaster. Let's get this sail furled and the boom secured. Send for the carpenters and have them report to me immediately."

There was no panic or fear in the chief mate's direction. The effect his voice had on Nearcus and Marcus and the entire crew was amazing. The rising panic ebbed away. The fear of the boat tipping over and sliding under the sea no longer existed. There was much work to do, but the chief's voice gave everyone confidence that all would be well. The storm might be fierce, but it was no match for the chief.

Under the fallen sail, Nearcus and Marcus were finally successful in getting free of the canvas. Marcus was the first to get to his feet and he reached down to help Nearcus stand. As the deck pitched and rolled, Marcus reached for the ship's rail to steady himself. In the total darkness Marcus did not see that the rail was missing, having been smashed by the falling mail sail boom. Marcus lost his balance and was leaning over the edge, about to fall overboard. He grasped Nearcus to stop his fall. The athlete tensed his body and resisted the slave's pull in a natural reaction that was the result of all his pankration training. With this strong support to hold onto, Marcus was saved from going into the sea.

Marcus stepped back, away from the deck's edge and turned to face Nearcus. Out of the dark, the slave saw two faces appear behind Nearcus's shoulders. Facing him was the very angry captain and the large young sailor who blamed Marcus for the earlier wind shift. The captain pushed Nearcus to the side and the youth lost his footing on the pitching deck and fell to his knees. The captain stepped forward to get just inches from the larger slave and said in a loud and mean voice, "Are you and your god the cause for this bad fortune? I demand to know! Tell me now or we will throw you to the sea!"

Just then a bolt of lightening flashed across the sky. It was so near the ship that the thunder sounded like an explosion overhead. In the light flash Nearcus clearly saw the three men above him. Marcus stood tall and erect, his face without fear. The short captain looked up at the slave with panic in his eyes and worry shaking his whole body. The young sailor crouched to the same height as the captain and reached for the officer's arm in fear. That scene witnessed in just a split second of lightening would stay in Nearcus's memory forever. At that moment he held Marcus in awe and wanted to be like him, brave and confident.

"You are the cause! You asked your god to destroy us! Why would you do that? You are an evil devil who brings nothing but misfortune to all of us! We beg you to jump into the sea and take your evil from us! Your presence on my ship has angered Poseidon and all the gods of the sea. They will torment this ship until you leave. Now save us! Leap into the sea!" the captain cried out in panic. As he pleaded, the large, strong sailor behind him was shaking and crying like a baby.

Nearcus took in all of this and it confused and angered him. How could these grown men quiver in the face of gods who mistreated them? When Nearcus had been let down and mistreated by the gods he had just spit and turned his back to them. He thought, "Maybe these adults know more than I do? Maybe it is not Marcus the gods are angry with, maybe it is me. Maybe everyone on the ship is in danger because of me."

Marcus continued to stand there without responding. The captain opened his mouth and started to curse Marcus when the chief mate arrived. Having heard the captain's shouting he had come to see what the commotion was about.

The chief spoke before the captain could continue, "Captain, I know you want a good report. The mast is still strong and the stays were not damaged by the poor seamanship in reefing the sail. The deck railing will be repaired by the carpenters in the morning. The sail is being furled and the boom lashed down. We will maintain steerage way by use of the jib until the storm passes. No casualties reported. All is under control, Captain."

Once again, the calm professional demeanor and voice of the chief had eased worry and chased away fear. The captain broke his glare at Marcus and turned to the chief and said, "Very well, Chief. I want this man watched and prohibited from praying to his gods. If the storm does not pass by mid-morning I will know this slave is responsible for our ill fortune."

The captain made his way across the pitching deck to the main cabin. The chief turned his glare to the seaman. Once the captain had moved far enough away not to be able to see or hear, the senior sailor put his face just inches from the seaman's nose and shouted, "You make an ass look smart! I warned you about going to the captain with your stupid ideas and silly fears! I cannot abide a slimy coward like you." The seaman continued to cower and seemed to fear the chief more than the tempest. The chief stepped back a foot and then continued, "You caused the captain to get involved so now you can carry out his orders. You must stand right here until mid-morning watching the slave. You must make sure he does not pray to his gods."

"But chief, how can I do that? He could pray without bowing his head!"

"You're the cause of that stupid order, so you are going to carry it out," the chief said as he turned to attend to his many other duties on this very rough night at sea.

As the chief finished speaking another bolt of lightening blasted across the black sky. Again the thunder broke over the tossing vessel like a wave crashing into the shore. This time a furious downpour of hard rain accompanied the flash and crash. The intensity of the rain made it grow even darker and more frightening. Nearcus was still on his knees and as the rain drenched his face he looked up at the men in front of him. This storm was a new experience for Nearcus. It was his first exposure to real danger, and it was not over yet. If he had been looking behind him he would have seen even more and greater danger hidden within the tangled sail that was draped over the deck cargo. He would have seen Dioxippus slowly and carefully making his way towards his back.

CHAPTER 7

The driving rain, the blowing sea foam, the wildly rocking deck and the fear shown by the crew all combined to make the night a perilous situation. Rather than attempt to stand up, Nearcus remained sitting on the deck. He reached for something to hold on to. In the dark his hands found the lashing ropes that held the deck cargo of olive oil barrels secured to the ship. These were strong lines that were taking the beating of the storm well. Nearcus decided that he was going to clutch these robes and put his face close to the deck to keep the rain and sea spray from stinging his eyes and nose until the morning came. All Nearcus wanted in life at this moment was for the sun to rise; he knew all would be better in the light.

Unfortunately, the position Nearcus had decided to hold until morning made him a perfect target for Dioxippus. With his face close to the deck, Nearcus could not see anything around him. Dioxippus was not sure of what he intended to do to Nearcus, but he was certain he needed to repay the younger boy for the great embarrassment he had suffered. Dioxippus did not know if Nearcus could swim, but the storm was a perfect opportunity to throw his teammate overboard to find out. Everyone would think he was swept away by the storm. But if that was not possible, then Dioxippus figured he could use the confusion to beat the younger boy severely. Dioxippus was determined that Nearcus was to suffer in some way before the sun rose again.

Marcus was still standing in front of the quivering young sailor. The slave saw that the seaman was no threat to him now that the captain had retreated. So Marcus calmly took a seat on the deck. With both legs crossed and his hands on each side to support him, Marcus was able to keep his position despite the chaotic movement of the deck. The young sailor just stood there, staring at the slave and fighting to keep his balance while not knowing what to do next. In the dark, he did not see the swift and agile figure slide behind Marcus.

Dioxippus slipped behind the olive oil barrels and held his position to wait for another flash of lightening in order to see what was around him. He did not have to wait long for very quickly another bolt lighted the sky, immediately followed by thunder's crash. In that split second of light, Dioxippus saw the sailor wobbling as he struggled to remain standing, the back of Marcus as the slave sat facing the other direction, and his prey, Nearcus, spread out face down on the deck the other side of the barrels. Deftly, with the sound of the heavy rain and wind masking his noise, Dioxippus moved closer to Nearcus. Once in position, the older boy timed his next action to the roll of the deck. As it rose up, Dioxippus rode up with it and upon the downward fall he lunged for Nearcus. He landed squarely on Nearcus's back. The surprise jolt and crushing weight forced Nearcus to exhale all of his breath. When he tried to draw more air into his lungs, the pressure of Dioxippus on his back made it next to impossible to breathe.

This time Nearcus knew it was not Marcus who had tackled him. This time Nearcus knew who his attacker was. And all fear left him because this time he knew he was going to fight Dioxippus without the handicap of a fever and a hole in his jaw. This time Nearcus was going to show the older bully that he picked on the wrong victim.

Instantly, Nearcus pulled his elbows under his chest and forced both his own body and Dioxippus to rise. This

70

enabled him to draw a full breath. Now that he had air in his lungs, with great speed that once again amazed Dioxippus, the young boy kicked his legs to the right to free them from his attacker. In one rapid motion, Nearcus next pulled his knees under him and twisted to his left until he could hook Dioxippus's waist with his left arm. Speedily Nearcus pulled his head from under the older boy's chest and with the same motion rolled onto Dioxippus's back. In less than a half second, Nearcus had used his speed to totally reverse the situation on his attacker, doing it so swiftly that Dioxippus did not sense what was happening and could not react. Next Nearcus rammed his left forearm under the older boy's chin. Nearcus cinched-up his choke hold tighter and tighter. The adrenaline pulsing through Nearcus's veins allowed him to apply sufficient pressure to his attacker's neck to bring about unconsciousness in just a matter of seconds. Once Dioxippus went limp, Nearcus did not release his choke hold as he would do in pankration competition. Rather, he just loosened it to allow Dioxippus to breathe, but Nearcus was not going to give up his advantage until the older boy understood that he did not wish to be his enemy.

The ruckus in the dark had gotten the attention of Marcus and his guard. The fight was so short that neither of them was able to react before it was over. Marcus shouted over the wind and rain, "Young Nearcus! Is everything alright?"

Nearcus did not answer. He was unsure what to say. After all, he had subdued his attacker for now, but everything was not alright if he would have to look over his shoulder for the rest of his life. Finally, the young boy said in a loud voice, "I am safe for now, but this man attacked me."

Marcus moved towards the sound of the voice. In just a few feet he reached the two athletes coupled in a wrestling posture. More by feel than sight, Marcus determined the position of the two combatants. As Marcus reached the boys,

71

Dioxippus regained consciousness and started to struggle. Nearcus reapplied pressure to his attacker's throat and said through clinched teeth, "Stop it or I will put you to sleep again!"

Dioxippus relaxed his body and tried to nod in understanding. He was having trouble keeping the heavy rain from his eyes and nose, so breathing was extremely difficult.

Marcus yelled a question at Dioxippus, "What are you doing? What are you trying to do?"

Between the rain and Nearcus's tight hold, Dioxippus was unable to answer. Nearcus finally answered his coach, "Dioxippus here felt I embarrassed him at the trials and he wanted to get even by throwing me overboard."

Marcus sat back in surprise and shock when he heard what was said. He could not believe that anyone would seek such severe harm to a competitor over being embarrassed. He knew that Dioxippus was a bully, but still the idea of harming a teammate over a perceived grudge was just too far-fetched for Marcus to comprehend. After a few moments of reflection on just how unbelievable Dioxippus's intentions were, Marcus was able to shout over the storm, "Dioxippus are you crazy? You would kill someone for embarrassing you?"

Upon hearing himself called crazy, the older boy got extremely angry and struggled to get free, but Nearcus held him in an inescapable hold. Nearcus ignored the point of Marcus's question and shouted to his captive, "I did not try to embarrass you! I was sick and passed out before I could make you submit!"

Nearcus felt Dioxippus relax upon hearing this. The older boy thought about what he had heard. He considered that maybe at the trials Nearcus was not trying to show that the only way Dioxippus could beat him was by Nearcus giving up and letting the older boy win. Maybe there was another reason Nearcus had quit the bout.

Upon feeling Dioxippus's muscles relax, Nearcus continued talking, "Can I let you go now? Are you going to stop trying to hurt me?"

Dioxippus nodded slowly. Nearcus cautiously released his hold on the older boy. Dioxippus moved to the side and rubbed his neck. Another flash of lightening illuminated the sky and another loud clap of nearby thunder immediately followed. This gave Marcus the opportunity to see the eyes of Dioxippus. He did not like what he saw there. The older boy was bitter and angry. Marcus was sure that Dioxippus still wanted to hurt Nearcus and only was behaving right now because he knew that Nearcus was good enough to win any fight that might be started. And Marcus sensed that Dioxippus was not the type of young man to do anything he would have to answer for in front of any adult. Marcus was sure that somewhere in Dioxippus's life he had developed a belief that he could only win by being a bully. Marcus felt anger and love towards the young man. He was angry that Dioxippus posed a threat to Nearcus and yet he felt great sadness that this sixteen-year old boy was so full of self-hate that he had to strike out at others to make himself feel big. Despite the seaman being only feet away, Marcus did pray to his god. Silently he asked God and Jesus to take the pain and hate from the heart of this bully.

Once he had finished talking to God, Marcus spoke to the boys, "You young men are teammates, here to represent Chios in the best possible fashion. Your families and neighbors want to take pride in you. How can they be proud if you are trying to hurt each other? You don't have to best friends, but you must cooperate. You understand?"

Nearcus and Dioxippus may have thought they were young adults before Marcus spoke to them. But after he was done, each was reminded that they were not fully grown yet and, though even a slave, Marcus was a man; someone who they realized knew more than them and that they must obey. Sitting in the dark, each with his own thoughts,

Nearcus and Dioxippus had the same desire. Both just wanted the rain to stop, the sun come up and the ship to stop rocking so much. They wanted to put this long, treacherous night behind them and start a new day afresh. In the sunlight and wearing dry clothes the world would look better and dark things would disappear. If only the sun would come up. And they were not alone in their hopes. Every person on that storm tossed ship wished the same thing. But none of them knew that they were about to find out that sometimes the daylight could be more treacherous than the night.

CHAPTER 8

The black night had slowly given way to a gray morning. The wind and rain and rough seas continued with just as much force, but in the early morning light things began to look more reasonable. The chief mate made rounds between all the working parties on deck that were repairing part of the previous night's damage. The deck hands cleared the sail by rolling it around the heavy, large boom that had crashed to the deck the night before. The carpenters directed other sailors on clearing away the crushed railing sections so that work could begin on the repairs. Other sailors built small tent-like structures over their cooking pots in order to start small fires to cook a hot breakfast. While the chief kept each sailor busy helping to complete all the necessary work to make the ship seaworthy again, the little captain strutted back and forth on the raised deck aft by the helmsman. The captain was angry and frightened and he was not very good at hiding his emotions. Whenever one of the crew would look to the aft deck he could sense the fear that engulfed the captain. Whenever a crew member would look at the chief, who was all business and calmly professional, he would get a sense of hope that maybe the situation was not that bad.

But the tempest continued to beat the ponto with large waves and driving winds. The rain from the low, gray clouds was so intense that often times the morning horizon was blotted out completely. In fact, three hours after sunrise the storm had only grown more severe. The crew was exhausted from working through the night and all morning. Their fatigue began to drain their hope of surviving, no matter how confident they were in the chief. The captain was afraid and so they felt they should be afraid as well.

Then something happened that made them even more terrified of the sea. The carpenter crew on the forward starboard side were concentrating on fitting a newly cut board into a missing section of the railing when it happened. Out of the dark and wild ocean a creature rocketed into the air so close to the ship that members of the working party could have touched it had they reached out over the edge of the ship. The creature was massive, with glistening black rubber for skin and a flat-nosed head around a gapping mouth full of razor sharp teeth. The creature rolled in the air as it shot past the ship, revealing its white underbelly just before it crashed into the angry waves.

For hundreds of years, sailors around the Mediterranean and Aegean Seas had heard stories of a giant fish that could leap from the water to smash ships and devour their crews in just a few mouthfuls. Stories abounded about mean and terrifying sea monsters with an intelligence and nastiness unmatched even by many of the gods. But after years of earning a living on the sea without ever seeing such a creature, most veteran sailors had come to believe that the Orca stories were just fables told to scare young seamen. The sight of this massive, black, fierce whale flying out of the angry sea and crashing down with such force that the ship shuddered and swayed when hit by the fish's wake was enough to scare everyone.

The forward carpenter crew ran from their station, scrambling over the cargo hatches and across the sail being furled on the deck. The fright on their faces was enough to scare all who saw them. Soon the entire crew was rapidly talking about what some of them had seen. The excited conversation and panic in those who had seen the Orca breech close aboard the vessel soon spread to the passengers assembled in the main cabin. Grown men began to wail and cry loudly in prayers to Poseidon to save them from this sea monster. On the aft deck, the captain stopped his pacing and stood perfectly still, frozen in one place with fear. In his mind he was sure that his ship was doomed and would soon be broken apart by this killer whale. He knew that someone onboard must have angered the gods to such a high degree that they are determined to sink this ship and drown—or have the Orca devour—all souls onboard. And the captain was sure he knew who was causing his ship's troubles.

"Bring that slave to me right now!" the captain bellowed above the noise of the storm and the panicked cries of the crew and passengers. Two of the sailors by the main cabin knew who the captain wanted and they quickly ran to where Marcus was sitting next to Nearcus. Without a single word they snatched the slave to his feet and pulled him aft.

Across the main deck the chief saw the two sailors dragging Marcus towards the captain who was standing by the helmsman. The chief knew that something terrible was about to happen to an innocent man. The chief did not believe that the storm was caused by gods and he was sure that the sea monster was just a big fish looking for food near the surface. In his mind he was surrounded by weak men who would rather blame their misfortune on non-existent gods than have to own their personal responsibility to work hard to achieve what they wanted. When he was a junior seaman he had seen how a mob's mentality can harm innocents. He had witnessed a young mother and her three-month old daughter thrown overboard at the height of a terrible storm by a panicked crew because it was believed that the baby's crying was a bad omen that irritated the gods. He clearly remembered how superstition and trusting your fate to gods resulted in the death of two innocents. It was a full twelve hours after the mother and daughter had been thrown overboard that the storm had ended. The chief knew that the average life of a severe sea squall in the Aegean Sea is less than twelve hours, so the killing of the innocent passengers did not make any difference in what happened. And the chief had made a promise to himself that he would fight superstition and brutality brought about by a stupid belief in gods and never let such a thing happen again if he could prevent it.

The chief pushed his way next to Marcus just as the captain finished pointing at the slave and accusing him of being the cause of the voyage's misfortunes. The captain screamed in a frightened voice, "Slave you are guilty of sabotaging this trip. You have angered Poseidon by praying to your slave god. Now you must renounce your god and pray to Poseidon to please the sea god and save us from the storm and sea monsters! Do it now!"

The chief could tell by looking into Marcus's calm face that this man was not intimidated by the demands and threats of the captain, nor did the slave worry about angering Poseidon. The chief knew that Marcus was not going to renounce his god; he could see it in the slave's face and demeanor. The chief was right. Marcus stood there silently and did nothing to answer the captain.

"You renounce your god and pray for Poseidon's forgiveness now! Either you turn Poseidon's wrath from us or we will please him by offering you as a sacrifice!" the captain shouted with even less control of his emotions. The captain was very frightened and showed himself to be a coward, unworthy of command. His fear was contagious and the entire crew pressed closer to Marcus. They all swayed with the movement of the pitching deck and jostled each other trying to get close enough to lay hands on Marcus. Standing right behind Marcus was Nearcus, pressed by the crowd of frightened adults towards his teacher and friend.

The chief knew he must act now or Marcus was doomed to be thrown into the sea. The chief climbed onto the aft deck and pushed his way to the captain's side. He was afraid that the frenzy of the crowd may have grown too intense to stop what was about to happen to Marcus. But the chief knew his captain well and had a plan on how to appease the fear of those onboard. The chief knew that the fear was born of ignorance, superstition and fatigue, but that did not make it any less dangerous for innocent Marcus — in fact, it probably made the slave's position even worse.

"Captain!" the chief shouted into the ear of his superior in order to be heard over the commotion of the storm and the shouts of the mob below. "Do not let this man be thrown overboard! It is clear what we are in the middle of! This slave's god has taken up battle with Poseidon and we are caught in the middle of it! If we throw this slave into the ocean then we have taken sides in the battle and what if his god is more powerful than Poseidon? We do not know about his god and so he may be even fiercer than an angry Poseidon. Our best hope is to stay out of a battle between the gods over this man! Let the gods war against each other — but let's not take sides because to do so would only make one of the gods our enemy!"

Upon hearing what his chief mate said, the captain grew sullen and silent. The last thing he wanted to do was make a god more powerful than Poseidon angry at him. The more he thought about what the chief said the more confused and undecided the captain became.

Nearcus was nearly swallowed by the crowd pushing him closer and closer to Marcus's back. The young athlete had only wanted to see the sights of Corinth and have an adventure off of Chios, but so far his trip has been full of terrible experiences. Now he was worried and confused about what will happen next. He thought things would be better in the morning, but they have grown worse; the weather so bad, the killer monster after the ship and the angry adults trying to please their gods by killing Marcus. Yet, one thing kept coming back into his mind. Marcus had said that Jesus had told him that they would reach Corinth. Nearcus thought, "Then your Jesus had better do something right now Marcus or you will never see Corinth."

"Captain," the chief mate said, "We should offer up this slave to the gods and let them decide what to do with him."

Upon hearing this, the captain turned to the chief and asked, "How?"

"Let us tie him to the boom and hoist him aloft with the mainsail. Leave him strapped to the top of the ship and tell the gods that they can decide what to do with him. Let Poseidon and this slave's god fight for his life. If he is still alive when the storm passes and there is no further sighting of the monster then we will know that his god has won this battle with Poseidon. If he is dead when we bring him down, then we know that Poseidon is more powerful. Either way, he is there for the gods to fight over and we will no longer be a part of the battle."

The captain had no ideas of his own. So he quickly nodded in agreement with the chief's solution. The chief immediately took charge of the situation and had Marcus brought to the base of the main mast. He explained what was to be done to appease the gods and the sailors eagerly prepared the boom to accept the slave.

Marcus's arms were spread wide and his wrists tightly bound to the large pole. The chief inspected the lashings and order them changed. Under the chief's direction, rope was used to lace the slave's entire arms, from shoulder to wrist, to the boom. A separate line was passed under Marcus's arms and tied to the pole. As the seaman finished their task, the chief brought a jar of fresh water to Marcus. The chief leaned closely by the slave's ear and told him privately, "Drink all of this. You will need it when the sun comes out again."

Marcus did as he was told, and after he had finished he told the chief, "Thank you, may the Lord bless you for your kindness."

The chief was surprised by the sincere words of a slave about to be crucified to the top of a tall mast in a terrible storm and left there until the danger had passed. He said into Marcus's ear again, "I did the best I could. I had them tie your entire arms and chest so you will not suffocate while you hang there. I hope your god can sustain you."

"My Lord can and he will. He will take us to Corinth."

When the rest of the rigging was complete, the chief stood back and gave the signal to raise the main sail. All crew members pulled on the main halyards in a coordinated rhythm of pull, grab more rope, and then pull together. Higher and higher the sail went up. With each unified jerk of the halyards Marcus felt pain run from under his arms to the base of his feet. Every time he was raised another foot the muscles in his shoulders burned with an even more intense fire. Marcus had never felt such pain in his entire life. Yet he did not cry out. He closed his eyes and did what the captain had ordered him not to do. He prayed to God. He did not ask for the pain to be taken from him. The slave actually gave thanks that God thought him worthy enough to suffer for his Christ. Jesus, who was sinless, had died on a cross. Marcus knew he was a sinner and yet God had selected him to share in the glory of His son. Yes, Marcus gave thanks.

On the rolling, pitching main deck the passengers stood looking up into the driving rain. They held onto whatever they could find and onto each other to steady themselves. No longer a shouting, jeering, panicked mob, they stood in silence and watched Marcus's fate. The calm, quiet peace they saw in his face puzzled them. Where was the anguish? Where were the fear and the pain? Where was the suffering?

Nearcus did not notice the rain anymore. The water beat against his face, but his eyes were fixated on his teacher. The young boy was confused and troubled. Three days ago he was chopping wood at his home. Now this morning he was being tossed about in a storm after a terrifying, sleepless night and he was looking at his mentor hung from the top of the mast as punishment for not worshipping Poseidon.

Nearcus deeply regretted ever wanting to see Corinth. However, he knew he was learning something. The gods are not fickle like he thought after he lost his bout at the trials; now he sees that they are useless and mean and arbitrary. The gods do not care about him or his family. Nearcus has learned that he will never ask a god for anything and that he will fight the rest of his life to keep the gods from having anything to do with his fate. The gods of his father fail his family continually. And even Marcus's god has failed him; he is hanging from the boom atop a tempest tossed ship. Nearcus knows that from now on he will fight the gods and take his life into his own hands. He will never let the gods play with him like they do with the captain and Marcus.

As Nearcus stared at Marcus he felt someone bump into him. He turned to see Dioxippus standing there, looking up at Marcus suspended high above the deck.

The older boy said, "Why doesn't your paedotribae cry out? He seems so calm? Where is his anger at his god? What kind of man is he?"

Nearcus did not answer Dioxippus, but slipped away from the bully quickly. From the other side of the deck, Nearcus looked at his team mate and saw that the older boy was not interested in him. Rather, Dioxippus kept his vision on Marcus.

Eventually, Dioxippus took a seat on the deck and spent hours in the heavy rain and rough seas just looking up at Marcus. On the pankratiast's face was no longer the scowl of a bully but the innocent curiosity of a young man who was seeing something he had never seen before.

CHAPTER 9

Hours passed and the storm continued to beat the ship. But late in the afternoon the wind shifted back to the northeast. Then the rain lessened from a torrent to a drizzle. Then it stopped completely and the wind grew less. After the wind stopped driving the seas the waves became smaller and the ship stopped being violently tossed about. The storm front had finally passed. With a steady wind from the northeast, the ponto was making excellent speed towards Corinth. The spirits of the crew begun to rise and the panic of the passengers passed as quickly as the storm died down.

On the deck in front of the mast sat Dioxippus, still looking up at Marcus. The young man had not moved from this position since he first sat down. He had watched Marcus rock side to side, swaying with the motion of the mast in the high winds and rough seas. He had seen Marcus gulp for air and shake his head to clear the water from his eyes as the rain continually pounded his face. On a couple of occasions during the long afternoon, Dioxippus thought that the slave had died. The man had hung limp in his bonds without moving for minutes. However, eventually Marcus would regain consciousness and lift his head to the sky once more. Dioxippus could tell that the slave was praying to his god. He wanted to know what Marcus was saying. Was he cursing his god for not helping him? Was he asking his god to reign down destruction on his tormenters? Was he forsaking his god and praying to Poseidon for help? How could he still be alive after all these hours? Dioxippus wanted to know so he had not left his position since the sail and Marcus had been raised.

Nearcus had returned to the spot on the deck where he and Marcus had made their home for the voyage. He sat there in the rain with his back to the olive oil barrels and he kept his chin and eyes down. He did not want the rain in his face and he did not want to think about Marcus. From his position just aft of the main mast he was not able to see Marcus suffering on the front of the sail. About every hour Nearcus went forward and looked up at Marcus to see if he was dead yet. Once he saw Marcus move, he returned to his spot on deck and lowered his chin again. When the rain lessened a little, Nearcus started to look out over the seas. He wanted to see the monster coming if the ship was attacked again. If the gods were going to send a creature to devour him, Nearcus wanted to see it coming so he could put up his best fight. Nearcus was mad at the gods and with his current attitude he knew that the gods would have to fight to take him.

Nearcus saw no monster. All he saw was the sea grow less violent and the waves diminish with each passing minute. Soon he stopped thinking about sea creatures and gods and thought of Marcus hanging atop the mast. Nearcus felt he should try to help his paedotribae and chaperone. So he left his spot on the deck to seek out the chief mate.

"Sir!" Nearcus said to the chief as the leader briskly walked forward on the deck. "Sir! I must speak to you!"

The chief brushed by Nearcus and said over his shoulder, "What is it young man? I am very busy."

"I don't want the captain to get in serious trouble, sir," Nearcus said in the hope of getting the chief's full attention. His choice of words worked and the chief stopped and turned to face the young athlete.

"What do you mean?"

"That slave hanging from the top of the mainsail belongs to a very wealthy and powerful merchant on Chios named Leonidas. The merchant is known across the island as a man who is very proud and protective of his property. I am afraid that if Leonidas lost a very valuable piece of property he would make serious trouble for the captain's cargo business. If that slave dies from what the captain has done, it will be very bad for business. Leonidas is not a man the captain wants as an enemy. Now that all is calm and there is no monster attacking the ship, can you ask the captain to cut the slave down in the hope that he is still alive?"

The chief looked deeply into Nearcus's eyes and thought to himself, "Here is a smart boy. Rather than plead for the slave's life, he has thought of a good reason for the captain to do what the boy wishes. Yes, this is an intelligent young man."

A small smile came over the chief's lips as he said to Nearcus, "I will see what can be done."

Nearcus lost sight of the chief who carried on with his duties. About fifteen minutes later the chief reappeared and ordered four sailors to climb the rigging to the main boom and to take along a long length of rope. Once aloft, the sailors tied the rope around Marcus's chest. Then they cut the ropes binding his arms and chest to the boom. Slowly they lowered the injured and suffering slave to the deck with the long rope. Now that the seas were calm and the sun was peacefully setting on the western horizon, none of the crew or passengers took any notice that Marcus was being freed. The danger had passed and the adults had no interest in a slave who had received what they thought was a just punishment.

Waiting to catch Marcus was Dioxippus, his arms stretched out to grab and guide the slave to a soft landing on the deck. The young man gently lowered the injured and exhausted Marcus onto his back and then Dioxippus removed the rope from around the slave's body. Then he rushed to a water cask nearby to get water for Marcus. He helped the paedotribae lift his head and sip from the cup. Just then, Nearcus approached the two lying on the deck hatch and knelt beside his teacher.

"Marcus, how do you feel?" said Nearcus.

Talking was very hard for the exhausted man so he chose his words very carefully. First he looked at Dioxippus and said, "Thank you and God bless you for your watch and the water." And then he looked at Nearcus and said, "I told you Jesus promised we would both reach Corinth."

After saying that, Marcus turned his head and closed his eyes and gave into much needed sleep. Without saying anything, Dioxippus and Nearcus who just hours before were fierce enemies, together lifted Marcus and carried him to the spot that was home for this terrible voyage. Carefully they laid the exhausted and injured slave down and covered him with robes from Nearcus's bag.

The two team mates then sat back and after watching Marcus sleep they looked at each other. Nearcus had been confused by the bully's vigil at the foot of the mast all afternoon and he still did not trust Dioxippus. But as he looked into Dioxippus's eyes he could sense something had changed. He no longer saw the angry, mean older boy he had fought before.

Dioxippus was not aware he might look differently to others. He only knew he was confused and curious about what he had seen that day. After hesitating for a minute, the older boy spoke.

"Tell me about your paedotribae. I want to know how he could be so calm when they seized him and how he could survive being crucified on the mast."

These questions were not what Nearcus expected to hear from his enemy. The bully he knew Dioxippus to be would have asked why Marcus had been such a fool to have let others take him. But now he wanted to know about how the slave was able to endure such punishment.

Nearcus thought for a moment and then answered, "Marcus was not born a slave; he was a young soldier in Thessalonica when he was taken captive."

Dioxippus nodded when he heard this for it made sense to him that the slave's bravery could come from having been trained as a soldier. Dioxippus used his eyes to express to his team mate to continue.

"I have known him for ten months. He belongs to Leonidas who loans him to our training camp to prepare athletes for the games. I know Marcus is very wise and that he has never asked me to do anything that could hurt me. He is supportive of what I want and has always helped me to reach my goals."

Dioxippus looked over both his shoulders and then leaned closer to Nearcus before he asked his next question for he did not want anyone else to hear what he was going to say, "Can you tell me about his god that he would die for?"

Nearcus also looked around the deck before he softly answered, "He says he belongs to Jehovah and Jesus the Nazarene. But that is all I know about them. Marcus said that they control the whole world."

"Are they only gods of slaves?"

"I don't know," Nearcus answered, "But I don't think so because Marcus said Jesus told him both of us would reach Corinth safely."

Dioxippus surprised Nearcus with what he said next, "Can I stay here with you tonight to guard over him? With the two of us, one can sleep while the other watches. It will be morning before we make port and I don't trust the crew or other adults. They may still try to throw him overboard in the night. Maybe this slave's Jesus could use our help to get him to Corinth safely."

Nearcus thought, "Last night, Dioxippus, you tried to throw me overboard and now you want to be here while I sleep?" But Nearcus thought that his team mate could be right about the crew or passengers still wanting to kill Marcus. So he nodded to Dioxippus that it would be alright, but to himself Nearcus decided to keep awake all night to watch Dioxippus.

Nearcus and Dioxippus cooked a dinner of grain and fish and shared it. Marcus continued to sleep without moving a muscle. After dark, Nearcus said he would sleep first and laid down with his head resting against a bag. He shut his eyes and pretended to sleep, but he kept alert to be ready should Dioxippus try anything. If he had known what the three of them would have to face on their trip to Corinth starting the next day, Nearcus would have slept as much as possible to prepare his strength for the challenges that lay ahead.

CHAPTER 10

Dioxippus was unable to sleep when it was his turn. Too many questions were racing through his mind and his thoughts were too confused to sleep. After a short while he gave up the effort and sat up. With Marcus lying peacefully between them, Dioxippus and Nearcus sat facing each other. This night was not as dark as the previous evening. Stars filled the ocean's canopy and a quarter moon shone low in the northern sky. The night was quiet. No screaming wind or pounding waves against the ponto; just a peaceful lapping sound of the small waves against the hull and intermittent creaking of the sail rigging that pulled against the steady, favorable breeze. All the passengers and most of the crew were asleep. Only the few sailors on watch stirred now and again as they made their rounds on the main deck. Now it was peaceful. Now it was the kind of trip that Nearcus had expected; but the tortured and broken body of Marcus before him made it impossible for Nearcus to enjoy his surroundings.

Dioxippus broke the stillness by softly sharing what was bothering him. He said, "I wish I had a trainer such as this man."

Nearcus looked at his team mate's silhouette across from him and listened as the young man shared his feelings. Not knowing how he should respond to a bully who felt he had to talk, Nearcus just nodded and gave a small grunt. That was all that was needed for the older boy to know his team mate was listening.

Dioxippus continued, "I used to have a paedotribae, but last year the leaders in our camp decided my teacher should work with another boy. So this year I had to train myself."

Nearcus did not want to talk to his enemy, but his curiosity caused him to speak. He asked, "Nobody helped you prepare?"

"I was the oldest at the camp and knew enough to prepare myself. I have been competing for over four years. The camp leaders thought I was too rough on the other boys so they tried to get me to quit. But I showed them. I beat them all."

Marcus coughed and this interrupted the boys' conversation. But the slave immediately returned to sleep.

Dioxippus pointed at Marcus and continued, "Look at how twisted his arms are. Do you think we should massage them? Would it help get the good blood back to his hands?"

"Good idea. Let's do it," Nearcus replied. Each boy took one of Marcus's arms and started to rub it in a long motion from the shoulder to the wrist. Marcus remained asleep as the boys continued to provide this aid.

Nearcus was learning how Dioxippus had become so mean and angry and he wanted to know more. He said, "Then I guess your camp leaders did not want you at the trials?"

Dioxippus kept his eyes on Marcus's arm as he continued to tell his story, "Yes, they made me pay my own way to the trials. The rest of the team was sponsored by the local city fathers, but I had to fund my own way."

Having lived at home his entire life, Nearcus had never been given any money for anything. His father took care of all financial matters. So Nearcus was curious where Dioxippus could get money to pay for his trip to the trials. He asked, "Where did you get the money?"

"I stole it," was Dioxippus's honest and direct reply. "I tried to get a job to earn the money, but the city fathers had conspired to keep me from finding any work. No one would hire me for anything. So the night before we left for the trials, I went into the wool merchant's home in the next village and while he and his family slept, I took money from his office."

Nearcus sat there in shock. He had never known a thief before, and he had never heard a thief talk so casually about stealing. Nearcus thought about how upset he would be if someone came into their house under the cover of darkness and took his father's money. Nearcus knew how terribly hard his father and he worked to earn that money. Nearcus was shocked to hear Dioxippus tell him that he stole another man's hard-earned money as if somehow that wool merchant owed it to Dioxippus.

"You stole the merchant's money?" Nearcus blurted out. "Why didn't your father just give you the money?"

Dioxippus hesitated before he answered. Talking about his father was difficult for the young man. "I don't live with my father anymore. He won't let me."

"Why not?" Nearcus asked before he thought about how it was truly none of his business.

"I got mad at him and beat him," Dioxippus said as he lowered his chin and shut his eyes for a moment. Then after a pause he continued, "I have a bad temper. Last year we fought over something—I can't even remember what it was about—and I got mad. When he turned his back on me I jumped him. Nearcus, I beat him very badly. He never recovered completely and now most of the day he sits in front of the house and looks out over the street. The neighbors see him and are reminded that he raised a bad son, a son who is a danger to everyone. Since then I have lived with an uncle in the country. That is why the city fathers did not want me on the pankration team."

"Your uncle would not give you the money to go to the trials?" Nearcus asked, still amazed at how different Dioxippus's life has been compared to his own.

"My uncle is also afraid of me. He has me live with his slaves and gives me food and a cot and that is all. Anything I want in life I must go out and take it myself."

As the two sat there in silence rubbing Marcus's arms, Nearcus was beginning to realize just how wonderful his life was at home. He missed not having a mother, but his father had always cared for him and encouraged him and protected him. Nearcus stopped thinking about his own dreams and plans just then and began to ponder what life must be like for Dioxippus.

"Did you have to steal the money to pay for this trip too?" Nearcus asked out of intense curiosity. His voice and tone were not judgmental but merely inquisitive.

"No. The island games committee has a fund to support any competitor who won a place on the island team but did not have the money to make the trip. I didn't have to steal to get here. I just had to beat you." After a short pause Dioxippus added, "I thought you quit at the trials to let me win because you knew my reputation and wanted to humiliate me. I don't need anybody's pity or anybody's help to get what I want."

The sharp edge and bitterness in Dioxippus's voice immediately transformed him in Nearcus's mind back into the hard, brutal bully he had known yesterday morning. The softer and more innocent young man Dioxippus had been since Marcus was hoisted to the top of the mast had slipped away. Nearcus kept silent and continued to rub the slave's arm.

Soon Dioxippus exhaled a slow, long breath and said in a much gentler voice, "I want to know why Marcus did not fight the crowd that was persecuting him. I know him to be a brave man. He proved it by the way he faced the danger and took the pain without crying out. I want to know the secret this slave has on how to become the master of others; how to take the power from those who hate you. I have never seen a man with such power."

No more was said between the two boys that night. They massaged Marcus's arms, kept a watchful eye out for others and took turns sleeping for short periods. However, no one approached the three travelers during the entire night.

As the twilight just before the dawn brightened the eastern horizon, Nearcus started a cooking fire to boil water. He used the hot water to make oatmeal from the grain in Marcus's sack. When it was ready, he gave a bowl to Dioxippus who ate it quickly. Nearcus then tried to rouse Marcus from a deep sleep. After some effort, the slave opened his eyes and looked around. He looked at Nearcus and then looked to his right and saw Dioxippus scooping the cereal into his mouth. Seeing Dioxippus, Marcus smiled. Then something happened that Nearcus had not seen before. He saw Dioxippus smile back at Marcus.

Marcus tried to move his arms to raise himself to a sitting position, but his limbs only partially responded to his wishes. Nearcus and Dioxippus reached over and helped the slave sit up. Marcus looked at his two arms and saw that they were still marked with deep grooves where the ropes had cut into him. He tried to move his arms but he could barely bend his elbows. There was great stiffness in his biceps and a burning pain ran from his finger-tips in both hands right to his neck and shoulders. Marcus quickly lowered his arms and rested his wrists on his thighs. The pain lessened when he relaxed his muscles.

Marcus smiled and said, "Not yet. Maybe later I can use them."

Dioxippus reached across the slave and took the full bowl of oatmeal from Nearcus's hand. He filled the spoon and lifted it to Marcus's lips. The slave let Dioxippus feed him and ate the first bite. Nearcus retrieved a cup of water and whenever Marcus nodded to him, Nearcus raised the cup to give the slave a sip. None of the crew or passengers saw this sight, but if they had it would have seemed strange that two free-born young men were serving a slave breakfast one spoonful and one sip at a time.

After breakfast was done, Nearcus cleaned the dishes and packed them away. He was sure that they would reach land before the mid-day meal so the utensils would not be needed onboard again. Dioxippus helped to move Marcus to a position where the slave faced the sun, his back leaning against the ship's rail. The warmth of the sunlight felt good on Marcus's face and neck. He shut his eyes and soaked in the curative powers of the fresh air and bright sun. He quietly said a prayer of thanksgiving for his life and the warmth on his face and body. As he did this, he slowly closed his hands into a fist and then opened them. He repeated this exercise many times as he tried to restore circulation to his arms.

Dioxippus could tell by the smile on the slave's face that Marcus was praying again. He watched as the paedotribae exercised his hands and wondered if now was a good time to ask Marcus about his gods. The young man was about to speak when there was a commotion raised on the foredeck. Shouts were heard from the crew and then many passengers rushed to the bow to learn what was happening. Dioxippus wondered if the sea creature had returned. He jumped to his feet and assumed a fighting stance. If it was the sea monster again and anyone came to throw Marcus overboard, he would have to go through Dioxippus. The pankratiast was ready to use all of his skill to defend the helpless slave sitting on the deck.

Nearcus jumped to his feet and looked forward. He heard laughter and excited cries coming from the bow and this bewildered him. Then he understood why everyone was so excited. Land had been spotted! The terrible, stormy, scary voyage was nearly over! Soon all would be safely on land!

"Dioxippus! Relax! They have spotted land!" Nearcus said to his team mate when he noticed the defensive position the older boy had taken.

Unlike Nearcus, Dioxippus did not smile upon hearing the news. He turned to Nearcus and said flatly, "Guard Marcus. I will go and retrieve my goods while everyone is forward and the cabin is empty." Then he trotted aft.

It was another four hours before the ponto reached the shore of the small village of Minoa, about thirty miles northeast of Corinth on the Megara plain. The winds of the storm had blown the ship right past Salamis and landed it on the northern shore of the Gulf of Saronicus. Despite missing their primary destination, the crew and passengers were happy to have survived the unseasonable storm and reach the other side of the Aegean Sea. The Romans had improved all roads in Greece so the cargo could be loaded onto carts and easily transported to Corinth from this village. Likewise, the passengers could arrange their own transportation to wherever their intended destination might be.

After the terrible events of the voyage, Nearcus and his slave chaperone were now just as unwelcome to join the rest of the Chios Isthmian Games cohort as Dioxippus. Two of the adult coaches of the team approached Dioxippus and held a conference with him; however they were too far away for Nearcus and Marcus to hear what was said. The coaches turned and walked away and Dioxippus returned to where Nearcus was helping the weakened Marcus stand on the pier.

"They want nothing to do with us now," said Dioxippus as he approached his new traveling companions. "We are to fend for ourselves and meet them at the start of the competition in three days. That is, if we can get there with no help from them. As far as they are concerned, it would be better if we did not show up."

"I don't understand. Didn't we earn the right to represent Chios at the games? What did we do that was wrong?" asked a shocked Nearcus.

Marcus answered the boy, "They do not want to be associated with a slave who was crucified for bringing the wrath of their gods down on them. They are embarrassed to be seen with me. Perhaps you should go with them and I will find my own way back to Leonidas."

Both boys looked at each other and shook their heads emphatically. Then Nearcus spoke first, "No, no Marcus! You are too weak to leave you here in a strange land alone. Besides, my father only let me come to Corinth if you were my chaperone. I cannot leave you."

"And I *will* not leave you," added Dioxippus. "They did not want me along to begin with anyway. I would rather travel with you."

Marcus looked deeply into each boy's eyes and saw a determination that showed both were maturing into responsible men very quickly. The slave especially felt the sting of Nearcus's words. Aegospotami and Leonidas had charged the slave with the sole responsibility of looking out for Nearcus. Marcus felt the trust placed in him by these men to be a significant honor. He felt that this responsibility was given him not only by these men, but by God. So he said a quick silent prayer and slowly nodded agreement to the boys.

"How are we going to get to Corinth?" Nearcus asked the obvious question. At twelve-years old and away from Chios for the first time in his life, he had no idea how to arrange travel plans. He looked around the waterfront of the village and it occurred to him that he had no idea which direction it was to anywhere, let alone Corinth.

Dioxippus opened his small leather valuables pouch hung on the belt over his tunic. He took out two golden-colored bronze coins. Showing them to his new traveling companions he said, "I only have these two dupondious and it is not even enough to buy us a small meal."

Marcus turned to Nearcus who was holding their travel sacks. "Young Nearcus, dig into that bag and find my valuables pouch and look in it."

Nearcus did as he was directed. He found what was left of the money his father had given to fund the trip to the games. Marcus looked at the coins in Nearcus's open hand and said, "We don't have enough for us to hire transportation and also pay for rooms and food in Corinth. I guess we will walk to the games."

"But how far is it and which way do we go?" asked Nearcus who was now a little frightened as well as confused.

"God will give us sufficient strength and He will guide us. Do not worry young Nearcus," answered a very weak, but confident Marcus.

Dioxippus saw that Marcus believed that his god would strengthen and guide them and this gave him great encouragement. But Nearcus had other feelings and said to himself, "Think what you like Marcus, but I will never but my faith in a god again."

Dioxippus took Marcus's arm to support him and this caused the slave to wince in pain.

"Oh, that hurts you! Sorry, would it be better if you walked by yourself?" the older boy said.

Hearing Dioxippus apologize was something that Nearcus thought he would never experience. He watched as Marcus smiled and answered, "Dioxippus you are a good man. I will be pleased to use our assistance."

Marcus and Dioxippus started down the main street of the village, not sure of the path ahead but confident they would reach their goal. Nearcus trailed behind, confused and unsure of what lay ahead.

The Greek coastal village was so small that there was only one road out of the hamlet. It led along the coast and

Marcus figured it would eventually join with a main thoroughfare that would lead southwesterly to Corinth. Upon reaching the town limits the road became narrower and rougher. But the weather was nice and the road easily traveled, so Marcus's spirits were high despite his painful arms and shoulders.

The sun was bright and directly overhead now. Marcus noticed an olive grove along the side of the road a few hundred yards ahead. The walking had helped him regain his appetite so he suggested to his two traveling companions that they stop under the shade of the trees and fix a mid-day meal. Nearcus and Dioxippus were also hungry so it was agreed that they would stop.

As Nearcus took the cooking pot and grain from the sack, Dioxippus searched for small firewood under the olive trees. After gathering a sufficient amount, he returned to the temporary camp.

As the boys went about preparing the meal, Marcus stepped behind a nearby tree that had a strong trunk and a low, sturdy branch shooting off to one side. When the boys could not see, Marcus placed his right wrist in the crook between the trunk and branch and then jerked his body away in a quick violent motion. When he did this, he felt his right shoulder pop. It was a very painful fix to his dislocated right shoulder made worse by his knowledge that he had to repeat it to reset his left shoulder as well. Quickly, before the boys noticed, he repeated the procedure and the pain was so intense on the left shoulder that he let out a small cry when it popped back into place.

His self-treatment complete, the slave returned to where the boys were starting the fire and sat down and leaned against a tree and rested with his eyes shut. He was a strong man and was rapidly regaining his strength after his ordeal, but he knew he really needed a couple more days of rest if possible before his body could start to completely recover. This short rest was a blessing, but he knew they would have to start traveling soon if they were to make it to the games on schedule. He prayed for stamina and strength and safety on their journey.

Marcus resting against the tree, and the boys busy with starting a small fire and heating the water were too occupied to see the eyes watching their every move from behind a tree ten yards away. Standing in the large shadow of the mature olive tree, with the trunk between her and the travelers, stood a woman dressed in dark clothes. She was perfectly still and extremely hard to see in her partially hidden position. Carefully she watched the trespassers make themselves at home on this land. She kept silent and just watched for now. But she had plans for this tiny band and soon she would put those plans into action.

CHAPTER 11

The three travelers relaxed in the shade after finishing a simple, but filling meal. Suddenly, Marcus opened his eyes when he heard a noise coming from behind him. He leaned forward and with great pain turned his head to see around the tree he was leaning against. In the small twigs that carpeted the ground beneath the olive trees he heard the rustling of many feet approaching. Now he saw a group of five men led by a woman dressed in black coming straight for them. Nearcus and Dioxippus also heard the strangers coming and quickly stood. Marcus struggled to get to his feet as well.

The boys and the slave stood there silently waiting for the customary greeting from the approaching band. But nothing was said; no "Greetings travelers! How may we help you on your journey?" that they would have heard from any strangers on Chios. The woman in the lead just motioned with her hand and the men surrounded the travelers. These were rough looking men and big enough that if they cared to, they could easily subdue the boys and weakened slave. But they just silently stood in a circle staring at the trespassers.

Marcus felt he had been polite long enough so he waited no longer for the proper greeting from his hosts. He spoke first, "Greetings. May I help you with something?"

The women looked Marcus up and down and waited a long time before she finally answered, "What is your business here? Why have you come onto this land?"

"We are travelers going to the Isthmian Games. We stopped under the shade of these trees for our mid-day meal." Marcus thought about seeking forgiveness for trespassing, but then thought better of doing so. He figured that no farmer would begrudge weary travelers the use of his trees' shade, and if a farmer did, then he was not worthy of an apology.

"Is that all of your business?" came the sharp reply from the stern lady in black.

Something inside of Marcus was bothering him. He felt the overpowering urge to say something that seemed inappropriate for the situation. But try as he might, it was impossible for him to fight this desire so before he realized what he was saying, he blurted out, "We are also here seeking to follow the will of God and his son, Jesus the Nazarene."

Nearcus and Dioxippus jerked their heads to look at Marcus. They were shocked by what he had said. Both thought to themselves, "Why would he admit that now? Didn't that get him hung on the mast already?"

Immediately upon hearing the name of Jesus the woman and her friends broke into large smiles! Their posture went from stiff and threatening to relaxed and welcoming. The woman asked, "Truly, my friends, are you followers of the Way?"

Marcus nodded. Nearcus and Dioxippus just stood there frozen in confusion at what was taking place before them.

"My name is Iliana and these are my slaves. We too all follow the Way. Welcome brothers in the Christ!" the woman continued. The slaves swarmed around the fellow slave to give a warm greeting to Marcus. But when they slapped his back in a welcoming gesture, Marcus fell to his knees in pain. Dioxippus rushed to the slave's side and stood over him to protect him from being touched again.

Dioxippus said forcefully, "He is hurt. They tortured him on our ship for praying to his god. Stand back from him."

"God has led you to us!" Iliana gasped to Marcus, "Is your name Marcus, the slave from Chios?"

Marcus was in great pain but in even greater confusion. He simply nodded in response to Iliana's question.

Iliana next spoke to Dioxippus, "Then are you Nearcus?"

Dioxippus shook his head and looked over at Nearcus who was still frozen in his position, a mere spectator of all that was happening around him.

"Nearcus?" Iliana said to the young boy. Nearcus nodded his head and when he did, the woman in black rushed to him and threw her arms around his neck and squeezed. She looked skyward and said in a soft voice, "Thank you, dear Lord! Thank you!"

Iliana released the very confused boy and stepped back, a wide smile beamed across her entire face. She laughed at the looks she was receiving from the strangers on her land. Then she explained her joy, "Five nights ago I had a dream—a vision really, in my sleep. The Lord said to me that soon a young boy would cross my path named Nearcus. I was to help him in anyway I could for he has been chosen by the Lord." Then she turned to Marcus and said to him, "Just last hour I was in the village and there all the talk by the sailors was of their terrible crossing because a slave named Marcus had prayed to God and the Nazarene to the displeasure of Poseidon. I heard of how they crucified you to appease the sea god, but you did not die. I was on my way home when I saw your camp here on my land. Oh! Thank you Lord! I am so blessed to have the privilege to help you on your travels!"

Nearcus was frightened. He was very frightened. Iliana said she had her vision five nights ago. That was the same day that he had heard the voice in the orchard saying he was chosen! This scared Nearcus terribly. His mind was full of questions. Chosen for what? Had he heard the voice of this god and his son? How could that be when Nearcus hated all gods and wanted nothing to do with them? Indeed, Nearcus was very confused, and very frightened.

It seemed to Nearcus that Marcus took this startling news with great ease. The slave also rolled his eyes to heaven and said aloud in a whisper just loud enough to be heard, "Thank you Dear Lord for answered prayer." Then Marcus spoke to Iliana, "Please meet our friend and companion, Dioxippus. He is a strong young man who has been very faithful and a great help to me."

Dioxippus remained stiff and did not smile when Iliana approached him and hugged him as well. She said, "Welcome Dioxippus, we are glad you are here with us." The young man who was feared but not loved nor welcomed in his own home did not know how to respond. So he just stood there with his arms by his side, confused about how to accept this genuine expression of welcome.

Dioxippus may have been confused about how to react to Iliana's embrace, but he had no doubt about his feelings concerning what Marcus had said. The words of this man he had only known for a couple of days had tremendous effect on the young pankratiast. Marcus was the first man who ever treated Dioxippus with friendship and respect and, even possibly in the young man's mind, love. Dioxippus carefully watched the slave because he wanted to learn more about a man who could love someone as bad as Dioxippus knew himself to be.

Iliana had her slaves gather up the belongings of the travelers and led the trio to her home on the far side of the orchard. It was a stone house with four rooms. Iliana's husband had been a successful olive grower who had built this house for his bride, Iliana, thirty years previously. Four years ago he had died in an accident in the fields and since then Iliana had run the business with the help of her five slaves. A talkative woman, Iliana filled the short walk with a running commentary about her life and her Lord. Upon reaching the house she continued her personal history.

"Oh, I am so sorry about the rude greeting we gave you! You see, it has been a difficult year in this region for followers of the Way. We have a body of believers that meet in my house on the Sabbath and the local leaders of the synagogue and the district governor often times try to intimidate us. In fact, just three years ago, four of our brothers and two of our sisters in the Christ were taken from us during the terrible times," Iliana said as she showed her guests to seats at an outside table and motioned for the slaves to bring water mixed with a little wine to drink. Then she continued, "The local population knows that we are not a threat to them and that we do not participate in unholy rituals and pagan sacrifices. You would be surprised by the rumors that have been spread about us by our enemies. They tell people that we drink the blood of sacrificial victims and that we plot to overthrow the government. But everyone around here knows that is not the case, so our local enemies have started to bring in strangers from Athens to persecute us. So now whenever we see strangers approach our home I am afraid we are not too hospitable until we have determined their intentions."

"We thank you for your faith and service and hospitality," Marcus said, "But soon we must start our journey again. These two strong young men must represent our island at the Isthmian Games. They are our pankratiasts and we must be there in three days. Can you tell me how long the walk is to Corinth?"

"It is a good three days walk, but you will not be walking!" said Iliana. "Stay with us and rest after your hard voyage. I will have Giorgos drive you in our olive cart to the games. The road from here to Corinth is good and it can be done in one long day's journey by cart."

Marcus was happy to accept the offer to rest. He had not shared with his young traveling companions, but with his severely wrenched and dislocated shoulders, he had dreaded the long walk and wished he could spend a day or more in bed to heal.

Marcus and Iliana sat at the table and shared stories about the Christians they knew and other churches they had visited. While they were engaged in joyous conversation, Nearcus caught the eye of Dioxippus. Without the two adults even noticing, the young men slipped away from the table and walked around the nearby grounds. In silence they watched the slaves hard at work tending to the trees. The workers were doing the spring pruning to shape the olive trees and ensure maximum fruit production later in the year. At his home, Nearcus called this part of the cycle of orchard farming the "cursing time." The branches of the trees scratched the arms all day long during this pruning and his father's slaves would curse about their pain continually. Yet here in the olive orchard, these men seemed very happy in their work and a couple even whistled! Nearcus found this quite amazing and moved closer to see if the slaves knew some secret trick that made it less painful. He hoped to learn something that his father could use to make life better at home.

Dioxippus maintained a sullen look on his face and he was very quiet as he accompanied Nearcus into the orchard. Dioxippus was glad for their good luck in coming across Iliana and the help she offered, but he still was very uneasy about the kindness shown to them. He had never experienced anything like it and this made him leery of the possible motives of these who called themselves followers of "the Way."

Nearcus was disappointed as he watched the slaves in the orchard. They were using the same method of pruning as his father had taught him. The only difference was in the attitude of the slaves. Rather than curse continually at the irritation of the short branches scratching their arms, these slaves ignored the pain and focused on the wonderful sunlight, beautiful weather and good companionship they

experienced on this afternoon. Having seen what he
wanted, Nearcus turned and strolled back towards the
house. Dioxippus turned and followed him.

"Do you know what this Way is that Iliana and Marcus
talk about?" Dioxippus broke the silence to ask his team
mate.

Nearcus answered by shaking his head and keeping his
eyes forward, not looking at Dioxippus. Nearcus was
wondering the same thing but inside he was conflicted. He
wanted to know how the slaves could be so content in their
work and how Marcus could bear up under such torture
without being bitter and why a widow such as Iliana was
full of overflowing joy. Yet he was afraid the answer might
involve having to believe that a god cared for him and
Nearcus was personally at war with all gods.

Soon they neared the table where Marcus and Iliana
continued to talk and laugh. Nearcus then responded to
Dioxippus's question, "I guess we might find out tonight. I
heard Iliana tell Marcus that this church was meeting at her
house this evening. But you should really ask Marcus."

Dioxippus knew that is what he should do if he really
wanted the answer, but he was hesitant to come right out
and ask Marcus about his god. While trying to find the
courage to ask about the Way, his thoughts were interrupted
when Marcus motioned for the two athletes to draw near to
him.

"In just a couple of days, God willing, you will be
representing your home island before thousands and
thousands of spectators at the famed Isthmian Games.
During our voyage you had to neglect your training. Now,
you must take advantage of this time we have been given to
prepare for what is ahead."

Dioxippus and Nearcus had their thoughts quickly
redirected by the paedotribae. Gone were questions about
gods and beliefs; back were thoughts of pankration
techniques and plans.

"Well, don't just stand there!" Marcus said to Nearcus. The twelve-year old had heard that phrase for the past ten months and knew exactly what was expected. Nearcus turned to his left and started a fast trot towards the orchards. Dioxippus saw Nearcus start running and with only a moment's hesitation figured out what the coach desired and joined his partner stride for stride.

Soon the athletes had reached the far side of the orchard near where they had camped for the mid-day meal. Upon reaching the road they turned to the left and continued their run.

Dioxippus asked, "How long does he have you run?"

"He expects us to return completed winded. So we go until we feel we cannot go any farther, and then we see if we can return without walking or stopping. If we return too soon it will tell him that we are not serious about our training."

Dioxippus had a thought and asked, "How would he know if we just sat under a tree for a long while and then ran back?"

Nearcus had never, ever even considered such a trick. Now that Dioxippus mentioned that option, Nearcus was amused that it had never crossed his mind previously. He smiled and said, "But I would know." Then he increased his pace slightly and Dioxippus had to strain to keep with him.

It felt good to Nearcus to run. He needed to stop thinking about all that had happened and to get back to something comfortable. And running was comfortable for Nearcus. To Nearcus the wind in his hair and the burning in his legs and lungs were a sign that he was accomplishing something that only he had control over. He determined how fast and how far he ran; not his father or his paedotribae or anyone else was in charge of him when he ran. Nearcus had discovered over the course of his training that it was during the running that he could think best and sort out his problems. After a half-hour of non-stop running all his problems seemed to fade away and it was just him and the run left. Running was a source of peace in this young boy's life.

Today's run was especially nice for Nearcus. He was running in strange territory and everything he saw and passed was new to him. He felt free and excited to explore these surroundings. Nearcus led the pair of athletes up one row of olive trees and then down another. They turned left and then right and then left again; all the while traveling farther and farther from Iliana's house. After forty-five minutes of this random pattern of running, Nearcus felt he was growing tired sufficiently that it would appropriate to start the return trip. He crossed over to the next row of trees and reversed his course. He ran a few hundred yards and then turned to the east. He ran a hundred yards farther and turned to the south. He led Dioxippus another hundred yards and then he stopped in his tracks.

A surprised Dioxippus nearly ran into the back of Nearcus and said, "Whoa! Why did we stop?"

"I am lost. I don't know the way back to Iliana's. Do you?"

"I was not paying attention. I was just following you," Dioxippus replied.

Nearcus and Dioxippus turned circles looking in all directions trying to see something that was familiar. But deep in the olive orchard all the trees looked the same. They remained quiet and listened for the sounds of the slaves working in the trees. It was silent; they heard nothing.

After a couple of minutes of quiet, Dioxippus said, "Let's head east. I think the road is that way, and once we find the road we can head south until we come to our old camp or the town. Then we can get directions."

Nearcus liked the idea so he nodded and immediately started running to the east. A few hundred yards later there still was no road and the boys were still just as lost. But their spirits were raised when they heard voices just over a slight rise ahead.

Nearcus stopped running and began a slow walk towards the voices. Just before the two boys reached the top of the rise and could see who was speaking they both heard something that made them stop and fall back a couple of steps.

The voice over the rise said in a very angry and authoritarian tone, "We will kill them and but an end to this once and for all. We shall finish what the emperor started three years ago. We will rid this area completely of all of them. They must be purged from our society before they can grow any stronger."

Another, deeper voice joined in, "Yes! Kill them all!"

Upon hearing this Dioxippus grabbed Nearcus's shoulders and pulled him to the ground. The two scrambled to hide behind a nearby olive tree.

"Who are they going to kill?" innocent Nearcus whispered to his team mate.

Dioxippus just shook his head. He did not know but he understood that ruthless men planning to kill do not want any witnesses to their plans. If they discovered the two boys he knew that they would be murdered too. Dioxippus pointed in the direction the two pankratiasts had come from and started to move as swiftly and quietly as possible. Nearcus followed as the boys stepped very carefully to keep from rustling the twigs and leaves on the ground. Despite their best efforts, Nearcus accidentally snapped a small branch that lay across an indentation in the ground. The noise caused the voices to pause.

Dioxippus and Nearcus heard one of the men yell, "What was that? Quick! Go take a look!"

Nearcus wanted to run as fast and as long and as far away as he possibly could. But just as he took his first step, Dioxippus grabbed him and guided him to a hiding place behind a fallen olive tree. Dioxippus instinctively knew that it was impossible to run without being seen in this neatly maintained orchard. Hiding was there best option and with luck the men would think they had heard an animal or bird.

The tree had fallen over years ago and small brush had grown over the trunk and between the branches that lay on the ground. Dioxippus put his fingers to his lips to tell Nearcus to keep from speaking and then he scooped out the dry brush next to the trunk and pushed Nearcus into the depression he had made. Then he covered the younger boy with the brush he had dug out. Next Dioxippus burrowed his way under the overgrown branches to hide himself as much as possible.

Nearcus remained totally still and he worried that the beating of his heart was so loud that it would draw the men right to them. Dioxippus felt exposed and sure he could be seen through the dry branches, but he dared not move because the rustle of the brush could be heard.

Both boys heard the men approaching their position. They were sure the men had seen them hide and were heading straight for them. They felt it was just a matter of moments before these killers pounced on them and ended their short lives.

CHAPTER 12

Marcus was beginning to wonder why the athletes were out so long. As Iliana continued talking about the growth of the church that met in her house, Marcus looked beyond her to see if the boys were coming into sight yet. He expected them to return within an hour and it had been nearly an hour and a half since they left. Finally he could ignore his concerns no longer and he interrupted his hostess.

"I wonder where the boys are. I hope they did not get lost out in the orchards."

Iliana looked skyward and could tell by the sun's position that it had been a good while since the athletes had departed. She saw that Marcus had a concerned expression on his face and so she got up from the table and walked towards the nearby field where the slaves were still pruning. She called for them to stop their work and to come to the house.

When the five laborers had assembled by the house, Iliana told them, "That is enough work for today. I want you to spread out and search for our two young guests. They went on a training run and should have returned by now. I am afraid that one olive tree might look like another to them and they got confused and lost. Giorgos, please organize the search to cover as much territory as possible before the sun sets. We must return our lost lambs to the fold before it is dark!"

Giorgos was the oldest and most able slave on the farm and since the death of Iliana's husband had taken on primary responsibility for ensuring the business was run successfully. He knew that the spring pruning schedule was very tight and that there really was no time in it to lose most of this afternoon's work to look for lost young men. But he was devoted to his master's family and could see that the welfare of these boys was important to Iliana because it was important to her guest, Marcus. Giorgos quickly changed his day's priorities and gathered the other four slaves around him. He assigned each of them a specific search area and directed that all report back no later than sunset whether they were successful or not. Giorgos decided that he would try a different method to find the lost pankratiasts. While the others searched their assigned sectors, he would follow the boy's tracks in the dirt through the orchards. He thought he could get a good general direction to search even if he eventually lost their tracks.

With everyone understanding their mission, each set off on the search. Marcus got up to join Giorgos but Iliana stopped him. She insisted that he remain with her. She told Marcus that she truly needed his company because she was not fond of being alone. In reality, she did not want to burden Giorgos with an injured man who would slow down the search. Giorgos was a swift runner and Marcus would only make it harder for him to find the boys.

Far from the house, Nearcus and Dioxippus remained absolutely still in their hiding places. The voices of the gang could no longer be heard, but the sound of their heavy steps through the twigs and leaves grew louder and louder. Nearcus was frightened and wanted to pray for help but he told himself it would do no good. "The gods don't care and they don't help," he thought. As he was thinking this he heard a loud crack just the other side of the log he was hiding behind. Nearcus held his breath and tried not to move a muscle. He knew that with one more step by the gang member the game would be over. He would be discovered and nabbed for sure.

Options raced through Nearcus's thoughts. He had uncontrollably reverted to his competition mindset. He was thinking very, very rapidly about his next moves. If the thug saw him, should he jump up and use his speed to kick the enemy in the face and then run away? Or should he try for his legs and a trip maneuver to get the opponent on the ground and go for a choke hold to subdue him? Many scenarios and options raced through Nearcus's mind. He was about to settle on one choice and jump into action when he heard something that totally surprised him.

"Ha! Ha! Ha!" laughed the thug in a hearty voice, "Look! Over there!"

His laugh was answered by two other men laughing. One shouted, "How did those sheep get out here in this orchard? Stupid animals!"

"I don't think they can tell anyone of our plans! Back to camp now," the first voice directed, he obviously being the leader. Nearcus and Dioxippus listened closely as the footsteps receded back over the rise. The first to stir from hiding was Dioxippus.

As he dug Nearcus out from his hiding place, Dioxippus whispered, "We must get clear of this place now while we have the chance."

Nearcus at first agreed and started to quietly and slowly walk to the west, away from the gang's camp. However, after only a few steps he stopped. He turned to Dioxippus and said, "It just occurred to me. What if these men were the Athenians hired to harass the followers of the Way? Iliana and her house could be the targets."

In his mind, Dioxippus agreed with the younger boy's logic, but he also thought, "What if they are the target? What has that to do with us? We just met these Christians." Before he could share his thoughts, Nearcus had turned to approach the rise that separated them from the gang's camp. Dioxippus stood there, frozen in indecision. Should he follow his foolhardy team mate or get as far away as he possibly could? He wrestled with this serious decision for nearly a full minute before the sixteen-year old made his choice.

Carefully, being as silent as possible, Dioxippus caught up with Nearcus and took the lead. As they approached the top of the rise, Dioxippus got on his hands and knees to continue. As he got even closer to the top, he started to crawl on his stomach, with Nearcus following him in the same fashion. Soon they were in a position where they could see the men as well as hear them. Both boys were hidden at the base of an old, wide olive tree. Dioxippus peeked around the trunk and got a glimpse of the camp layout then pulled his head back into hiding. Nearcus remained on his stomach and listened intently to what they heard."

"Are you sure of the way there? We don't want to fall upon innocent Greeks because we got the wrong farm," said the leader of the gang to the other six who were sitting in a circle, reclining against olive tree trunks or stretched out completely on the ground, leaning on one elbow.

Another of the gang answered, "I have the map right here in my bag. It is very clear on how to get to the farm from here. I am sure we will have no trouble finding the place even in the dark."

"Well," the leader said, "no sense in tipping our hand by arriving early. We don't want to show until every last one of them has arrived. It promises to be a tiring night so I am going to rest now and I recommend you do the same. We will leave in another hour or so."

Dioxippus watched as the men settled into sleeping positions. However, his sights were fixed on one particular item, the sack with the map in it. If his suspicions were correct, these thugs were planning to raid the Christian meeting at Iliana's house this evening and kill everyone there. The thought of innocent victims dying because of their beliefs did not truly bother Dioxippus because he did not know these Christians. But tonight Marcus would be at Iliana's house and the thought of these men killing his friend did bother the young man.

Dioxippus leaned near to Nearcus's ear and quietly whispered, "If we get that sack with the map in it we can find out if they are planning to attack Iliana's this evening. And if they are, the map will guide us so we can get there first to warn Marcus and the others."

Nearcus knew that Dioxippus was right, but he did not see how they could steal the sack without getting caught. He nodded to indicate that he understood the logic, but his eyes were full of questions on how to accomplish this feat.

Dioxippus saw the questions in Nearcus's eyes and said, "I know how to get the sack. Follow me."

Slowly and very quietly the two boys slide backwards to where they could not be seen from the gang's camp before they stood and carefully retreated a good distance away. Dioxippus there explained his plan to Nearcus. The younger boy thought it foolhardy and very dangerous. He did not see how Dioxippus could execute his plan without getting caught. When Nearcus told him his opinion of the plan, Dioxippus backed up two steps before he spoke.

"We must do something. Do you have a better plan?"

In all honesty, Nearcus did not have a better plan, so he shook his head. Then he remembered something that Marcus had taught him during his months of training. The paedotribae had taught Nearcus to use faints and misdirection to get an opponent out of position. Once the man you are fighting has taken your bait, he will be susceptible to your attack if you can strike with great speed.

Nearcus's eyes grew wider as this thought became a plan in his head. He said, "Maybe there is a way to get that sack. Those men do not look to be the best athletes. I doubt any of them can run more than a few hundred yards before they are winded"

Dioxippus nodded in agreement and as an indication for Nearcus to continue. The younger boy completed his idea, "I am faster than you and I know I can out run all of them. If I can get them to jump up and chase me, maybe the sack will be left behind for you to nab."

"That's a big maybe, Nearcus."

"Well, once I get their attention and everyone is looking at me, maybe you can run in from the back and snatch the bag and take off the other direction. If they are all focused on me, then you should get enough of a head start to get away, I think."

Dioxippus knew that Nearcus's plan was risky, but he had to admit it probably had a better chance of success than his own plan of trying to crawl in while they slept and lift the bag from the side of the man with the map. So, he nodded and when he did, the two boys agreed on a plan that they both felt was more likely to fail than succeed. Both were thinking the same thing, "If only we had not gotten lost, we could just run back and warn Marcus and the others."

But they were lost and they both knew they had a duty to perform, even if it cost them their lives. Dioxippus surprised Nearcus by reaching out his hand. Nearcus looked at it and then grasped Dioxippus's elbow with his own hand and they shook arms. Then Dioxippus turned and went to position himself as closely as possible to the sack with the map in it. Nearcus watched his new friend move quietly through the orchard around to the left of the rise. Once Dioxippus was out of sight, Nearcus started up the rise to position himself to attract the gang.

Once both boys were in position, Nearcus took a deep breath and started to stand up to be seen, but before he could complete this maneuver he heard a loud noise behind him and their plans immediately changed. The next hour would be one of the most memorable in these two boys' entire lives.

CHAPTER 13

"Nearcus! Dioxippus!" came shouts from a distance. "Where are you?"

Giorgos had followed the boys confusing tracks as best he could, but once he lost their footsteps on the orchard floor, he had continued in a northeasterly direction shouting their names. Now he had arrived close enough for his shouts to be heard by both the boys and the gang members.

"Nearcus! Dioxippus! Can you hear me?" Giorgos continued to shout across the orchard. Nearcus turned his head swiftly in the direction of the shouting. Then he looked back towards the gang's camp. He saw all the men stir from their resting positions and jump to their feet. The leader motioned for the men to take cover and try to hide from the approaching stranger. He wanted to remain undetected as long as possible so his gang would not lose the element of surprise when they attacked. He thought that perhaps this shouting stranger would pass by without discovering their camp.

Nearcus's thoughts were racing in the sharp, focused manner he had before each pankration bout. He popped to his feet and shouted as loudly as he possibly could, "I am over here! I have found a band of robbers and murderers!"

As Nearcus said this he watched the leader of the gang. As the young boy anticipated, his shout drew an immediate reaction from the leader,

"Get that boy! He knows too much!" the leader yelled as he sprang from his hiding place and charged up the small hill towards Nearcus. The others in the gang immediately

117

followed him. There was a mad scramble to the top of the rise as the six men hustled to capture Nearcus.

Seeing the commotion, Dioxippus recognized his chance to grab the sack with the map in it. As the entire gang focused on young Nearcus shouting at the top of the hill, no one paid any attention to their belongings spread out across the camp. Dioxippus dashed into the camp while all the men were looking the other way at Nearcus. He snatched the sack and ran back into the orchard without being seen.

Dioxippus crouched behind a big tree fifty yards from the gang and pulled the map from the sack. It did not take very long for him to see that his suspicions were correct. The target of these murderers was the Christian house church that met at Iliana's. He stuffed the map back into the sack and then peeked around the tree trunk. No one was near him, but the noise coming from the chase of Nearcus could be heard. Shouts of "Get him!" and "There he goes!" echoed across the orchard. Recognizing that the plan had worked, Dioxippus took advantage of his opportunity to escape. Using the information he had seen on the map, the young man knew the best way to reach Iliana's house was to head south until he came to a small road, then turn right and the road would lead to a pathway that approached the house from the east. He scanned all directions to once again ensure the way was clear, and then Dioxippus started to sprint through the olive trees. He was tired from the previous training run, but his lungs and legs felt fine as he ran for a purpose now. He ran to save Marcus.

Once Nearcus was certain that all the gang members were focused on him and had started to pursue him, he turned and ran due west. The leader of the gang was the first to reach the top of the rise and when he scanned the orchard he immediately caught sight of Nearcus running through the trees about fifteen yards ahead of him.

"There he goes! Get him!" the leader shouted as he took off running after Nearcus. The rest of the gang members soon caught the leader and the swifter of the party pulled ahead to close on the fleeing young man.

Just twenty yards to the south, Giorgos heard the commotion ahead of him and stopped. He ceased his yelling and watched the chase pass in front of him. He immediately recognized the pursued as Nearcus and it was obvious to Giorgos that the young man was running for his life. The slave also noticed gang members reaching into small sacks hanging from their tunic belts and pulling out good sized stones. Two of the thugs stopped and loaded their slings with the stones and twirled the leather straps over their heads. Then both simultaneously let go their stones which went flying directly at Nearcus. One stone hit an olive tree limb and fell to the ground. The other stone barely missed Nearcus's skull and landed with a tremendous thud against a tree trunk next to the running youth. Giorgos was unarmed and not in a position to give aid to the young pankratiast. But he could pray to his god. Giorgos dropped to his knees right where he stood and prayed for a heavenly protective barrier to surround the innocent young man running for his life. He asked God to send a legion of angels to deflect the stones now being hurled through the air at Nearcus, and he prayed for special strength to fill and sustain the boy's body. He prayed with great faith that Nearcus could run faster than he had ever run before and to not grow weary as the chase continued.

Nearcus did not know about Giorgos's prayers, but he did hear the stones whizzing by his ears and striking the trees around him. Faster and faster he pushed his body. He ran in a straight line down a row of olive trees. Every now and again he jumped to the other side of the row of trees, but he kept his direction westerly. He knew that if he turned in any way his pursuers could cut the corner and gain on him.

Nearcus's plan was to force these men to run faster and longer than he was able if they wanted to catch him.

Nearcus did not even look behind him because he thought it might slow him down. If he had, the sight of the gang leader's short sword flashing in the sinking sun as the thug waved it in anger would have frightened him. But despite the long run he had completed earlier in the afternoon, Nearcus felt strong and fast. He heard the stones from the slings striking the trees all around him and he knew from the damage that was being done to the trees that if one hit him squarely in the head it could possibly kill him. All Nearcus could do was run as fast and as far as his twelve-year old legs would carry him. He expected to be struck by a deadly stone any second, but they all were just slightly off target and missed him. And so Nearcus ran on and on.

Giorgos finished his prayer and jumped to his feet and started to follow the gang to be in position if there was an opportunity to help Nearcus later. Just then, about thirty yards to his right, he saw a figure moving through the orchard heading in a southerly direction. It took a couple of seconds, but eventually Giorgos recognized the moving figure. It was Dioxippus running through the orchard. Giorgos ran to intercept him, finally reaching him a few rows of trees to the south.

"Dioxippus!" Giorgos said loudly as he caught up to the boy.

The young man was surprised to hear his name and he whirled around and assumed a fighting stance.

"Dioxippus, it is Giorgos, from Iliana's household."

The boy looked at the slave and then upon recognizing Giorgos, he ran to meet him.

"I have the map and I know their plans!" Dioxippus blurted out.

"What do you mean?"

"We must get to your mistress's house quickly. They plan on attacking the church meeting tonight and killing everyone there!"

Giorgos grabbed the excited young man by the shoulders and looked sternly into his eyes. What he saw there was fear and concern and the truth. This boy was not telling some story. He truly believed what he was saying.

Dioxippus reached into the sack he was carrying and pulled out the map. He showed it to Giorgos, who quickly reviewed it. The slave immediately recognized that it was marked with clear directions to Iliana's home.

"Come with me. This map shows the most traveled way there, but I know the shortest. We must get there and prepare for our enemies' attack," Giorgos said hurriedly.

"I got the map because Nearcus drew the gang away. We must get him help!" Dioxippus quickly blurted out.

"Nearcus is in better hands than ours or any man's," the slave responded as he started off at a quick pace in a southwesterly direction. "That boy can run! He was pulling away from the gang when I last saw him and angels were providing him a safe escort."

Dioxippus was confused by the talk of angelic protection, but he had to agree with Giorgos that Nearcus truly could run! Besides, he thought, if Nearcus cannot out run the gang, then there really is nothing he and the slave could do to help. It was better to get to Marcus, he thought, because Marcus would know the best thing to do. Marcus would know how to help Nearcus. So, Dioxippus fell in behind the slave as they weaved their way through the orchard on the shortest path to Iliana's house.

The sun was setting as the first of Iliana's slaves returned from their searches for the lost boys. Over the next half hour, one by one the four slaves returned and reported no luck in finding the pankratiasts. With each report, Marcus had grown more worried about what could have happened to them. He now prayed that Giorgos might have had better success in finding them.

While Marcus stood outside the house and scanned the orchards to the north, Iliana was busy making preparations for the regular mid-week service of the brothers and sisters of the Way. She laid out bread and drink and dates and pomegranates for the members. Chairs and benches were brought out and set in the clearing near the house entrance. A fire was prepared in the center of the seats to be set ablaze once it was too dark to see.

Soon, the first of the believers arrived. A middle aged man with his young wife and infant son walked up the path from the main road. Iliana greeted them with a warm smile and showed them to the table loaded with refreshments. The slaves had washed themselves after their day's work and search and now were helping Iliana to host the worshippers arriving.

In just a quarter hour, another seven men and five women and eight children had arrived. Marcus noticed the assembly growing, but he maintained his vigil to the north looking and praying to see the arrival of his lost boys. Then suddenly his hope soared! Running through the olive orchard he saw two figures coming straight for the house. At first he thought it was Nearcus and Dioxippus, but soon he recognized the one in front as Giorgos. When Marcus finally saw Dioxippus clearly, he ran to the young man and forgetting the pain in his arms he hugged him. Dioxippus did something he had not done in a very long time, he hugged back and it felt very good to him. He was only seven years old when his mother was taken away and that was the last time he remembered ever being hugged. Just now, for the first time in such a long time, he felt wanted and missed. Dioxippus forgot about the danger and the peril Nearcus was in for just a second while Marcus greeted him with a hug.

"Dioxippus, you are safe! Praise God!" Marcus uttered in all sincerity, "Where is Nearcus?"

Dioxippus and Giorgos explained what had happened and how Nearcus was running for his life when they came back to warn of a planned mass murder at the meeting.

What happened next, truly shocked Dioxippus. Rather than arm themselves or flee to their homes, the Christians gathered around the fire and knelt down in prayer! The leader of the church, a tall man of over sixty years of age named Filaretos, stood by the now blazing fire and lifted his hands and face to the sky. He led the entire congregation in a prayer first for Nearcus to be saved and then for the murderous gang to change their ways and embrace the "Way." Dioxippus had seen many men pray in his life to the idols found all over Chios, but they never trusted their lives to the gods! These people were asking their god to deliver them from the murderers and they believed he would with a faith so strong that they were not going to flee or fight. A strange feeling came over Dioxippus as he heard the fervency of Filaretos's prayer. Dioxippus started to believe that this Jesus could actually save them!

A mile to the northwest, the leader of the murderous gang was completely exhausted and fell to his knees. He could not chase this boy any more. This tough leader of cut throats was gasping for air and a sharp pain pierced his right side so intensely that he could no longer stand, let alone run. Other men in the gang were farther ahead of the leader but when they noticed he had given up the chase, they too stopped and walked back to him.

"We will never catch that boy," the leader gasped, "I say good riddance. I haven't run so much since a Roman garrison chased me for stealing a merchant's purse."

The rest of the gang collapsed around the leader and all were breathing heavily; none of them able to say much until they rested more.

Finally, the leader asked the two with the leather sling shots, "I thought you two were the best marksmen with a sling in all of Greece. That is what you told me when I recruited you. How come you couldn't hit a boy running in a straight line only twenty yards right in front of you?"

"I don't know. Something strange was happening out there. I know I had a good bead on him many times when I let the stone fly, but they all hit the tree trunks or limbs," said the younger of the two sling hurlers.

"Yes, there's something strange in these woods," added the other hurler.

"The only thing strange is that I believed you two when you bragged about how good you are," chided the leader.

"What do we do now?" asked another of the gang.

"Show me that map and let's get our bearings," replied the leader.

It was only then that the keeper of the map noticed his sack was missing. He said in a frightened voice, "I can't find it. I must have dropped it when we were running. I don't know where it is."

The leader spit in disgust. He was not only angry over the loss of the map, but because this night's business was going totally wrong. A long moment passed while he thought of what to do next. Finally he shrugged his shoulders and said, "This has gotten too hard. We're not getting paid enough for all of these problems. Let's find our way out of here and locate an inn where we can get some strong wine. There is always next week if they want us to attack the Christians. But tonight is a bust so let's go make the best of what is left of it."

All of the gang smiled and nodded in agreement. They were too tired and too lost to continue with their original plans. The leader's suggestion to go get drunk instead was a welcome decision. After five more minutes of resting, they got up and started to find their way through the orchard in the darkness, looking to enjoy themselves rather than to commit murder.

CHAPTER 14

It was more than a mile after his pursuers gave up the chase before Nearcus stopped running. He crouched behind a tree and listened. The only sound was the rustle of the wind through the olive orchard as the evening breeze rolled in from the nearby sea. He heard no footsteps or voices and he saw no lights in any direction. Much to his relief and shock, he was not injured by any of the dozen rocks slung at him during the chase. He leaned against the tree trunk and allowed his breathing to slowly return to normal. He honestly felt as if he could sprint another mile if he had to, but he was relieved that it was not necessary. His main concern right now was that he was still lost, and now he was lost farther from Iliana's house.

As Nearcus sat in the dark and gathered his thoughts, Marcus was meeting with Filaretos and Giorgos. The church meeting had continued despite the threat of murderers falling upon the congregation, but now it was over and the Christians were making their way back to their homes, all rejoicing at being safe and thanking Jesus for his protection. Marcus was anxious to search for Nearcus and he told the other two men that he planned to leave immediately. They counseled that it would be better to wait until morning to hunt for the missing boy, but Marcus had enough waiting and doing nothing. Aegospotami had entrusted his son to Marcus and the slave felt he had let the father down. Marcus wanted to find Nearcus now!

Giorgos said to the anxious paedotribae, "It will be very difficult in the dark as there are no lights in the orchards and no moon this evening. However, the sky is clear and the stars are bright so we might have a chance to locate him. I suggest I take us to where I last saw him and we start there. He was running west through the orchard. I doubt that he would turn to one side if he was trying to put as much distance between him and the gang chasing him. So we should go to where I saw him and head west from there."

When Dioxippus saw the three men leaving the yard and heading north into the orchards, he ran to join them. Marcus was going to send the young man back to wait at the house, but when he saw the look of determination on Dioxippus's face, he decided the boy deserved to join the search. The four men, the oldest over sixty and youngest just sixteen trotted through the trees with Giorgos in the lead, carrying the only torch they were using.

Nearcus did not want to return the way he had come. He was afraid that the murderous gang might still be in that direction. Yet he knew that if he continued to the west, he must be going farther from Iliana's house. But he was also very curious to know if the plan had worked and Dioxippus had been able to snatch the map and if so, were they right and Iliana's house church was the target. It was his curiosity that overcame his fear of the gang, so he decided that his best course was to move four rows of trees to the south and then walk very quietly easterly. By doing this he hoped that if the gang was still after him they would be in his original row of trees. Nearcus hoped that if he moved very carefully and dashed from tree to tree in the dark four rows to the south he could escape detection should he hear the gang ahead.

After nearly a quarter hour, Nearcus had yet to see or hear anyone so he stopped dashing between trees and just walked at a slow pace down the orchard row. He had concluded that the gang must have given up chasing him and went away, so he strolled through the black night thinking about food. He had missed the evening meal and after all his physical trials of the day, he was very, very hungry and thirsty. As his thoughts dwelled on the hope of getting some food and drink in the near future, he heard something move just ahead of him on his left.

Panic flooded Nearcus's thoughts and he dropped to his stomach. Then he crawled to the nearest tree trunk for cover. Once there he froze in position and listened carefully. He heard the leaves rustle and he could dimly see movement ahead. There was definitely someone there and they were trying to stay hidden. He could see two of them crawl on their knees between the trees about twenty yards away. Nearcus thought to himself, "I have nearly walked into a trap! They are lying in wait for me!"

Nearcus peeked around the tree trunk and saw the figures move again and they looked to be closing his position rapidly and quietly. He did not think they had seen him yet, so Nearcus decided to use the night and the tree to hide until they passed in their search for him. Looking up, the boy saw that the bottom branches on the olive tree were low enough that it would be an easy climb to hide in the sprouting limbs. He had grown up climbing the smaller mastic gum trees in his father's orchards so it was an easy matter for him to grasp a limb and swing himself high into these branches.

Once in his hiding place, Nearcus's competitive mind once again raced with options just as it always did in a pankration bouts. His immediate plan was to remain still in the tree and hopefully the murderers will move on their way, never spying his hiding place. Nearcus figured that the gang had split up into teams of two and had spread out to search for him. If this was the case, then it would be better to let them pass without getting into a fight that might attract the rest of the gang to him. "But," he thought, "if they see me then I will pounce on the nearest one and take off running again. I outran them once and I will do it again.

This time I will head east and try to reach a town or someplace I can get help."

As the two figures approached in the dark and shadows of the thick orchard, Nearcus felt fear rising within him. He was very frightened yet at the same time determined not to give up without trying to win. Just as the two dark figures were about under his tree, Nearcus heard the first sound from them.

The sound was, "Baa." Looking straight down Nearcus saw for the first time that these two figures were the sheep that had earlier distracted the gang! He felt foolish over the fear he had experienced and the thought of him hiding in a tree from two sheep was embarrassing and funny to him. For the first time since he yelled at the gang to attract their attention, Nearcus said something out loud, "I must look the fool!" And then he laughed loudly at himself.

Nearcus dropped from the tree and started moving easterly again. Soon he saw something moving in the distance he knew could not be more sheep. A torch was moving through the orchard coming toward him but slightly north of his route. Nearcus was not laughing anymore. He was sure this was the gang searching the orchard for him. He thought of hiding in a tree again, but he rejected the idea as being too risky. The light was far enough away that Nearcus was sure he could start running to the south and put enough distance between him and the murderers to escape. He began to run, but at a much slower pace than before because it was difficult to see at night under the canopy of olive trees that nearly plotted out the stars.

Filaretos had begun to feel his advanced years. He said to his fellow searchers, "I am afraid I am holding you younger men back. I will rest here and then head back if that is fine with you."

The others nodded and Giorgos approached the church elder and said, "The tree rows are laid out north to south and east to west." Then the slave pointed to the south and continued, "When you feel ready, just walk this direction for nearly a mile. Don't leave this row until you see the lights of Iliana's house on your right. Then just go to the light. It will be the first light you will see."

Filaretos smiled and said in a grandfatherly voice, "Yes, I know Giorgos. I have been traveling through these orchards since before you were born."

Giorgos smiled back at the old man and said, "God be with you."

"And God be with you in your search for the boy who was not raised here."

Marcus was anxious to start searching again. He was thankful that the elder had decided to return because, in fact, he was slowing the group. Giorgos raised his torch and pointed it to the east and said to Marcus and Dioxippus, "Who we seek is this way."

As Iliana's slave led the way, Dioxippus had a thought he did not share with the two men, "Yes, and the men we do not seek could be this way as well. But we will know soon enough."

Nearcus had covered a few hundred yards when he stopped and looked behind him. He saw the light moving in the same easterly direction and he smiled. The gang had not seen him turn south to avoid them.

Suddenly, Nearcus felt an overwhelming weakness. It was as if his strength had drained out of his toes. He was exhausted and too weak to continue. He took a seat next to a tree trunk and put his head between his up-raised knees. Nearcus was light headed from a lack of food and water and from the energy he had used to battle fear and to run beyond his limits. Without any advance warning, his body had just quit on him. He thought, "Wherever my strength had come from today, it is spent now. I should have rested for longer when I had lost them. I should have..." His thoughts stopped there as he rolled over onto his side and closed his eyes. Thoughts and plans would have to wait for a later time. Right now he had to sleep. He could not stop himself from falling into a deep slumber.

Filaretos had to stop a couple of times as he walked in the dark towards Iliana's house. Each time, he rested for a few minutes then started walking again. Rather than being frightened by being alone in the dark when a gang of murderers could be in the area, he enjoyed the solitude and fresh breeze on his face. He did not feel alone. He talked aloud to his god, Jesus, as he traveled. He thanked his Savior for cleansing him from sin and he thanked him for the chance to have this time to pray and lift up the cares of those in the church. He was walking and talking with Jesus as if the Lord was physically right next to him. Filaretos did this regularly and tonight it was especially sweet to him. He felt fulfilled and happy to have the Lord as his guide on this dark night.

In fact, Filaretos felt that his god was giving him specific directions at that very instant to deviate from the path Giorgos had set for his return to Iliana's. The old man stopped in his tracks and said aloud, "Lord, you lead and I will follow. You are in control." Then he turned to his right and went directly away from his previous destination. He did not know why the Lord wanted him to travel to the west but he was in such close communication with Jesus that Filaretos was certain that he must go this new direction. He said to himself, "This should be interesting!"

CHAPTER 15

Nearcus was stirred from his deep sleep by the sounds of wild shouts coming from just a dozen yards to his west. He opened his eyes and saw a tree burning, the light of the blaze made the shadows of the olive trees around it even darker and the bright light hid the distant stars in the sky. Around the tree stood six men, three of them holding burning torches and all of them holding jugs or bottles of wine. In the light of the fire it was easy for Nearcus to recognize the gang of murderers he had previously escaped. He was shocked by how close they were to where he had been sleeping. He wondered, "How is it that they did not see me?"

The answer to his question came when he looked at the burning olive tree. Tied to the trunk of the tree was a tall, old man. The gang had set the branches of the tree afire over the old man's head. Soon the flames would consume the branches and start down the trunk. When this happened, the old man would die a brutal and grotesque death.

The gang stood around, obviously all drunk with much wine, shouting and jeering at the old man. They yelled over the noise of the crackling fire that was rapidly consuming the old tree, "Old preacher man where is your god now? How is your Jesus going to save you from this?"

Nearcus saw that the old man's face was red from the heat of the fire just a foot above his head. The young pankratiast was lying on his stomach and scooted to his left to gain cover behind a tree trunk. He was so close that he clearly saw the old man's eyes. He did not see fear in those eyes; he saw a peace and confidence, even happiness, which was totally out of place for the situation. What he saw in the man's eyes had a remarkable effect on the boy. Inside, Nearcus began to feel he must do something, but he had no idea what he could do.

Filaretos had found his stroll with his Jesus to be more interesting than he could ever imagine. He had been surprised when he walked into the gang of drunks who were passed out in an orchard clearing. They had stirred and cursed the church leader for waking them. Then the leader had asked a question that Filaretos knew he had to answer truthfully. The leader had asked if Filaretos was a believer in Jesus and a follower of the Way. Filareto's answer resulted in the gang becoming violent and murderous again. Still drunk from earlier in the evening, they continued to consume the bottles of wine they had brought with them. First they had beaten the old man and then tied him to the tree trunk so they could use him as a target to practice throwing their knives and slinging their stones. Filaretos had been stuck twice in one arm and once in his lower right leg with the knives and four stones had found their mark on his chest and shoulders. When one of the gang members had approached Filaretos to retrieve his knife that was sticking out of the old man's leg, he was careless with his torch and accidentally set the tree limbs on fire. The thug had jumped back and fallen down. This had caused the rest of the gang to laugh heartily. The leader had cheered when he saw the tree catch fire. He and his men had become focused on watching the flames and waiting for the fire to burn Filaretos to death.

Now Nearcus shifted his focus from the old man's eyes to the blood oozing from his knife wounds. He looked more closely and saw that one knife was still stuck in Filaretos right shin. This gave the fast young pankratiast an idea on what he could do to save the old man from a horrible death.

Near him was the gang member who had started the fire and then fallen down. This thug was obviously more drunk than the others and he had edged away from the burning tree to a spot where he could sit down without being laughed at. This spot was just a few feet from Nearcus's hiding place. The man sat there with his legs spread in front of him and hands to his sides, one still holding a partly consumed bottle of wine. Nearcus noticed that all eyes were on the burning tree and the gory execution of the old Christian and sitting in front of him was an opponent in the perfect position to be tackled from behind. Nearcus instantly left his hiding place and after just three quick steps he jumped on the gang member's back. The pankratiast applied a choke hold with such force and skill that the man was unconscious in just seconds. Nearcus rolled the man to his side and grabbed the drunk's floppy straw hat and wine bottle. Then the tall twelve-year old, took large rapid strides towards the burning tree. He hoped the rest of the gang paid him little attention, thinking he was one of their cohorts.

By now the larger tree limbs were beginning to fall to the ground in a fiery rain. Nearcus ignored the cinders and branches falling around him and the tremendous heat the raging fire was giving off. His months of intense training had taught him to ignore pain and other distractions when he was engaged in a fight. He kept his focus on his objective and ignored everything else. His objective was to reach the knife in the old man's leg. This ability to concentrate was why Nearcus was the best pankratiast of any age on Chios and it was this ability that permitted him to dodge the falling, flaming branches and reach the knife. He grasped the knife handle with his right hand and pulled it out quickly. Nearcus then jumped to the back of the tree and cut the ropes holding Filaretos to the trunk. Just as he succeeded in cutting the last rope, Nearcus heard a thundering crack over his head. He looked up to see what was happening and the heat of the fire burned his eyebrows completely off.

Nearcus reached around the trunk and grabbed the old man's arm and pulled Filaretos to his side of the tree.

The leader of the gang began to get sober very quickly when he realized that it was a stranger in his friend's hat who had run towards the burning tree. When the leader saw the ropes fall from Filaretos's chest he became extremely angry that someone was spoiling his brutal fun. He stepped towards the tree trunk to stop the stranger when he heard the same loud crack in the top of the tree. Looking up, the leader saw the entire top half of the tree leaping with flames thirty feet high that were being blown by the on-shore wind right in his direction. The top of the tree tottered and then fell rapidly towards the drunks standing dumbfounded and completely frozen by the awesome sight over their heads.

A couple of seconds later, the fiery mass of branches and cinders came crashing around them. Two of the gang ran to safety just before they were engulfed by the raging ball of fire, but the rest of the gang was trapped in the inferno. They screamed and cried out as the heat seared their skin and set their hair on fire. Each of them ran from the flames, stripping their flaming tunics from their bodies as they made it to open space. They dropped to the ground and rolled until the flames were out, but they were in such wretched pain their cries could be heard for hundreds of yards. Despite their painful suffering, all of the gang survived the crashing, flaming tree except for the leader. As the tree lay on the ground being consumed by a tremendous fire, there was no sight of the leader anywhere. He was gone.

Nearcus and Filaretos were not under the tree when it fell over. They were able to run to safety as the tree fell away from them. Filaretos could only travel a short distance before he collapsed into Nearcus's arms. The boy dragged the large old man behind a tree trunk and sat with him, looking out for the gang who he figured would be searching for them. When he heard the screams from the gang members it did not take long for Nearcus to realize what had happened. As he watched the tree rapidly burn out, he spied a couple of figures helping others leave to the east, opposite of where he was hiding with Filaretos.

Now Nearcus knew he had to do something to help this injured and bleeding old man. As he examined this stranger to determine which wound was the worst and needed attention first, Nearcus was surprised by what he heard.

"You must be Nearcus, my boy," Filaretos said through clinched teeth but with smiling lips.

Nearcus was exhausted, lost and burned and yet the fact that this old stranger knew his name was the biggest shock of the night. Yet, all Nearcus could do in response was nod and ask, "Who are you?"

"Just a servant of Jesus who was saved by his hand."

Nearcus's forehead really stung from the burns he had received saving this old man's life, and now he was being told that he did not do anything—it was Jesus who had saved this stranger! Nearcus's attitude became even bitterer towards all gods. He thought, "They don't do anything, but people give them the credit for being saved!"

But then in the light of the dying fire Nearcus saw Filaretos's eyes and again there was that peace and happiness in them despite what had happened to him and the pain he must be suffering from his wounds and burns. Nearcus stared into the old man's eyes and began to question whether he had saved the man alone or, perhaps, there was some other power working this night that Nearcus could not explain.

CHAPTER 16

Dioxippus and the two slaves had seen an orange glow coming from a part of the orchard to their south. Immediately, Giorgos thought that the murderers had reached Iliana's house and had set it ablaze. Just as he thought this, the three searchers saw gigantic flames leap high into the sky above the glowing light.

"They have reached the house and have set it afire!" Giorgos shouted.

"Then they have either caught Nearcus or given up the chase and carried out their plans," Marcus said.

Dioxippus nodded and sincerely wished that Nearcus had outrun the murderers and gotten away. But he, too, found himself caring about Iliana and the others who might be suffering a vicious attack by the gang.

With nothing else said, all three men changed their original direction and ran towards the fire. They raced through the orchard and it did not take very long for them to reach the burning tree. They stopped a short distance away to survey the situation. Giorgos was relieved to see that the house was not on fire and that only one old olive tree was being consumed. Yet, he was confused so he scanned the orchard in an attempt to learn more about what had happened. Looking to his left, hidden in the dark shadow of a tree trunk he saw two figures lying on the ground. Giorgos reached out his arm and tapped Marcus on the shoulder and pointed to the two figures. Marcus did the same to Dioxippus and the three men moved towards the figures.

Upon reaching the men in the shadows, they saw Nearcus pressing one hand against the leg wound of Filaretos and with his other hand he was trying to stop the bleeding of the more severe of the two stab wounds in the old man's arm. Nearcus looked up when he saw the three approach, not sure of just who they might be; not sure if they were friend or foe. But he knew he must keep pressure on the bleeding wounds of this old man regardless of the approaching strangers' intentions.

Nearcus could not recognize who was standing in front of him because the fire was behind their backs so their faces were hidden in shadows. Before the boy could react or say anything he heard a voice that made his heart leap and his strength return.

"Nearcus! My wonderful student! You are alive!" exclaimed Marcus upon recognizing the young pankratiast.

Giorgos rushed to the side of Filaretos and, seeing the old man bleeding badly, the slave reached into his belt pouch and pulled a piece of cloth from it. Ripping the cloth in half, he handed one piece to Nearcus, and then Giorgos used the other half to wrap the old man's arm wounds. He said, "Use this on the leg and press very hard. We must stop the bleeding."

Nearcus did as he was directed and Dioxippus knelt down to help him.

Marcus took the arm bandage from Giorgos's hands and said, "You know the way. Run for help and medical aid. We'll tend to him here."

Giorgos nodded and sprinted off into the dark orchard.

"What happened here?" Marcus asked Nearcus.

Before the boy could respond, Filaretos spoke, "I was set upon by the gang of drunken murderers and they beat me and tied me to the tree. The tree was set on fire and I prayed for salvation from the pain, then out of the night Jesus sent Nearcus running to my aid. He cut me loose and saved me from burning! God crashed the burning tree onto the gang

137

and sent my tormenters scurrying for the cover of darkness, their tails between their legs! Praise be to God and his son, my savior, Jesus!"

Marcus responded, "Praise be to God." Then he looked Nearcus in the eyes and said, "You have done well this evening."

Nearcus kept pressure on the leg wound of Filaretos and pondered what the old man had said. He questioned to himself, "Who is this Jesus who gets so much credit and causes such devotion and worship from Marcus, Iliana and this old man?"

By the time the morning's first light appeared, Filaretos was resting comfortably in Iliana's house, his wounds bandaged and his stomach full of nutritious soup. The tree had finished burning and Iliana and her slaves were thankful that the fire had not spread to any other trees in the orchard.

Nearcus, Marcus and Dioxippus were asleep on the ground under a nearby tree. Exhausted by the night's great adventure, the trio slept soundly despite being on the bare ground. They were not awakened until Iliana nudged their feet with her toe to offer them breakfast.

The three were all very hungry, for they had used all of their energy in racing through the orchard the night before, so a morning meal felt wonderful to them. Sitting under the tree, scooping mush into their mouths from a common, large bowl, Marcus was the first to speak.

"Well, Nearcus," he said, "you said you wanted to travel to see exciting new things. Has it been exciting enough for you so far?"

All three laughed, and then Nearcus spoke, "After the voyage we had and the events of last night, I am afraid to think what is in store for us in Corinth!"

They were in high spirits and still laughing when Iliana returned and said, "Nearcus, Filaretos is awake now and would like to speak to you."

Nearcus stood and followed the woman into her house. He was shown to the room where the church elder was lying on a bed, his head propped up so that he could eat. His leg and arm were wrapped in large bandages and his face was smeared with oil to help relieve the pain of the burns that had scarred his forehead and cheeks. When Filaretos saw Nearcus enter, a large smile came over his face and his eyes took on a sincere twinkle. He motioned for Nearcus to draw near and to sit on a chair by the bed. Nearcus did as requested and sat down.

"Nearcus!" the old man said with a laugh, "You look a sight with no eyebrows and a red forehead!"

Nearcus had a little pain from his burns, but he figured it was slight compared to the pain this old man must be experiencing. So he smiled in response to the light-hearted comment made by Filaretos.

Seeing that he had set the boy at ease, Filaretos began to speak of the reason behind asking Nearcus to visit him, "Do you have any gods you pray to regularly?"

It seemed a very personal question to Nearcus, but when a boy is addressed by an old man on Chios, the boy must respond with the truth and not question the motive behind the elder's comments. So Nearcus said, "I don't pray to gods anymore."

"Why not?"

"They don't have anything to do with me and I don't have anything to do with them."

"You have been disappointed by the gods?" asked Filaretos.

Nearcus nodded and was about to add that he doubted that the gods even existed and if they did, they were too fickle to base your life upon. However, before he could speak the old man asked another difficult question.

"I know why the gods have disappointed you. Would you like to know why?"

In fact, Nearcus did want to know why the gods seemed to be at war with him. He thought, "If this old man can truly tell me why the gods have cast me aside, then I want to know." The boy nodded and his eyes gave Filaretos permission to continue.

"Many men believe in and pray to many gods. Men want to know why things happen the way they do. They want to know why some years there is enough rain for a good harvest yet other years there is not enough rain to save the crops. They want to know why some of their children die young and others become strong and help their fathers. They want to know why some bad men prosper while some good men suffer. So they look for answers from a source that is greater than themselves. Does this make sense to you?"

Nearcus actually did find this to make sense, so he nodded in agreement.

Filaretos continued, "You have found out at a very young age what many grown men never discover. Praying to wood or stone statues, whether they are small in your own home or in great temples in great cities does nothing to bring the rain, or save children or bring justice to bad men. You see, if a god is the creation of man's hands, how can this god do anything greater than a man can do?"

Filaretos paused to let the weight of what he shared with this twelve-year old boy settle into Nearcus's mind. After he saw in the boy's eyes that he understood, the elder continued.

"I no longer pray to man-made gods. I pray to the only true god, the maker of heaven, the earth and the sea. He existed before the earth and he will always exist. And, this is what I called you in here to say to you. I asked that you come to me so I can tell you Nearcus that this one, true God loves you! He loves you personally! There is nothing you can do to make him love you and there is nothing you can do to stop him from loving you!"

Nearcus would have scoffed to himself about what the old man was telling him except that he had seen Filaretos eyes when the elder was about to die a horrible death by being burned alive. The vision of what he had seen in Filaretos's eyes last night kept bothering Nearcus. He asked himself, "How could he have been so calm and joyous with the fire just above his head? How can I become so brave and happy?" For Nearcus knew he was bitter with the gods and everything in his life seemed to be getting so difficult. He had lost at the trials because of a bad tooth. He had made enemies of his teammates and one had even tried to kill him. His dream voyage to seeing the wonderful sights of the big city had become a nightmare. He had been cast aside to make his own way to the games and then hunted like prey by those who wanted to kill him. And now this old man was telling him that a supreme god actually loved him! "Ridiculous!" Nearcus thought.

Seeing the bitterness, disbelief and confusion in Nearcus's eyes, Filaretos added, "Do you think being there last night to save my life was by accident? Or were you chosen to be in that position for a purpose?"

"Chosen!" That word flashed through Nearcus's thoughts. His eyes grew wide as he pondered that word. Once again he was being told that he was "chosen." This time it was not a voice in the orchard as he sat under a tree. This time it was not from the lips of an old woman dressed in black on the side of the road. This time it was from a strange old man lying in bed suffering from near fatal wounds who had escaped a horrible death just hours before. In Nearcus's mind he kept shouting to himself in great frustration, "Chosen! Chosen for what and chosen by whom?"

Before Nearcus could answer Filaretos, the old man laid his head back and let his eyes close. The elder lay there perfectly still. Nearcus thought he had died, the torture and wounds having been too much for the old man. The boy

141

then saw Filaretos's chest rise just a little and then fall and then rise again. The old man was still breathing, but he was no longer awake. Nearcus silently stood and left the room. Iliana was in the next room and looked up at the boy as he crossed to the exterior door.

Nearcus looked at Iliana and said, "He is sleeping now." Then he went outside and withdrew from the slaves and Dioxippus to a secluded spot in the nearby orchard. He wanted to be alone to consider what Filaretos had said.

Nearcus thought, "Just suppose that this old man is right. Just suppose that there is one supreme god who does love me. And just suppose that this god had chosen me to be or do something for him in Corinth. What am I expected to do about this? What am I to do?"

The rest of the day Nearcus was quiet. He did not start conversations or seek out the company of his traveling companions or hosts. He had a lot on his mind. So it was a relief when late in the afternoon Marcus called the two pankratiasts to his side.

"In two days the games begin and we must get you young men ready to compete at your best," Marcus shared with them. "I think we can agree that yesterday you got in enough running!"

Nearcus and Dioxippus nodded and smiled, the elder boy even offered a chuckle in response.

"Let's work on grappling today," continued Marcus. "Come, let's find a suitable field and work to get the rust off of your moves and balance."

Soon, Marcus was supervising the boys' training in a small nearby field that had a bed of thick grass. Nearcus knew that Marcus was a tough task-master and that he worked his students very hard. This was new to Dioxippus who had been training himself for the past year and would take a break whenever he felt he needed to. Marcus, however, did not give rest periods. He drove the boys through drills and exercises one right after another. It was not until the evening meal was being prepared that he called a stop to the training and dismissed the boys.

"You are lucky to have Marcus as your paedotribae," Dioxippus said to Nearcus as the two boys rested in the shade of a nearby tree waiting to be called to dinner. "After today I can see why you are so good. You have had the very best training."

Nearcus nodded and thought, "Yes, I do have the best coach on Chios. I don't know how Dioxippus got ready for the trials by training himself. It must have been a terrible way to prepare."

"Can I ask you a question, Nearcus?" Dioxippus asked with hesitation.

Nearcus nodded.

"Why did the old man want to see you this morning?"

"He wanted to tell me about his god."

"What did he say?" Dioxippus asked with a very serious tone as he turned to face his team mate.

"He said his god was the only true god in the whole world."

Dioxippus had heard Filaretos say something similar at the church meeting last night. Hearing it a second time was just as odd to him as it was the first. Everyone knows that there are many, many gods in the world. How could the old man think such foolishness?

"Oh, yeah," Nearcus continued, "And he said that this one true god loved me personally."

When he heard that a god—especially an all-powerful god—could love a human, Dioxippus felt a strange feeling overcome him. To be loved was something he longed for with all his heart.

Without saying another word to Nearcus, the elder boy stood and went directly to Iliana's house. He walked through the front room and pulled back the drape that hung across the entrance to the bedroom where Filaretos was recovering. He quietly entered the room and sat by the bed

143

where Filaretos was sleeping. Dioxippus sat there in silence waiting for the church elder to awaken. Dioxippus wanted to know about any god who could love a bad person — about any god who could love *him*.

CHAPTER 17

It had been dawn when the trio of travelers had left with Giorgos for the long trip to Corinth. Now it was mid-morning and the small horse that pulled the wooden-wheeled cart was being rested on the side of the road. Giorgos had brought oats for the horse to supplement any feed that might be found on the roadside. As the horse ate the oats from an old small basket the slave held to it's nose, Nearcus, Marcus and Dioxippus reclined in the shade of a grape vine that had grown very high over an old stone wall.

None of the travelers talked much that morning. Marcus had awakened with tremendous stiffness in his shoulders and he was unable to raise his arms more than a few inches and every time he twisted or bent at the waist a frown and pain showed on his face. He dealt with the discomfort by restricting his movements to the absolute minimum necessary for the time being. Conversation was not easy when you are in pain.

Nearcus did not speak much because his thoughts were on their destination. His spirits were rising because he thought that maybe this horrible trip was starting to become the wonderful experience of seeing Corinth that he had dreamed of for so long. He centered his thoughts on the sights he would see and what it must be like to be in a city so crowed that it had over twice the entire population of his home island. There was a saying in all of Greece that "it is not every man's fortune to visit Corinth." Nearcus was anxious to learn why everyone said that. At last it looked to him that he will have the chance to become one of the fortunate men actually to visit Corinth. In the back of his thoughts was the confusion about being "chosen," but with each mile the travelers grew closer to Corinth, Nearcus was able to push that question farther back into the deep recesses of his mind.

Dioxippus had been quiet all morning because he was still in a state of grace. Something had happened to him that he could not believe or describe. For the first time in his entire life he felt whole; he felt loved entirely. He had talked to Filaretos and learned that Jesus had come to earth to take away his past sins so that Dioxippus could receive the full love of his creator. This knowledge was overwhelming to the sixteen-year old who had been kicked out of his house and banished to the slave quarters by his father and uncle. When the church elder had shared how Jesus had sacrificed himself for Dioxippus and that this son of god would have done it solely for him alone if no others had ever believed in him, the young man was excited beyond description. Filaretos had introduced him to a man who had lived perfectly and then rose from the dead to prove he was the true son of the one true god. And this one true god loved Dioxippus personally!

All through the night and this morning Dioxippus's thoughts were lost in this knowledge that he was worth so much that a sin-less man, the true son of god, would die for him. With this knowledge came excitement and a peace in his heart that Dioxippus had always wanted but had never found. The bitterness and hatred he had felt towards everyone was washed away when he met Jesus in that room with that suffering old man.

Soon the horse was sufficiently rested to resume the journey to Corinth. The Romans had paved the road a few years before and now it was used much more than in previous times. So, as the travelers got closer to Corinth the traffic on the road got heavier. By the late afternoon the traffic was thick enough that the cart was slowed to where it would have been faster to walk to the city. As the travelers approached Corinth on the Coastal Road that led to the city from the northeast, they first saw the great Acrocorinth which seemed to hover above the whole city. On top of this jagged 2,000 foot hill were the sacred shrines to the goddesses Aphrodite and Demeter. Next Nearcus and Dioxippus were impressed by the Temple of Apollo and near it the sacred springs of the Pierenne where Greeks had come for centuries to worship and be healed by the waters. Nearcus was truly excited about these fascinating sights that for many years he had dreamed of seeing. Now he was here and the experience was everything he dreamed it would be.

About two hours before sunset, Giorgos had the cart near their destination after navigating through the narrow streets and around many other carts, selling stalls, piles of trash, citizens who gathered in the middle of the road to talk and refused to move for the traffic, and squads of Roman soldiers that patrolled the city. Finally, the travelers reached their destination. The slave parked the cart in front of a large, impressive stone house squeezed between two large shops with their attached warehouses located on a busy thoroughfare in the western district of Corinth. Giorgos told his passengers to wait in the cart and to protect the horse from thieves, and then he went to the gate that separated the house's entrance courtyard from the street.

Nearcus thought that Giorgos was joking when he told them to guard the horse. He thought, "Who would try to steal a horse that is attached to a cart that we are sitting in?"

But then Nearcus began to think that maybe it was not a joke. Since they had entered the city, his head had been constantly swiveling from side to side as he tried to take in all that he saw. There was great activity on every street and around every corner something new and different appeared. Nearcus had never seen so many people in one place at one time and they all seemed to be moving so fast! There were merchants shouting at passers-by to buy their wares and others were rushing with arms full of fine linen or fruit or bags of meal or leather hides, tanned and ready to be made into sandals and furniture; all were hurrying with something in their arms that just had to be delivered to a buyer quickly! Not only items that could be transported in men's arms or small carts blocked the streets. Nearcus was surprised when Giorgos turned a corner and their route was blocked by a very large marble stone being moved through the city streets to a building sight.

The streets were not only crowded with the activity of commerce, but also by competing ideas. On each corner of each street there were the shouters! Men dressed in formal togas standing on stones or chairs and shouting about one thing or another! Most were talking about how the city fathers were wonderful and had arranged the games as a tribute to Poseidon. Others shouted continuously about the greatness of Emperor Nero and how he was a god that should be worshiped. Still others shouted to attract many of the visitors who had come to Corinth to attend the Isthmian Games to see the temples of Apollo, Athena, Aphrodite and Asclepius. Many shouted to attract those who wanted to wager a bet on different athletes to win different events at the games. Nearcus had never seen such activity or heard such racket before and his eyes, ears and mind were nearly overwhelmed by it all. He began to think that it was indeed possible for Marcus, Dioxippus and he to be distracted by something new and amazing long enough for a thief to actually loosen the horse's harness and steal the animal while they sat in the cart!

Nearcus forced himself to keep one eye on the horse, but it was difficult because there was just so much to see. Soon, Giorgos returned and took the horse's bit in his hand and led the horse and cart through the house's courtyard gate. Once inside, the slave securely shut the gate behind them. Marcus, Dioxippus and Nearcus climbed out of the cart and followed Giorgos into the fine house. There waiting at the door was a female slave named Iro. She was only sixteen but already fully grown. Her smile was welcoming as she reached for the bags in the hands of the travelers. Then she led them into a large room that was lighted by the sun through large doors on three sides. As Iro disappeared with the bags through a door on the right, a stately woman dressed in an expensive stolla covered by a detailed palla draped over her shoulder entered from the left.

"Hello travelers! I am so glad I can help you on your journey!" said the woman as if she was being more than just polite; it sounded as if she truly meant what she said. In her hand was a piece of paper and she lifted it as she said, "My name is Garifallia and welcome to my home. My dear sister in the Christ, Iliana, has asked me to offer you hospitality while you compete in the games. I am happy to do so. Please consider my home to be your home as long as you are in the city."

"You are very gracious," Marcus said, "May I introduce the Chios youth pankration competitors, Nearcus and Dioxippus."

The two boys nodded in a sign of respect and then Marcus continued, saying something that surprised Nearcus, "Dioxippus here is a new man. Last night he joined us in following the Way!"

Upon hearing this, Garifallia beamed with joy and crossed the room and gave Dioxippus a hug with her right arm around his shoulders. It was only then that the visitors noticed that Garifallia had no left arm under her palla. Nearcus wondered if his hostess had been born without the limb or if she lost it later, and if so, when and how did it happen. But boys in Chios are taught manners and to never ask personal questions of a lady, especially one who is your hostess, so Nearcus kept his questions to himself.

Dioxippus was a little uneasy when he was introduced as a new follower of the Way, but deep down inside it felt good. What happened next felt even better.

"Then we must celebrate the return of a lost lamb! I will have our church meet tonight to welcome you to Corinth! I want to show you that not all in Corinth live down to the reputation of this wicked city!" Garifallia's was happy and warm and it made all the men in the room feel welcome and special. She had that effect not only on men, but on women too. As the hostess of one of the largest house churches in one of the largest cities in the Roman empire, Garifallia had evidenced her gifts of hospitality and organization for over fifteen years. She called for her slaves and then she dispatched them to announce a special church gathering around the evening meal to be served within the hour. Her ability to assemble a large group, organize a meal for them all and help her guests settle was remarkable, but merely a display of her leadership talents.

Soon the great room of the house and the entrance courtyard were filled with two dozen church members. They gathered around the travelers and asked them about their journey. Nearcus had never seen Marcus so talkative before. The slave was at ease among these strangers in the big city and easily shared the torturous voyage and the perilous night in the orchards. At every turn of the story members of the church would say, "Praise the Lord!" or "Thank you, Jesus!"

After Marcus had told of their travels to date, the Christians wanted to know about Dioxippus and how he came to believe in their Savior, Jesus. Dioxippus was very shy about sharing such a personal experience, especially because he had learned in his hard life that if you open up to others about your feelings they will hurt you. But he felt a strange, warming power within that enabled him to ignore his past experiences with strangers and his family and to trust these who surrounded him. He was sure he could feel their love for him and this gave him confidence to obey the urge he had inside to talk about his experience when

Filaretos had shared the story of Jesus, the Son of the one true God with him just yesterday.

Nearcus watched as all the members of the church who had gathered in that house hung on every word that Dioxippus said. Again there were many exclamations of "Praise the Lord!" and "Thank you, Jesus!" Nearcus was confused about all of this and in his mind the impressions of all the many and great things he had seen that day swirled around and around. So, he quietly slipped out of the main room and made his way through the crowd to the front of the courtyard by the street. There, just to the side of the gate was a small, one-horse stable where Giorgos was feeding the horse and rubbing it down in preparation for his long trip back to Iliana's tomorrow.

"Well hello young Nearcus," Giorgos greeted him as he walked around to the front of the horse. "It is pretty crowded in there, isn't it?"

Nearcus picked up a handful of oats from the feed bag and offered them to the horse as he responded, "It is crowded everywhere in this city! I have never seen so many people."

Giorgos smiled and moved to the side of the horse and picked up a brush to curry the animal. He stroked the horse's flanks as he talked, "Garifallia is an amazing woman. In just minutes she can gather an entire houseful of people and feed them all. And she does it with only three slaves and one arm. I have never known a woman like her."

Nearcus was curious so he asked, "How did she lose her arm?

Giorgos continued to groom the horse as he answered, "About three years ago Rome burned and many blamed the Emperor. So to deflect criticism from himself, Nero accused the Christians of starting the fire and of defiling the gods and their temples. For awhile it was a really bad time to be a Christian. Most of the trouble was there in Rome, but some of the hatred and fear did spread to the colonies. Since

Corinth is a hub on the direct trade route to and from Rome, some of that trouble came here. Garifallia is a pretty important person here in Corinth. She has built a successful business in trading fine linens and she is a Christian. Her business competitors used the persecution to try and put her out of business. They accused her of all sorts of lies and brought her before the Roman governor who dismissed all the charges as being vicious falsehoods. But this is an evil city and its reputation as the worst in the empire is well earned. When her competitors could not get the Roman government to put her out of business they gathered a mob of drunkards and superstitious criminals to drag her off to the temple of Palaimon and demanded that she renounce Jesus the Nazarene and worship Apollo and his fellow gods and goddesses. Do you know what she did?"

Nearcus had stopped feeding the horse and was totally enthralled with the tale, so he shook his head and said quickly, "No, tell me."

"She just smiled at them! This got them so angry that they charged her and lifted her over their heads and ran to the top of the temple steps. Then they threw her into the sacrificial pit where she landed on the old bones of animals that had been slaughtered in ceremonies. One of the larger bones from a bull pierced her left arm so deeply that it nearly cut it off just above the elbow."

Nearcus grimaced when he heard how Garifallia had been maimed. Giorgos saw this pained look on the boy's face and stopped his horse grooming to face Nearcus. Then he continued, "She would have bled to death right there with the mob screaming at her but the Lord came to her rescue. The earth quaked violently and the frightened mob screamed and ran from the temple. They did not know if they had displeased Apollo or Palaimon by throwing her into the sacrificial pit or if her god was so powerful that he shook the earth in rage. Regardless, they all left in a hurry! Seeing them scatter, a passing Roman patrol ran to investigate what had happened. Leading the patrol was a centurian who is a member of the church that meets at Garifallia's house. He jumped into the pit and tied off what was left of her arm. He had his squad take her home where the rest of the arm was cut off and she healed well enough."

"Why didn't she just pretend to worship Apollo and deny her god? If her god forgives those who do wrong, why couldn't she just say anything to get to safety and then ask for forgiveness later?" Nearcus asked. He was thinking of what it would be like to go through life without an arm just because you wouldn't say certain words at a certain time.

"I guess Jesus wants to be a friend to those who are a friend to him. A true friend does not desert another just because it is convenient or safer to do so."

Nearcus was about to argue that a true friend would not want another to be maimed for the rest of his life over just a few words, but they were interrupted by the arrival of Garifallia. Being the good hostess she had noticed that one of guests of honor had slipped away and she came to find Nearcus.

The graceful lady spoke as she approached, "Nearcus, did you get enough to eat? I know it must be tiring to have such a commotion after such a long journey, but the church members will be leaving soon and you will have quiet to get your rest for the night. It will be dark soon and so all of them must be leaving to be off the streets before the night starts in Corinth."

This raised a question in Nearcus's mind and he asked. "Why must they be in their homes by dark? Is there a law about being on the streets at night?"

"Oh! I wish there was!" responded Garifallia, "It would be grand to have peace during the night. No, we just find it best to avoid those who want to do their business in the dark."

Nearcus had a questioning look on his face. He was not following what his hostess was saying.

Unlike Garifallia who had lived her whole life in a big city, Giorgos understood the simple farm background of Nearcus and explained, "Nearcus, men who do evil prefer to do it under the cover of darkness. All evil avoids the light because it does not want to be seen."

Nearcus wondered what evil he was referring to. What happened on the streets of Corinth at night that grown men made an effort to be indoors before the sun went down? In a matter of hours he would find out.

CHAPTER 18

That night Giorgos slept in the small stall with the horse. It was not a very good horse, but its importance to Iliana's business was vital. It was the only horse the farm owned. It was used to haul the cart through the orchard during harvest time and then it hauled the olives to market. Without the horse, it would be terribly hard for the business to remain successful. So, Giorgos watched over the horse very closely. Whenever he came to the city with the horse he slept with it at night. He was careful not to let anyone steal the precious animal and he always left the city as soon as he was able. To Giorgos, the city was nothing but a place where bad things happened. On the farm, bad men who wanted to cause harm had to travel a great distance to reach Iliana and Giorgos and the rest of the household. But in the city, these bad men were just a few feet away, just beyond the latched gate near the stable. So, as usual, on this night Giorgos slept in the stable to protect the horse and to preserve the success of Iliana's business which he was devoted to doing for her.

While Giorgos drifted off to sleep he thought of the long, lonely journey he had tomorrow. He planned on getting a very early start in order to avoid as much congestion as he could and get clear of the city as quickly as possible. While he was planning his activities and timetable, he heard a noise the made him sit-up with a jolt. He heard the latch on the gate being opened. It was being opened slowly, but Giorgos was sure he knew the sound of the bolt being slid to the side. He thought that a thief was entering the courtyard from the street to steal his horse. Quietly, the slave moved to the end of the stable and peered into the darkness. He was right, the gate was open just enough for a person to slip through it. But Giorgos could not see anyone in the courtyard. There was no movement or sound. He thought he should be able to hear footsteps on the cobblestones that covered the courtyard, but there was only silence.

He heard the horse stomp a leg and when he turned to look at the animal he felt something hard strike him on the back of the head. Giorgos fell to his knees from the force of the blow. He was staggered and dizzy but still alert. He reached in front of him and placed his hands on the ground, then lowered himself to the straw that covered the floor of the stable. He thought, "Just a couple of seconds lying down to clear my head then I can get up and fight."

As Giorgos lay there he heard light footsteps running across the courtyard cobblestones. When he opened his eyes, he saw the horse's hind hoofs and beyond them the large, dirty feet of a man wearing old, torn sandals. The slave tried to rise to fight the thief that was taking his precious animal, but the blow to his head made it impossible for him to regain his balance. He rose to his hands and knees but that was as far as he could go before sinking back to a prone position in the hay. Giorgos reached out his left arm and grabbed the right rear leg of the horse and held on with all the strength he could manage. But the horse kicked the slave's hand free with little effort.

Giorgos was in a panic and angry that he could not make his body fight the thief. He lay there with his head on the ground, his face turned to his left and his eyes open. He was so, so dizzy, yet he could still see the feet of the thief and the horse. And then he saw another set of feet! These were much smaller and feminine. They rushed up behind the man's feet and Giorgos heard a girl shout, "Stop! Thief! Help! Help!"

The injured slave recognized the voice of Iro, the young slave of Garifallia's. She had seen the intruder and rushed to stop him from stealing Giorgos's horse.

"She is a brave girl," Giorgos thought, "and she is screaming loudly enough to wake the dead! Come Marcus! Come Dioxippus! Come someone quick!" But Giorgos knew there was not anyone in the household who was a match for this thief. The only male slave Garifallia owned was very old and supervised the other female house slaves. He could barely walk, let alone fight a mean thief. Marcus was injured and could barely raise his arms, and Dioxippus and Nearcus were only boys, also no match for this obviously bold, vicious and hardened criminal.

What Giorgos saw next made him even madder and more desperate to get up and fight. The horse stopped moving backward, but the men's feet were now facing Iro's feet. Then the girl's feet were lifted in the air and her screams became muffled. Giorgos knew he was seeing the thief choosing to ignore the horse and, instead, grab the slave girl to carry her off. Giorgos could see the girl's small feet frantically kicking as there were suspended six-inches off of the stable floor. The thief had his hand over her mouth but Giorgos could tell she was angrily screaming as the man moved towards the courtyard gate, his new prize in his arms.

The sound of bare feet rapidly slapping against the cobblestones was great news to Giorgos. It meant that someone from the house had been stirred and was running to stop the kidnapping.

"Stop! Stop! Put her down!"

Giorgos recognized the voice of the man shouting. But it was not a man; it was a twelve-year old boy. It was Nearcus. He was the first to respond.

The thief was having difficulty with the squirming, angry female slave. She was quite pretty and a young girl like this would fetch top dollar if he got her to Athens and sold her at the slave market there. He did not want to damage his prize, but he was being chased and her fighting was slowing him down so he slammed his right fist into her jaw and she went limp. Now he could make good his escape without having a squirming girl fight him at each step.

Nearcus had jumped from his bed and thrown his tunic over his head and raced out to see what the commotion was about. He had seen a very large, burly man leaving the courtyard with Iro in his arms. Instinctively, Nearcus raced to help the girl. Barefoot and still a little asleep, Nearcus was not fit to engage in a fight with a man very much larger than himself. Yet he knew something must be done and he was the only one around to do it. He thought, "Where is Marcus? Where is Giorgos?" But these thoughts passed quickly as the thief left the courtyard and ran down the narrow street. Nearcus knew he had to keep them in sight. So he ran barefoot through the nearly deserted, dirty Corinthian street. At the corner, the thief had turned right with Iro still vigorously fighting her abductor. Nearcus followed, and because of his greater speed, the boy was rapidly gaining on the thief who was slowed by carrying his squirming captive. When Nearcus saw the thief hit Iro, his fear was replaced by anger. He ran even faster.

Now that Iro was no longer slowing the thief, he ran faster and it was harder for Nearcus to close on him. The thief obviously knew the city well. He turned down one street and then into another and then up an alley and then down narrow steps. Nearcus was totally lost, but he kept the thief and Iro in sight. There were others on the street but they paid no attention to a large man carrying an unconscious girl and being chased by a twelve-year old boy. After all, this was the night in Corinth and evil things were seen regularly. No one was going to interfere in another man's nightly business.

Nearcus followed the thief around a sharp turn and suddenly found himself on a street full of lights. In front of each establishment was a bright torch burning. Many men and only a handful of women walked in and out of the open doors of each business. Nearcus slowed to a trot as he made his way through the crowded business area, still keeping the thief in his sight. He saw the burly man stop at a shop and pound on a door. It opened slightly and after a short exchange with someone behind the shop door, the thief moved quickly down the street to the far end.

Nearcus wondered what shops would be open this late in the night, but his question was answered when he came to the first one. Inside were boisterous men lifting wooden goblets and pouring wine down their throats. There was no food to be seen, just drink everywhere. The next open door Nearcus passed had the same scene. The young boy wondered how these men could be up late drinking and still get to their jobs when the sun came up. But then he understood what Giorgos had said about evil business being the trade of the night. These men did not work day jobs. They came out at night to reek havoc on the city by stealing and attacking citizens.

Suddenly, Nearcus felt at risk. Until now he had been focused on catching the thief and helping Iro escape. But now, surrounded by a street full of evil men he became frightened at what might happen to him. He stopped trotting and froze just a few yards down the street. In the distance he saw the thief with Iro over his shoulder. The thief turned and looked right into Nearcus's eyes and then smirked, as if he was saying, "You lose, boy. This is my place and now I am safe and I can do anything I want to this girl."

Nearcus went from frightened to angry again in an instant. One of the reasons he was the best pankratiast on Chios was that he hated to lose—at anything! He gave a quick thought of returning to get Marcus or to find a Roman patrol, but this passed from his mind when he realized that he had no idea where he was. How could he find Marcus and how could he lead help back here?

The young man started down the street with his eyes fixed on the doorway the thief had entered at the far end of the street. Nearcus had no plan and he was not trying to think of one just yet. His emotions were driving him to do something and he would figure out what he could do as he went. Drunken men and even those not drunk took notice of the tall boy who had no business being on this street at night. Some made lewd comments to Nearcus while others just looked him up and down slowly and then turned away with a disgusted expression. Nearcus kept his eyes focused on his destination and pretended not to notice the evil men that surrounded him.

About twenty yards from his objective, Nearcus stepped on something sharp. He looked down and it was a shard of a broken clay mug that some drunk had thrown in the street after finishing his drink. The pointy piece of pottery did significant damage to the bottom of Nearcus's right heel. A one-half inch gash was opened and blood began to flow from it. It hurt, but Nearcus was not going to stop to attend to it. He was afraid that if he stopped moving on this street some of these evil men would get it in their mind to abuse him. So the young pankratiast did as he had always done in a bout, he ignored the injury and its pain and kept moving forward.

Soon he was at the door where the thief had taken Iro. He looked in and saw that it was not a drinking establishment. It appeared more like a merchant's place of business with a small room that had a couple of wooden chairs against the wall. On a small table near the back of the room was a single candle that gave off a dim, smoky light that left dark corners where men could be sitting. Nearcus hesitated while he tried to sort out the many thoughts in his mind, "You need to come up with a plan for this bout. Do you attack right away from the front or look for other options? Look over there. Is that a man in the shadows? Where could the thief have taken Iro? Are there rooms through that curtain on the side? Think! Nearcus! You need a plan and you need it right now!"

While straining to look in the corner shadows before entering the room, a plan finally came to the young competitor. If the shadows could hide attackers, then they could hide him as well. Nearcus took a step back and looked up and down the street. No one was paying attention to him any longer. To his left he saw a slight opening between the buildings. Quickly and quietly he slid into the narrow slit that separated the building where the thief had entered and the neighboring stone warehouse. It was pitch black in this hiding place and Nearcus had to feel his way forward as he could see nothing. Sliding sideways, moving his left foot ahead a little and then following with his right foot, he was able to go nearly ten feet into the crevasse. He stopped there because he heard voices coming from behind the wall in front of him. They were deep voices and it sounded like maybe three or four were speaking. The volume of the conversation grew louder and louder as the men began to shout at each other. Now Nearcus could clearly hear what was being said.

"You would do better selling her to me right now!"

"I could get a lot more for her in Athens!"

"Yes, but you would have to pay to transport her there and if she escaped or killed herself, you would get nothing. And a little less now is better than a lot of nothing later."

"But you are offering me practically nothing for her!"

"Of course I am. She is known in this city and it wouldn't be long before someone sees her and then all is lost. I have a caravan going to Rome tomorrow morning. I will send her there and that is how I will make a profit. But it costs a lot to send her that far so my profit will be small."

The voices grew quieter and Nearcus did not hear what the thief said in response to the slave merchant's offer. He decided that he needed to get behind the building and see if he could sneak in from the back. Nearcus tried to slide farther back into the small space between the buildings but soon it was too narrow to continue. He had to retrace his steps to return to the main street. As he reached the entrance to the street he jumped back into the shadows when he saw the thief leaving the building and pass directly in front of his hiding place. The thief was counting coins in his hands while he frowned, obviously not satisfied with the small price he had received from the slave merchant.

Nearcus was relieved that the large, burly thief had left. He hoped that the slave merchant was a much smaller man—a man more his own size in case he had to fight to release Iro. Nearcus was revising his plans now. His first thought was to try to return to Garifallia's house and lead them to the slave merchant. She could have the Roman authorities force the return of her property, but if that did not work then it might be possible for Garifallia to buy Iro back. However, Nearcus rejected this plan for two reasons: the first was because it could take him a long time to find his way back to the house in the dark and the second was the imminent departure of Iro. Dawn was just a couple of hours away, and the slave merchant could be moving his product at anytime to link up with a caravan on the edge of the city. Nearcus was not sure what he should do, but he was certain of only a couple of facts. He was here now and Iro was here in this building now. Whatever he did, Nearcus knew he must do it before the sun came up.

The young pankratiast was out of ideas on how to beat this problem—this opponent—he was facing. Whenever he had reached this situation in a real bout back on Chios he would revert to a very basic tactic—he would charge directly at his opponent. Having reached the decision that there was no other option, Nearcus stepped out of his hiding place and went to the open door of the slave trader's business. With a bold swagger that he used to try and hide his fear, Nearcus entered the small, poorly lighted room. He expected to find himself surrounded by men hidden in the dark corners, but to his surprise he was all alone in the room. Nearcus only hesitated for a quick second before he put his chest out and chin up and stepped through the curtain covering the back exit to the room.

Upon entering the room he saw a large table with one burning candle at its center. Around the table were four men, sitting on benches drinking from large mugs. The room smelled of sweat, wine, garbage and vomit. Its stone floor was strewn with half-eaten fruit covered with crawling insects. The stench of the rotten left-over lamb and ham next to it made Nearcus's stomach flop over and the urge to vomit nearly overcome his senses. The four men all looked at him with violence and malice in their drunken eyes.

"What do you want little boy?" sneered the man sitting at the far end of the table. Nearcus recognized the voice as that of the slave merchant he had heard yelling previously.

"I have come to purchase the slave girl you got tonight," Nearcus said, trying to sound grown-up but having little success at it.

"What is that wench to you? Your sister or something?" asked the largest, meanest looking man in the room.

"I want to buy her back for her owner who is a powerful person in this city." Nearcus could tell by the reaction of the men around the table that he had said the wrong thing. All the men looked at each other and then the slave merchant nodded.

Immediately the men rushed Nearcus and before the boy could react he was held tightly by this evil crew. The only damage he was able to inflict before being subdued was to kick the leader in the chest with his bleeding foot. The slave trader looked down at the bloody spot on his tunic and became very angry.

"Look what you did you insolent pup! You have soiled my best tunic!" The next thing Nearcus felt was a massive fist crash into his jaw. He thought it must have come from the large man on his left. The man hit the perfect spot to make the nearly healed hole in the boy's jaw burst open and spurt blood which quickly filled Nearcus's mouth. The blood ran out between his lips and covered his chin and flowed over the front of his tunic. This result of one punch surprised the men and they stood there with their mouths gaping as they watched Nearcus bleed profusely.

The big man who had hit Nearcus started to laugh loudly at seeing the damage he had caused with only one punch. The others joined him in laughing at Nearcus who was stunned by the massive pain racing through his jaw.

"This boy must be a walking sack of blood! You poke him anywhere and blood comes spraying out!" laughed one of the other men.

"Enough fun," said the merchant in a very business like voice, "Take him to the holding cave and we will send him to Rome with the others. Maybe he will have healed by the time they reach the city and then he can bring a good price."

Suddenly, a canvas bag covered Nearcus's head and he was pushed and pulled through a door at the side of the room and then down a hall, then down steps, then down another hall, then down more steps. After five minutes of these twists, turns and steps he heard a wooden door being opened. Next he was pushed violently into a room where he landed on the rough earth floor and the limbs of other bodies. Once he heard the door closed and locked behind him he removed the bag from his head. He looked around and saw that he had been deposited in a small cave where fourteen others were crowded together. It was much cooler than the night air he had just come from so Nearcus figured it must be deep below ground. The single candle that was perched on a small ledge of the wall opposite him was of such poor quality that the upper half of the cave was filled with the black smoke it gave off. But without it, all of them would be sitting in total darkness.

And right now, Nearcus felt as if his life had been thrown into darkness. A week ago he was sitting in a field, under a tree when he had heard a voice tell him that he was chosen. Now he sat here in an underground cave as a captive about to be transported to Rome to be sold as a slave. And his jaw hurt again and was bleeding. And his foot hurt and was bleeding. And his heart hurt and his hope was nearly gone.

He touched his jaw and gently cradled it in his left hand. Nearcus felt darker and lower than the cave that held him captive.

CHAPTER 19

Giorgos was still lying on the stable cobblestones when Marcus reached him. Dioxippus and Garifallia soon followed and they helped Giorgos sit up. Although he was still dizzy he was able to tell them what had happened. Upon hearing that Nearcus had taken after the thief, Marcus jumped to his feet and went to the open courtyard gate. He ran into the middle of the street and looked both ways. It was deserted at this hour of the early morning and he saw nothing of his student. Marcus returned to the others and shook his head to indicate that he had seen no one.

Garifallia was a woman with a quick mind who formulated solutions rapidly. She sent her old male slave to gather members of her house church once again. She told her female slave to bring her paper and pen. On the paper she hurriedly wrote a plea to the leaders of the other house churches to join them in the search for Iro and Nearcus. Garifallia placed her hand on the slave's head and prayed that God would protect her as she traveled the streets of Corinth just before dawn. Her slave then ran to the nearest house church with the message. Soon that church had passed the request along to the next closest church and this daisy chain of communication continued throughout the early morning. By the time the sun was just beginning to appear, hundreds of Christians were on the street making inquiries to find the lost slave and pankratiast.

Those Christians who could not join the search gathered in homes to pray for the safety and recovery of Iro and

Nearcus. Their prayers were intense and specific. They petitioned God to save the lost children.

Nearcus was unaware of what was being done to help him. He felt like the earth had swallowed him whole and that his life from here on would be one of destitution. He felt like he had lost his father, his sister, his home and his future. His competitive attitude to face all challenges with the confidence that he could win was ebbing from him rapidly.

Just when he felt at his lowest a hand softly touched his shoulder. Then he heard a voice that could have come from an angel.

"Nearcus, we will be fine. Don't worry," Iro said softly in his ear. Then she took the hem of her stolla and ripped off a large piece of the linen. She neatly folded the cloth and indicated that Nearcus should open his mouth. With the touch of a gentle nurse she applied the cloth to the bleeding hole in the back of Nearcus's jaw.

As she tended to his wound, Nearcus got a close look at Iro for the first time. He thought to himself that although her features were plain, there was a very beautiful quality about her that was truly attractive. It was her manner and her graceful way of doing the ordinary. He had seen Iro fight like a wild cat when she was being taken, but now she was a soft, cuddly kitten as she treated his injuries. While she gently kept pressure on his jaw to stop the blood flow, he had a thought that seemed very out-of-place to him. He forgot about his situation—about being cast into a hole in the ground and being sold into a lifetime of slavery—long enough to realize that he had seen and experienced more on this adventure than he realized. Since his mother's death years ago, Nearcus had no real contact with women. He would see the wives of other farmers keeping their homes and supporting their husbands, but he gave them little thought. On Chios he had never come across women like Iliana or Garifallia or even Iro. These were strong women who did not need to depend on a man to accomplish much in life. "Why was that?" he wondered.

"Clamp down on this now and I think the bleeding will stop," Iro said as she removed her hand from Nearcus's mouth, leaving the cloth positioned over the hole.

"Thank you," Nearcus said through clinched teeth.

"Were you the one chasing us?" the young girl asked in her soft, warm voice.

Nearcus nodded.

"Thank you, but I wish you had not gotten into this trouble over me. I will be all right whatever happens. I have a spirit that watches over me and protects me from real harm."

Nearcus nodded again; he was getting used to hearing about the god these Christians worshiped. It figured to him that as a member of Garifallia's household she would be a follower of the Way as well.

Iro could see the pain and fear and anger and confusion in Nearcus's eyes. She saw a twelve-year old boy trying to face his troubles like a man. This moved her to feel compassion for a troubled soul in a position he did not understand. She reached out and gently took his hand and held it with both her hands. She just sat there with him in the dimly lighted cave and held his hand, not saying a word but just being there with and for him.

Nearcus forgot about the others in the cave. He forgot about the danger he was in. He forgot about the dreaded future that lay ahead of him if he was sold as a slave in Rome. He remembered his mother holding his hand when he was little and had awoken from a nightmare. He remembered the feel of her hard hands being able to gently melt away his fear and confusion. He remembered how he felt loved and secure when his mother held his hand.

Nearcus shut his eyes and let the touch of Iro's hands folded around his carry him to a better time and to calm his fears. He opened his eyes after five minutes and looked at

Iro's face. Her eyes were shut but her lips were moving very slightly, as if she was talking but no words were coming out.

"What are you doing, Iro" Nearcus asked in a quiet, confidential voice so that none of the others in the cave could hear.

Iro opened her dark brown eyes and said, "I am praying for you."

"What are you praying for? That I can find a way to get us free?"

"Oh no!" she smiled as she responded. Her smile came more from her eyes than from her lips. "I am praying that you will feel better and that Jesus can take away your fear and provide you peace in your heart."

Nearcus started to draw his hand away from hers when he heard this, but he stopped before his hand was free. His body froze as a flood of thoughts crashed over him. He saw the faces of all the Christians he had met on this adventure. Marcus hanging on the top of the mast. Iliana praising God that she had found Nearcus. Filaretos's eyes when he was tied to the burning tree. Garifallia's peace and love after losing her arm for being a Christian. Even the change and newly found peace in the eyes of Dioxippus. And now, here is Iro praying for him while they are imprisoned in a cave! It suddenly hit Nearcus that all of these people had something they thought was worth living for and, even more importantly, worth dying for. And what did Nearcus have? Confusion and fear and a self-confidence that got him thrown into this situation. And he had his own personal war with the gods.

"How can Jesus help me in here?" Nearcus asked before he realized he had even spoken.

"Dear Nearcus, we are all children of God who Jesus loved so much that he was willing to be the bridge for us to reach our Father in heaven. God cannot be joined with anything that is unclean—He is holy, so he can only be with who is holy. When we sin we are unclean—we are not holy.

So how can God gather us up as his children and be with us when we are sinners? The only way we can become holy is for our sin to be judged and punished. Jesus came from God to take on all of our sin and to be punished unto death for us. He had never sinned, so he was not crucified for his own sin, but for my sin...and for your sin. He loved us so much that he died in our place. But here is the good news! After Jesus died for us, he rose from the dead! He defeated death and now lives to help us each day. So we do not need to fear death and we can rejoice in our current life because we know Jesus loves us so much that he will never let anything overtake us that is beyond his power to help us endure."

Iro stopped here because she wanted to be sure that Nearcus understood what she had shared. She watched his eyes and in them she saw him trying to comprehend what it all meant. Iro silently prayed, "Dear Jesus send the Comforter to Nearcus and help him now."

Iro's words felt like solid blows landing against the shell around Nearcus's heart. He had built that shell to protect him from the fickleness and disappointment found in his father's gods. Now this slave girl was saying things that made sense to Nearcus, but he did not want to believe her. He hated being bitter, but he was frightened of becoming a believer and then finding out that this god was like all the others so many adults worshiped. Still, there seemed to be a strong force pushing Nearcus to the edge of his disbelief. In his heart he felt a great challenge. He wanted to believe that there was a supreme God who loved him personally and wanted to guide and protect him, but he had been disappointed by all the other gods so it was very difficult for him to accept any god by faith.

Iro sensed Nearcus's moment of decision. She did not know what more to say when a thought entered her mind and she blurted out, "Nearcus, don't be fooled by all the stories about Apollo and Poseidon and all the other gods that men have made. Here is a secret about those gods that adults won't tell you. All those gods are made up—they don't really exist. That is why they always disappoint."

Those words sparked an explosion of light in Nearcus's heart. In an instant, everything in life was clear to him—everything was now illuminated! He had long suspected that the gods that man had created did not exist! Now he knew he was right! He knew that there was a force pulling him through events in his life—especially over the past week—and Iro has explained who that force has been! Nearcus wanted to believe that there was only one true God and the push he felt to make the decision to believe seemed overpowering now. He found it hard to find breath to ask his next question, "What must I do to become a Christian?"

Iro's face grew into a smile of happiness and answered, "Just ask Jesus to forgive you of your sins and promise to worship Him and His Father. Soon he will send the Holy Spirit to fill your heart and then your spirit will know that you belong to the Christ forever."

Nearcus was ready to believe and he knew that what he was about to do would change his life forever. He took a deep breath, held it and then exhaled slowly. As he did, he prayed in a very soft voice, "Jesus forgive me for my sins and help me to believe in you."

Inside, the strong push he felt behind him suddenly left and it was replaced with a lighter-than-air feeling. Nearcus was free of the heavy burden of his unbelief and bitterness towards gods he had thought were warring against him. Nearcus felt a strange warming in his heart. He did not know what it was, but later he would describe it as his new awareness of true, divine love.

The outside conditions remained the same. Nearcus was sitting in a dark dungeon, about to be sold into slavery, with a hole in his mouth and a deeply cut heel that was still bleeding. But inside he was in a whole new world of light and love. He was truly happy and thrilled to know a God who was real and who really loved him. He sat there with a sparkle in his eyes and a silly grin on his face. He looked so content and happy that Iro laughed out loud at his appearance!

Nearcus laughed with her. The others in the cave were mystified and some were irritated at the laughter under such dismal circumstances. A couple of the others shouted for the two young people to quiet down and to sleep. They said there was nothing to laugh at in this dark, cold cave.

But Nearcus felt warm and glowing throughout his body and soul. It was as if the dungeon had started to flame with light! He wanted to share what he had just learned and he gave a quick thought about telling the others in the cave that there was nothing to worry about—God loves them and he reigns over all!

Before he could say anything, all ears turned to the door as the sound of footsteps approached from down the hall. Light soon shone beneath the door and the sound of the lock being opened followed. As the door opened the four men who had earlier beat Nearcus were there with clubs and swords.

"Alright! Everyone up!" the slave merchant shouted. "Grab your things and follow me. Don't try anything or you will be beat until you wish for death! Let's go! Hurry it up!"

Nearcus was nearest the door and started to stand to lead the way, but Iro pulled on his arm to stay with her and let others go first. As the group left the cave, the narrow hallway forced them to travel in pairs. Each pair was separated by a couple of feet from the one in front of them. The men escorting them were positioned with the slave trader at the front and the biggest, meanest man at the rear. The other two guards were spaced among the pairs heading up the hall. Nearcus and Iro were right behind the second guard, who kept turning his head to watch those behind him as well as those in front.

The hallway was dark with the only light coming from the candles held by the four guards. As the group progressed up the narrow, dark passageway, the space between pairs grew greater and the line spread out. Soon, the guards lost sight of some of the pairs for just an instant as the hall twisted and turned. All the slaves and the guards kept a close eye on the rocky floor because it was uneven and easily could cause them to trip. While looking at the ground, Nearcus was amused to see his own bloody footprints he had left when they had brought him to the cave. His thoughts were on the bloody sacrifice that his newly found savior, Jesus, had made for him and Nearcus thought it appropriate that he was walking a new path stained by blood.

As the guard ahead of Iro and him climbed a couple of steps carved into the cave floor, Nearcus raised his eyes to watch him. When he did, he saw something that puzzled him for just a second but then immediately gave him a bold idea. He saw that his bloody footsteps led into the darkness to the right while the line of slaves and guards was heading down a hall to the left. Nearcus immediately understood that the slaves were being taken someplace other than the slave trader's rooms. These underground passages must lead to different places. Nearcus grabbed Iro's arm and pretended to trip on the steps. This slowed the couple and permitted the guard in front to move around the corner ahead and out of sight for just a second. As soon as the guard disappeared from sight, Nearcus pulled Iro into the darkness to their right. The couple behind them was looking down at the steps and did not notice Nearcus and Iro duck into the dark passageway. When the slaves looked up upon reaching the top of the steps they saw the guard's light shining from around the corner to the left and followed it.

Nearcus held Iro with one arm and placed his other hand against the cave wall. As quickly as he could in the pitch black he moved forward by sliding his hand along the cave wall as a guide. Once they were ten yards into the dark,

Nearcus stopped and stood still, listening for the guards. He heard nothing but the sound of footsteps growing fainter.

"We must move quickly before they realize we are missing," Nearcus whispered to Iro, finally saying something to the young slave who had followed him without question or hesitation.

"Do you know where this leads?" she asked in an even quieter whisper.

Nearcus pulled her forward as he slowly proceeded in the dark, his right hand sliding over the side of the cave. He answered, "It should take us to the merchant's business and the street."

The young boy from Chios was calm; surprisingly calm it seemed to him considering the perilous situation they were in. But his mind was still racing as he thought of what might lie ahead. "What if there were other men in the shop? What if there were other tunnels that led off of this one and he went down the wrong one? What if the guards caught up with them? Should he fight them?"

Iro spoke in the dark, "God will guide you, Nearcus. Do not worry."

Nearcus felt as if Iro could read his thoughts! But her words gave him confidence and he appreciated them. He squeezed her hand in response.

The couple twisted to the left and then the right and tripped on steps leading upward and both were totally lost in the absolute darkness. This went on for five minutes that seemed to Nearcus to be nearer an hour. Then he saw something that made his heart leap! Ahead of him he saw the faint glow of light! They must be nearing the surface and freedom! With the light as a reference, Nearcus was able to move faster. He increased their pace and the light grew brighter as they grew closer. Suddenly Nearcus saw shadows move across the light! There must be men ahead and they are coming toward Iro and him! Nearcus halted his advance and pressed himself against the cave wall, guiding Iro to do the same.

"What is it?" she asked.

"I don't know. I think someone is coming."

CHAPTER 20

Aggelos was a tent maker in the industrial heart of Corinth near the port. He had been a Christian longer than nearly every member of the local churches. In fact, Aggelos had been a co-worker with the one who was called Paul, the Apostle. Together, Paul and Aggelos had spent many hours sitting and talking together while sewing tents by hand when Paul lived for eighteen months in the city.

A large man with fiercely strong hands and arms, Aggelos had a natural scowl on his face that was made more frightening by the many pock marks that scarred his cheeks and nose. A disease when he was younger had left him with a face that looked as if dozens of birds had pecked at him and torn bits of his flesh free to feed their chicks. It was not surprising that Aggelos frightened all who met him for the first time. His size and strength and scowl and scars were quite intimidating to strangers. However, members of the Christian church knew him to be a man of kindness and light. Whenever he talked of his savior, Jesus, his scowl would turn to the widest smile imaginable and his happy demeanor would brighten any meeting.

Aggelos had a very rough past; before he met Paul and the Christ, he was well known in the tough neighborhoods of the meanest parts of the city. When he would get drunk he would get mean and everyone knew to steer clear of the big tent maker. Even now, his reputation as one of the meanest and toughest men in the city still remained among those evil men who conducted their business at night.

When Aggelos was awakened from his night's sleep with the news that Iro had been kidnapped, he immediately went to his friend's Garifallia's home. After talking to Giorgos, the tent maker had a good idea where the thief would take a slave girl to sell her for gold. There were only five places where merchants regularly dealt in stolen slaves and Aggelos knew all of them from his wild youth. As the other church members spread out to search the city's streets, Aggelos went directly to the five slave traders he knew would be the destination of a thief with a stolen slave to sell.

At the first three traders Aggelos had to pound on their locked doors and get the men out of bed. Each of them was afraid of the hulking man who was in a great hurry and frightened by his intensity and size and disposition. Each assured Aggelos that they had not seen Iro or heard of any other merchant buying her. Upon departing, Aggelos gave each of them a look so fierce that they understood that if they had lied to him, he would return and make them pay. Aggelos would never harm them, but his previous reputation and size and scowl made them all believe that he surely would do them great harm if they crossed him.

Aggelos's next stop was the street known throughout Corinth as "thieves' alley." The last two illegal slave merchants were located on this roadway that contained shops of every vice known to man. The only time of day that this street was quiet was just before dawn. The previous night's parties were nearly over and it was too early to start the new day's evil ruckus. Aggelos beat on the locked door of the first trader at the near end of the street. Eventually a small man with one eye that looked to his right and another that looked straight ahead came and opened the door.

"What do you want at this hour...Aggelos?" asked the merchant, now frightened because he had recognized the tent maker as the hooligan who formerly terrorized "thieves' alley."

"Tell me, little man, did you buy a sixteen-year old slave girl last night?"

"No, I did no business last night," the trader said and then added, "But..."

Aggelos leaned into the doorway, his face just inches from the scared little man, "But what? Do you know where she is?"

"I had a man—a known thief—come by last night and offer me a young, black-haired girl but I refused to consider it. That man has burned me before by selling me slaves that I had to return later."

"Where did he go?"

"Try my competitor down the street. He will buy anybody from anybody."

Aggelos turned and started running down the street. He did not even take time to give the slave trader his leering look before he left. Aggelos felt he knew where Iro was and nothing was going to stop him from retrieving her.

Aggelos was surprised when he came to the shop at the end of the street. He did not have to bang on a door to wake the merchant; in fact, the front door was wide open and no one was in sight. He walked across the small room at the front of the shop and threw back the curtain to the back room. His large frame nearly filled the entire door, but there was no one there to intimidate. Aggelos looked around the room and saw the small doorway to the right. He strode across the room, easily tossing the wooden table and benches out of his way to reach the door quickly. Violently pushing the curtain to the side he peered into the dark hallway. Looking around, he found a candle he had knocked on the floor. He went to the other room and lighted the candle using the one still burning in there. Aggelos returned to the small hallway and started down the hall looking for the merchant and answers.

As he started down the narrow hallway, Aggelos had to squeeze his tight frame through some of the smaller parts of the passage. At one point it grew so narrow and steep that the large man had to stop and turn around to proceed backwards.

Farther down this same passageway, Nearcus and Iro kept pressed against the rocky, damp walls. Nearcus saw the shadow of the figure coming closer and he tried to devise a plan. He couldn't go back because the guards would capture them again. The passageway was too narrow to put up a good fight. Try as he might, he could not come up with a good option.

The man coming down the hall was nearly upon them. Having passed the narrowest part, the man turned to face forward again. As he did this the candle light illuminated his face and when she saw it, Iro rushed from her position behind Nearcus and quickly reached the large tent maker.

"Aggelos! Aggelos! You have come for us!" she shouted with great joy.

Nearcus stood there dumbfounded as he watched Iro throw her arms around the gigantic neck of the tent maker. She seemed to disappear as the great man wrapped her in his massive arms.

"Iro! You are well! Praise God! Praise God!"

Iro stepped back from Aggelos and turned to face Nearcus. Then she said, "This is Nearcus. He chased the thief and found me. Nearcus, this is our friend, Aggelos the tent maker! God sent him to save us!"

Nearcus was so relieved. Just seconds before he had thought that they were in dire circumstances and now everything was different. He spoke, "Sir, we escaped from the slavers but they might be coming at any time. Can we go?"

Aggelos laughed and said, "That is an excellent idea! Let's get you two back to Garifallia's and we can talk there!"

Nearcus was amazed at how near he had been to the home of Garifallia. With all the twisting and turning in the dark when he was chasing the thief, the boy was convinced they must have traveled at least a mile. However, it only took about ten minutes to walk back to the courtyard gate. There they were met by Marcus, Giorgos, Garifallia and many members of the church. When Marcus saw Nearcus approaching he threw open the gate and rushed to grab him in a great hug, his painful shoulders easily forgotten in his joy to see his lost student.

"Praise God you are safe! I am going to have to attach a tether to you until I can return you to your father. Everyday you get lost and I worry that I have failed in my duty to Leonidas and Aegospotami!" the slave said in only a half-joking manner.

Iro quickly responded to Marcus, "Oh! But Marcus he was not lost this time! No, he was found...by the Lord!"

Marcus stepped back and looked deeply into Nearcus's eyes. He saw a special light flashing there and he knew Nearcus had decided to follow Jesus. Slowly, Marcus raised his right hand and extended it to Nearcus and said, "Welcome home, brother Nearcus."

The boy reached for the slaves arm and the two shook arms in a formal manner. Inside, Nearcus felt excited and happy. He could not understand why, but he felt like he had settled something in his life that had been bothering him for a long time. He no longer felt bitter at idols and events. He felt whole and satisfied that he understood why he was alive. There was only one question that still bothered him. What was he chosen to do in Corinth?

Arm in arm Marcus and Nearcus crossed the courtyard and entered Garifallia's house. Standing in the door was Dioxippus who joined them by putting his arm around Marcus and the trio strode into the great room together.

Tonight the opening ceremonies for the games would begin and tomorrow the pankratiasts would represent Chios on the competition field. Then for the next days they would contend with the tremendous rigors of the battles that would continue morning and afternoon. But all of that was not to start for a dozen hours. Right now, both the boys wanted to spend this day learning about the Way and more about Jesus from Marcus and the other Christians gathered at Garifallia's.

CHAPTER 21

It was a day that Nearcus and Dioxippus would remember the rest of their lives. The boys were like sponges soaking up the knowledge shared about the Way from Marcus, Aggelos and Garifallia. Both boys peppered the adults with question after question about Jesus and Jehovah, the single true God. Each answer would lead them to another question.

Shortly after the mid-day meal, Dioxippus had learned enough about being a Christian that he asked, "Can I be baptized now?"

"Yes! Me too!" excitedly added Nearcus.

Marcus looked at Garifallia who looked at Aggelos and then the tent maker said, "I think that is a wonderful suggestion!"

Giorgos had remained another day before starting his long trip back to the olive orchards. He needed to recover from the blow to his head that morning and he did not want to leave so late that he would have to travel the roads in the dark. Consequently, Giorgos was able to load the boys, Marcus and Aggelos into the cart and transport them all to the springs located in a small valley in the foothills about two miles south of the city. There, in the waist deep water of this quiet spring pool, far from the crowds of the city, Aggelos baptized Nearcus and Dioxippus that very afternoon.

Nearcus was feeling happy and complete when they returned to Garifallia's house. What he found in Jesus was so much more than he had ever hoped to experience on this

once-in-a-lifetime trip to Corinth. Competing in the
Isthmian Games the next day seemed much less important
than it did when he started this adventure. When he left
home, he had been excited about the evening ceremonies
that opened the games. His father and Leonidas had told
him of the grand traditions and spectacular events that
surrounded the start of these games that were over five-
hundred years old. Nearcus had been enthralled with the
tales of the rituals and importance of the ceremonies.
However, now they all seemed trivial compared to the love
he felt from a god who came as a man to take Nearcus's
punishment for him. So it did not surprise him too much
when Aggelos called Dioxippus, Marcus and him aside just
before the evening meal to speak to them about what lay
ahead for the next few days.

"Tonight are the Mystical Rites of the cult of Palaimon,"
the tent maker said with a very stern voice, his scowl having
returned to his face. "It is expected that all participants in the
games partake in the rites. Have you heard what is
involved?"

Both boys shook their heads indicating they had no clue
what was to happen that night. Marcus just sat there very
still.

Aggelos continued, "These men worship a god named
Palaimon, who they claim was, like Jesus, a man who died
and was raised as a god—a hero who is the ideal for those
participating in the games. If they ask you to express your
fidelity and belief in Palaimon what will you do?"

Nearcus looked at Dioxippus, but the older boy kept his
eyes locked on Aggelos and said immediately and firmly, "I
worship only God and his only son, Jesus."

The scowl on Aggelos face melted into a warm smile.
Then the tent maker looked at Nearcus. There was a long
pause before Nearcus spoke. He was confused about what
was being said by Aggelos. Were the boys to go to the
ceremony or not? Were they to compete to represent their

island and its honor in the games or not? Did they suffer the trials of this trip to get here and then not even compete?

Aggelos lost his smile while waiting for Nearcus to answer. But rather than show disappointment in the young Christian's hesitation, the tent maker said in a fatherly voice, "Let us hope you don't have to make the choice between worshiping an idol or not competing. Tonight, you can attend the ceremonies as spectators. The games are really secular in nature, and only the traditionalists attach any religious significance to them. There will be many athletes there and it should be easy for you to keep to the back of the rites and not have to go forward to honor the idol. You probably can remain apart from any of the religious aspects of the ceremony and not bend your knee to any idol. The most crucial part of the ceremony is actually done in total darkness. At the Temple of Palaimon there is a crypt where all the athletes take an oath to do their best and not cheat. You can avoid this because it is done in the dark and no one will know if you go forward or not. The biggest decision you must make is not what happens at the pagan ceremonies tonight. As I explained, you will probably be able to attend without denying Christ unless you are asked specifically to worship an idol. But tomorrow morning poses a big problem."

Aggelos paused here and the boys leaned forward to learn what was to happen in the morning that could be a problem for them.

Marcus, who had remained silent until now, spoke, "You mean the oath on the Temple and Alter of Poseidon?"

The tent maker nodded and then asked, "What are your plans about this, Marcus?"

Before the slave could respond, Nearcus asked, "You mean like we did at the trials to Apollo?"

Marcus nodded and said, "But it is much more formal at the games. All the trainers, officials and athletes must swear by the Temple of Poseidon that they will not use any unlawful means to win. If you do not take this oath, then you cannot compete."

Dioxippus interrupted, "Then I won't compete. I am not going to worship an idol just to participate in any games!"

"How are you going to pay back the games commission on Chios who funded you to come here to represent the island if you refuse to compete?" Marcus asked Dioxippus.

"I don't care. I won't deny Jesus for anybody."

Both Marcus and Aggelos were mature Christians and in their hearts they were proud and pleased by the strength of this new brother's-in-Christ devotion and faith.

Aggelos addressed these visitors from a small rural island, "I had many discussions with the Apostle Paul concerning situations like this. And since he has actually seen Jesus, would you like to hear what he says?"

Now all three travelers leaned forward to learn what would be the best course to take.

"Paul said that we should not be burdened by the superstitions and restrictions that others live their lives by. We should do all we can to get along with others while never denying Christ's sacrifice for us. He said we were free to eat meat sold in the markets that had previously been sacrificed to idols provided we understood that it was just meat and that there was nothing holy about it because the idols were just man-made gods. In this case, since the mandatory ceremonies tonight are the official opening of the games I think you are free to attend as long as you understand that there is nothing in their empty superstitions. I feel Paul would also say that it is only right that followers of the Way state that they will not cheat or do anything unlawful to win at the games. You can stand before anyone and state that you promise to be honest. But we know you cannot swear to it by Apollo or Poseidon or any other false god."

"What are you suggesting then Aggelos?" asked Marcus, "That we take the oath but without mentioning Poseidon?"

Aggelos nodded and added, "You can try that. There will be so many athletes and trainers there tomorrow it might not be noticed that you fail to swear by Poseidon."

Something about this suggestion did not sit right with Dioxippus. He had a question in his mind, "But don't we say we will be faithful to Poseidon just by standing with the others as the oath to his Temple is said?"

Nearcus wanted to compete in the games. He wanted to do it very much. He did not know that asking Jesus to be his personal Savior would cost him his chance to represent his father and Chios at the Isthmian Games. He looked at Marcus with a confused expression.

Marcus could see the torment in the minds and hearts of Nearcus and Dioxippus. The slave had no clear answer to the dilemma himself. So he said, "Thank you Aggelos, your counsel has been very wise. I don't know what we shall do, but I think Jesus is faithful and will provide us the right answers when or if the situation develops where we must choose."

That made sense to Dioxippus and it gave hope to Nearcus that maybe he could participate in the games. Aggelos nodded and finished the conversation by saying, "Amen."

That night the crowds were tremendous at the Palaimonion. The opening ceremonies for the games were always well attended by Greeks from around the Aegean. Athenians were given special privileges and had reserved positions near the temple altar. Intermingled with the spectators were the athletes dressed in simple tunics and sandals. The entire assembly area was illuminated by specially made lamps. Each lamp was shaped like a wheel and handmade, some being quite large with many smaller lamps attached to them. Big or small, all burned expensive oil. There were hundreds of these distinct lamps that were brought forward for dedication by the priests. There was a pit in front of the altar where the priests had started a small fire. As each wheel was brought forward, worshippers would take a small lamp from it and pour oil into the pit. The fire would flame higher with each contribution.

At the height of the evening's celebration, after all the oil had been sacrificed in the fire, a large black bull was brought to the altar by four men. The bull was decorated with gilded horns and hooves and garlands of flowers were hung around its neck. The crowd screamed as the bull was positioned near the fiery pit. The chief priest then pulled a long-handled axe from behind the altar. He raised the axe over his head and with one quick blow he struck the neck of the bull. The poor animal fell to its knees and then rolled over on its side. In a matter of minutes it stopped kicking and struggling once all of its blood had poured out over the altar base and into the fiery pit. Once it stopped moving, the four men heaved the carcass into the fire where it was rapidly consumed by the flames. The crowd was in a near frenzy, shouting praises to Palaimon and laughing in celebration of the official start of the games.

Nearcus, Marcus and Dioxippus were at the very back of the crowd, far away from the altar. All three stood silently by and watched the people get excited over the killing of a dumb animal. Nearcus was interested in the ruckus, but it upset him in his heart. He felt like he was watching grown-ups pretending to find meaning in the cruelty of sacrificing a bull to a god who did not exist. These were Greeks, who were a people proud of their intellect and philosophy, and yet it seemed to this twelve-year-old boy that they were nothing but a lost mob this evening. Even though this crowd was made up of many of the finest citizens in the city, in his heart Nearcus felt they were just as lonely as the drunkards he had encountered in Thieves' Alley last night.

As the fire in the pit died down, the athletes were told to gather at the front of the crowd. Once the fire died completely, they were to move around the pit and touch the altar and pledge an oath to Palaimon that they would act honorably during the games. Nearcus and Dioxippus did not make a movement to go forward.

Just then they were surprised by the senior coach of the adult Chios team appearing suddenly on their right. Seeing the two boys he went to them and grabbed each by an arm.

"So you two mischief makers actually made it here. I am surprised. Let's go forward so you can take your oath," said the coach.

Neither of the boys had a chance to say anything before the coach led them forward. A short time later they found themselves at the end of the line of athletes waiting for total darkness before they could proceed to the altar. Once in line, the coach remained right by their side. Nearcus was afraid he was going to escort them to the altar when it was their turn. How was he going to avoid this oath to a pagan god?

Marcus had followed the boys and the coach to the front of the crowd. Once the boys were in line, he approached the coach. Grabbing the coach by the arm, Marcus led the man back into the crowd while shouting at him.

"What did you mean leaving us to get here by ourselves? Who is going to pay for our expenses—our lodging, our meals, our travel costs! What gave you the right to leave us like that?" Marcus badgered the coach as he led him farther and farther away from the athletes. Soon the coach was moving quickly to the far side of the crowd in an effort to get away from this angry slave!

Nearcus and Dioxippus smiled at each other. The last flickering flames in the sacrificial pit died down and with their demise the entire square and temple went completely dark. Now the line of athletes started to move forward towards the altar; that is, all the athletes except the two at the end of the line. Nearcus and Dioxippus easily slipped back into the crowd. In the total darkness they made their way through the crowd to the opposite end of the pit and soon were mingling with the athletes who had completed their oath and were waiting for others to finish.

The first trial of their faith at the games was over. God had provided a way for them to avoid denying Jesus. But the big test was to come tomorrow.

CHAPTER 22

It surprised Nearcus that he had slept so well through the night. He was well rested and anxious to start the day's bouts. His jaw only hurt a little and his heel could now bear his full weight when he walked. For some reason he had not experienced any pre-fight nerves throughout the night. This was unusual, for Nearcus normally found it hard to fall asleep the night before a competition.

However, that was not the case for Dioxippus. He had found it very difficult to get any rest during the night. He laid awake all night looking into the dark and worrying about the oath to Poseidon and how he would be able to avoid swearing by an idol. At the morning meal, Dioxippus looked tired and worried.

"You had trouble sleeping, Brother Dioxippus?" Marcus asked at breakfast.

Dioxippus nodded, keeping his bloodshot eyes down, looking at his meal of boiled oats and hard bread.

"Just remember," Marcus continued, "Whatever happens, it will be over in a couple of hours. Do not worry. Jesus will never abandon or forsake you."

The lack of sleep made Dioxippus irritable and even thoughts of his Savior did not make him feel any better. He was in a sour mood and he was going to stay in this mood for the day.

Nearcus's refreshed and positive mood this morning only irritated Dioxippus even more. The younger boy was smiling and confident, excited about the chance to compete. He thanked Iro as she served the meal and complimented

Garifallia on the nice flowers that had been cut and set on the table. He smiled at Marcus and, generally, was in a very happy mood.

"When do we leave for the stadium, Marcus?" Nearcus asked his coach.

"Shortly after we finish eating. We want to get there in time to find and join up with the rest of the Chios team."

Dioxippus threw his spoon down on the table and abruptly stood, pushing his seat back quickly as he stormed out of the room. Marcus and Nearcus looked at each other and shook their heads. Once Dioxippus was no longer near enough to hear, Marcus said, "He is troubled by this morning's oath to Poseidon."

Nearcus nodded and for the first time since he had awakened, Nearcus remembered what Aggelos had shared last night. How was the young pankratiast and Christian going to get past this requirement to publicly worship an idol? For just an instant, Nearcus's happy mood left him, but it soon returned as he pushed the dilemma facing him into the back of his mind. He decided to concentrate on the bouts and not the religious ceremonies of the day.

When Marcus, Dioxippus and Nearcus departed Garifallia's house to make their way to the stadium they were surprised by the crowds already clogging the streets at this early hour. Garifallia had prayed for them at the courtyard gate before they left. She also insisted that Iro accompany them as a guide, and now all four were pushing and pressing through the pedestrians, horses and carts that all seemed to be heading for the stadium. At one point, Nearcus got distracted by the sight of two women fighting on a side street and when he turned back to follow Marcus he could not see his coach. In a momentary panic Nearcus thought he had gotten lost again! But very quickly he saw the black hair of Iro bobbing up and down a few yards in front of him and he was able to rejoin his little band.

Once they reached the stadium, Marcus was glad they had started so early. It took nearly an hour before they could locate the little area where the Chios team had set their gear and organized a miniature base camp for the athletes to use during the next few days. Each team from the many corners of Greece had done the same and the entire area on the flat land surrounding the stadium to the east and south was a maze of cliques of athletes and their gear. Once they finally located the specific little camp for the Chios athletes, Marcus established a little area just for his two youth pankratiasts. He set their water jug, robes, oil jar and several towels he had brought in a square with a small clear area in the middle. The other competitors from Chios ignored the efforts of Marcus and also ignored the two outcast youths. All the adult and other youth athletes gave a very cold reception to these three. Nothing was said to them and none greeted them with even a smile or nod.

An hour later, the head team coach approached the Chios camping area and stood in its center. "We must assemble in the stadium for the opening procedures. Right after the oaths the first events will commence. This morning the sprints will be run first. All short distance runners come in your robes and pre-oiled to compete. You will take the oval as soon as the ceremony is over. First the adult division will go and then the youth races will be immediately following. Now let's go."

All the athletes not competing in the sprints dressed in their tunics and sandals, while the sprinters got ready to race. As the team made its way to the stadium field along with the thousand other competitors, Nearcus was feeling happy. He thought, "With so many athletes saying the oath to Poseidon at the same time, no one will notice when I swear to God to do my best and not to cheat and not swear by Poseidon. Yes, this will be no problem at all. I guess Jesus will truly make it possible for me to compete after all."

Dioxippus and Marcus moved along with the crowd going to the stadium field with the same thoughts. Marcus even offered a prayer of thanksgiving as they shuffled towards the oath ceremony.

Nearcus was awe struck when he entered the stadium. In the seats carved into one side of the hill to the west were over 20,000 spectators. To the north, standing on a small hill were another 10,000 and to the southwest, standing thirty deep were another 10,000 Greeks assembled to watch the opening day of the games. These 40,000 spectators were shouting praises for the athletes and to Apollo and Poseidon and they yelled in support of their own home cities. The sight of so many people gathered in one place and the sound of so many spectators shocked young Nearcus. He had never imagined it would be like this. The couple of hundred spectators who had witnessed the trials had been the largest crowd he had ever seen in his life while living on small Chios. Now it seemed to him that everyone in the entire world must have gathered to see these games!

Dioxippus was also impressed. His mood had begun to lighten when he realized that the thousand athletes would be saying the oath together and no one would know that he was going to worship the only true God and not Poseidon or any other man-made idol. Now with the roar of the thousands assembled on all sides of him as he entered the stadium area his spirits were lifted even higher. This was going to be a great day after all!

Marcus was too busy keeping track of his two athletes in the mass of people pushing to enter the stadium to be in awe of the spectacle. Nearcus was his responsibility and he must supervise the boy, especially in such a confusing environment like this. So Marcus reached out and grabbed the sleeve of Nearcus's tunic and held tightly to it. He told Dioxippus to grab hold of Nearcus's other sleeve so that all three could keep together when the crowd movement was pulling them apart.

Soon the crush of the crowd eased as the athletes moved through the tunnels that led to the stadium field and there was more room to spread out. Nearcus, Dioxippus and Marcus stood on the side of the Chios team, slightly separated from the others from their home island. It was not long before the entire field was filled with participants and trumpets blared from the platform at the southern end of the stadium. Nearcus and all the athletes and coaches turned to face the platform. The crowd noise peaked as all cheered the start of the games. The noise was nothing like Nearcus, a boy raised in a rural orchard on a small island, had ever experienced in his life. And the roar kept going and going and getting louder and louder. Nearcus turned in a slow circle, his eyes wide and his mouth open as he stood there amazed and speechless by the sights and sounds. This was so much more than he had ever imagined when he dreamed of coming to Corinth.

The trumpets sounded again and finally the crowd began to grow quiet. The city leaders, both Roman and Greek stepped forward on the platform and raised their hands. This caused the crowd to cheer again and this time the athletes joined in the shouts. Even in the large horde of athletes assembled on the field, Nearcus, Marcus and Dioxippus were noticeable because they were the only ones not cheering. Marcus was too focused on his athletes to care what was happening on the platform. Dioxippus did not participate because he was not sure if the crowd was cheering or worshiping the men raising their hands. Nearcus was the youngest person on the competition field and these events had him frozen in awe. So these three stood still while all others waved their hands and shouted. The only person who seemed to notice the trio was the head coach of their own Chios team. He cheered with his arm raised, but he did not look towards the platform; he kept his eyes on the three troublemakers on his team.

When the leaders on the platform dropped their arms the crowd began to quiet down. Soon the noise was low enough that the Roman city ruler could address those in attendance. He had a loud voice and was heard by many, but Nearcus was too far away to clearly hear what was said. But, like the rest of the athletes on his team, he stood there in silence and gave his full attention to the Roman, pretending he could understand him.

After the Roman finished speaking, a Greek dressed in a priest's robes came to the front of the platform. The Christians knew that now was the time that the oath would be administered. When the priest raised his right hand high over his head everyone on the field did the same; everyone except Nearcus, Dioxippus and Marcus.

The competitors and coaches, who were close enough to the platform to hear, repeated the oath after the priest said it. The oath then flowed back over the crowded field with athletes and coaches repeating what they heard said by those in front of them.

"I do solemnly swear by the Alter of Poseidon that I will perform the duties of the office I hold in these games in accordance with the rules set forth and that I will use no unlawful means to gain a victory or bring dishonor upon the great god Poseidon."

Nearcus, Marcus and Dioxippus repeated only part of this oath. They said out loud, "I do solemnly promise by the Lord Jesus Christ that I will perform the duties of the office I hold in these games in accordance with the rules set forth and that I will use no unlawful means to gain a victory."

No one seemed to notice the changes they made to the oath. A hundred athletes and coaches surrounded their immediate area and all were repeating the oath in a loud voice. It was nearly impossible to distinguish what the Christians said from what all the others yelled.

It was nearly impossible—but Lysander, the head coach of the Chios team did notice! He kept his eyes on the troublemakers and when he noticed they had not raised their hands he had moved closer to them. Standing directly behind them, he heard how they modified the oath to the Altar of Poseidon. This was what he had been seeking in his efforts to finally rid the team of what he considered radical troublemakers.

The oath being complete, all the athletes except the sprinters left the field of play and moved to the northeastern edge of the stadium to watch the competition. Lysander ensured his sprinters had reported to the starting area and then he went directly to the officials' platform at the south end of the complex. He hurriedly scaled the steps to the top and having rushed so much he was out of breath when he arrived.

"Mr. Senior Official!" he cried between taking big gulps of air, "Mr. Senior Official we have a problem!"

CHAPTER 23

Marcus saw them coming first. Lysander was in the lead and he was followed by three games officials dressed in formal togas. The four men rapidly approached the Christians.

"There! These are the ones I told you about!" Lysander said as he pointed at Nearcus, Marcus and Dioxippus. "They did not take the oath on the Altar of Poseidon! They are law breakers and have violated the rules of the game! They must be punished!"

Nearcus felt his heart sink into his stomach. His excitement and wonder at being in Corinth and at the chance to actually participate in the games quickly left him. He was numb with disappointment and, oddly, he also felt guilty of something. He felt as if he had been caught doing something wrong and he did not know why.

Marcus's eyes grew narrow and penetrating as he locked Lysander in an angry gaze. He thought, "What a small man! He cares nothing about the reputation of our home. He only wants to force his authority on everyone he can. Since we did not do exactly what he wanted, he has tried to eliminate us from the games. Now he is even reporting his own countrymen — members of his own team — to the authorities just so he can feel superior and punish these boys because of me." Marcus was really angry at what Lysander had done.

Dioxippus stepped forward and confronted the head coach. The young man stood his ground and challenged the adult to move any closer. But Lysander was a politician and a coward who did not like to fight battles he was not sure he could win. So the head coach stepped to the side and did not threaten to move beyond the bold Dioxippus.

"Is it true that you failed to take the oath before the games?" asked the senior official while looking directly into Marcus's eyes.

"We swore we would follow the rules and not cheat to get an unlawful advantage."

"By whom did you swear this?"

Dioxippus was glad that this direct question was asked. He had felt dirty trying to hide his loyalty to the one god who truly loved him. He spoke clearly and loudly, "We took our oath on the one, true living God and his son, Jesus of Nazareth!"

The senior official turned to the other two that had accompanied him to investigate the charge brought by Lysander. The officials had heard about Christians before. They were quite familiar with the claims that their god was the only true being and that it was more powerful than any other god. The senior official wished that the boys and their coach would merely say the words of the proper oath so that the games could continue with religion just set aside during the competition. But here were these Christians who had to bring their god into the proceedings. It irritated the senior official that he had to deal with such a problem.

"It is a rule that you take the oath on the Altar of Poseidon. Won't your god allow you to just say the words so we can get on with the games?"

Upon hearing this question, Nearcus was reminded of what he had thought when he heard how Garifallia had lost her arm. But now, for some reason he could not explain, Nearcus understood why she could not deny the Christ, even for a minute and even to save herself. Nearcus was frightened by this realization and he knew in his heart now that his dream of competing in the games was lost. He would not give honor to a false god and so he would not be allowed to participate. He thought of the disappointment this will cause his father and his sister. He thought about the months and months of hard training that will have been for nothing. He thought about the trials he had suffered on the trip to get here. But he knew in his heart, that he could never deny Jesus as his savior. Something had been given him by the Lord that Nearcus never wanted to lose — whatever the cost.

Marcus looked at Nearcus and Dioxippus. He knew that this was a decision point in their lives. Both of the new Christians looked back into Marcus's eyes and then shook their heads slowly. Dioxippus then raised his chin up and stood as tall as he could. Nearcus dropped his head down and put his hands over his eyes to hide the tears that were forming in them.

Marcus looked at the senior official who was sympathetic to what the boys had just been forced to give up because of the actions of Lysander. The older man turned and shook his head as he faced the other two officials. Lysander showed a big smile as if he had won a fight himself. The officials took a couple of steps away and then stopped. The senior official spoke quietly to the other two.

"It is a shame that their silly religion will deprive the games of one of the best young pankratiasts in a long time. I heard much about this Nearcus from those who saw him at the trials," said the senior official.

"Yes, his absence will affect the quality of the games this year and that is especially troublesome after the last games' results. You remember that many people left those games disappointed because the competition in the pankration was so weak," added one of the other officials.

The third official raised the forefinger on his right hand as if he had just thought of a good idea and said, "Maybe we can keep the crowd interest through the last day if we could arrange a grudge match against the gods' chosen representatives?"

The senior official smiled widely and patted the other official on the back and then all three turned and came back to the Christians.

"This is not my first encounter with you Christians," said the senior official. "You truly believe that there is only one god, and that Poseidon and Apollo and all the rest do not exist. Is that right?"

All three Christians nodded.

"Personally I cannot believe that. There has been too much evidence in my long life that there are many gods who influence men. Some gods are more powerful than others and some are kinder to us than others, but all the gods have some power and some involvement with us. How can you say that they do not exist and that you worship the only true god?"

Before any of the Christians could answer, the senior official quickly continued.

"If there really is only one god, and that is your Jehovah, then he must be all powerful since the earth, the seas, the rains, the harvest and the birth of children all come from him—since he does not share these powers with any other gods. Isn't that so?"

Marcus responded for all three Christians, "God is one, there is no other god. He works with great power in the lives of those that love him."

That is exactly what the senior official was trying to get the Christians to say.

"I propose to you a demonstration of your god's power. On the last day of the games we celebrate the victors of the contests. The champion pankratiast is especially honored as the ideal athlete chosen by Poseidon to be the best in the world. There will be over 40,000 Greeks and Romans in the stadium who do not believe your god has any power. Would you be willing to show them that he does exist and is the most powerful?"

Marcus knew he had stepped into a trap set by the senior official. If he agreed to put one of his Christian students against the pankration champion it would be an easy victory for the heathen athlete. God would appear to be weak and not equal to their idols. If Marcus refused the offer to show the strength of God, then it would be told throughout all of Corinth that the Christian god is too weak and so frightened that he won't even do battle against the forces of the real gods. And this story would be carried back to all corners of Greece by the spectators who had traveled to Corinth to see the games.

Marcus knew he needed wisdom and he needed it right now. He said a silent prayer, "Dear Jesus, you promised to give me the right words when challenged about my faith in you. Help me now to say what you want."

Marcus opened his mouth and he started to answer the senior official's challenge with a quote from the Hebrew Scriptures that said man shall not tempt the Lord God. But before he could get this response past his lips he blurted out something else, "Can Poseidon's ideal beat a twelve-year old boy?"

Nearcus and Dioxippus snapped their heads around to look at Marcus. Both were stunned by what Marcus was suggesting! Nearcus was the youngest competitor at the games! How could he defeat the toughest, best adult pankratiast in all of Greece?

Nearcus reacted to this suggestion by shaking his head. He was thinking only one thought right now; he was thinking of the voice in the orchard that had said, "In Corinth you will be chosen."

The officials and Lysander laughed out loud. A young boy against the best man! Indeed, this was even better than they had hoped for when they baited the Christians. The easy victory by an athlete who worships Poseidon will let all of Greece know that Christians and their God are phonies!

The senior official quickly spoke, not wanting to give Marcus a chance to back out of the arrangement, "Then it is done. On the last day of the games your young pankratiast will fight the games champion and we will see what gods are powerful and which are just foolish men's dreams!"

Lysander and the officials turned and walked away laughing and feeling very smug that they were able to put the Christians in a position where they had to lose.

Nearcus felt numb all over. What had just happened? What was he to do now?

CHAPTER 24

Garifallia had listened silently to Marcus as he explained what had happened at the games. Then she sent for Aggelos before she would respond in any way. Aggelos sat his massive frame on a bench in Garifallia's great room and listened without showing any emotion as Marcus repeated the challenge he had accepted to defend the power and might of the Lord against the beliefs of the pagans. There was a long silence before Aggelos or Garifallia responded.

"You say you were about to quote the Scriptures about man not tempting God when they challenged you? That would have been a wonderful answer. Why did you not say it?" the husky tent maker asked.

"I honestly do not know why I did not say it. It was in my mind and I opened my mouth to speak it when suddenly something else came out. It was as if I no longer had control of my tongue. I truly believe the Spirit pushed what I did say from my lips," answered Marcus.

"Are you honestly saying that you feel the Lord wants this match in front of a stadium full of unbelievers?" Garifallia asked in a very sincere and puzzled tone.

"You know the young athlete, Marcus. Does he have any chance against an experienced adult champion-level pankratiast?" Aggelos wanted to know.

"I have never seen a youth who is better. But against a muscular and experienced adult, it will take a miracle for him to win."

Nearcus and Dioxippus were standing to the side, against the wall to keep from interfering with the adults' conversation. However, upon hearing Marcus's honest assessment of his chances, Nearcus felt he must add something to their discussion.

"I can win…with the Lord's help," the young athlete said quietly but with confidence.

Before Garifallia and Aggelos could say anything, Marcus held his hand up to stop them from challenging the youth and his statement. Marcus knew Nearcus extremely well and he could read the athlete's emotions with great accuracy. Marcus could tell that Nearcus was not offering bravado but that he was very serious and the paedotribae wanted to know where this confidence came from. So, in a serious coach-to-athlete voice, Marcus asked, "Nearcus why do you feel that way?"

"Because I was chosen to defend the Lord's name before all of Corinth and when I win, His name will be praised throughout Greece and the whole Roman Empire."

The three adults looked into the eyes of this baby Christian and each saw that Nearcus deeply believed what he said. None said anything.

Nearcus now felt he should share for the first time about his experience in the orchard. "The afternoon before I was unexpectedly whisked away to represent Chios at these games I was sitting under a mastic tree in my father's orchard. I heard a voice clearly speak to me saying, 'In Corinth you will be chosen.' I did not know it at the time, but that was the voice of the Lord telling me what he had planned for me. I look at the events since I heard that voice, and it only has been through a truly miraculous path that I arrived at that meeting with the Isthmian Games officials this morning."

Marcus thought about the series of steps and trials that they had endured and overcome to make it to the games. He agreed with Nearcus that it could only have been through the hand of God that they were in the position this morning to receive a challenge to defend the name of the Christ.

"I am with you, Nearcus," Marcus responded very slowly and with deep emotion and assurance.

Aggelos had his doubts. He saw the risk if Nearcus lost. He was fully aware that the Corinthian church was struggling again. Some of the believers had started to turn to believing other leaders who were not strong in their knowledge of the faith. The church was breaking into different sects that followed one local leader or another and their faith in their leaders was supplanting their faith in Jesus. If Nearcus took the field as the grand finale of the games and was easily beaten by the adult pankration champion, then the church would split into even more fractions as weak leaders could start to preach that their kind of faith was true while that of Nearcus and Garifallia and others was weak and in error.

But then Aggelos had a glorious thought! What if young Nearcus *did* win? It would give the entire church in Greece and beyond the boost it needed right now to stand firm against pagan idol worshipers! It would unify the church and energize it like nothing since the personal presence and preaching of the Apostle Paul! But how can a twelve-year old boy be victorious? But what if he was—just imagine what it would mean if he did win!

"What do you think of the situation, sister Garifallia?" Aggelos asked.

"I don't know what to think. I need to pray about this—I need to pray deeply about this. If the Spirit is in it, then how can we be against it? But is the Spirit leading down this path? I need to pray and pray and pray for an answer," Garifallia said as she shook her head and turned to retire to her private room in the back of the house. She hoped to receive a clear answer before news of this challenge was spread throughout the games' attendees and the city. If she was convinced that Marcus and Nearcus were misinterpreting what the Spirit was directing, then it would be possible for them to slip quietly out of the city and a short note sent to the senior official saying the slave had spoken without authority.

Aggelos watched Garifallia withdraw to her room and then turned to face Marcus and the boys. "I think we all need to pray harder than we ever have prayed before."

Then the tent maker exited through the front courtyard. Marcus felt the old Christian and his hostess were right; much prayer was truly needed. But he also knew that much information was needed to properly prepare Nearcus to compete on the final day. So, the paedotribae led his two athletes back to the stadium. This time they went as spectators. They went to watch the men compete in the pankration. Marcus wanted Nearcus to study his potential opponents. The slave hoped that they could detect a weakness in each of the best fighters who might win the championship.

Lysander had forced Nearcus and Dioxippus to be expelled from the competition, but he could not prevent them from attending as spectators. When the head coach saw Marcus and the boys standing on the edge of the pankration field, he pointed to them. He said something to the competitor next to him. The competitor repeated what he heard to those near him who also passed it on. Soon the entire area around the field was buzzing with the news of Nearcus and his personal god fighting against the adult champion on the last day of the games. From the pankration area this news spread to the sprinting and long distance racing sections. Before the afternoon was over, most of the 40,000 in attendance at the games knew of the battle between the representative of the Greek gods and the Christian.

Marcus, Nearcus and Dioxippus returned to Garifallia's house for the evening meal. At the table, Garifallia said she had heard from spectators returning from the day's events at the stadium about the planned match between the new champion and the Christian boy.

"I prayed continuously all afternoon for guidance. I was sure the Spirit told me to advise you to leave the city and not to put the good name of the Christ and His followers in jeopardy by participating in this match. But now that is not possible because everyone is aware of the challenge and if you withdraw it would be worse than being beaten. A valiant effort done with dignity and a good heart can be effective even if the final result is a loss."

Nearcus put down his spoon and interrupted his senior and hostess, "But I am going to win." He did not say this as if he was boasting. He said it as if it was already a historical fact.

Garifallia looked at Marcus with great concern and doubt in her eyes. Marcus returned her gaze and then looked down at his plate and continued eating.

"I have prayed too," Dioxippus said, joining the conversation. "Nearcus will win. The Lord has assured me of this."

Nearcus looked as his team mate and smiled. They both nodded and smiled and continued eating heartily.

Marcus kept eating as he said, "Well, there you have it. I guess it must be settled. Nearcus will win."

After saying this, he looked up and into Garifallia's confused eyes and she saw that the slave was just as confused, but that he was going to support his athletes no matter what.

That night Nearcus and Dioxippus had a restful and sound sleep. The adults hardly slept at all. They were worried, but the boys were confident in their Jesus. In the early morning, Marcus was still awake when he heard the boys doing exercises in the courtyard. Before he could get to them to ask what they were doing, the athletes had left the courtyard and were running down the nearly deserted streets. They hoped to complete a long run before breakfast was served. They knew that Nearcus's training must resume in earnest if he was to be ready to win at the end of the week. On this eventful trip to Corinth, the two boys had gone from enemies to fast friends and it showed as they playfully pushed and teased each other while they ran.

An hour later, the pair returned both covered in sweat, but both also smiling and happy in their exercise. It felt good to shut out all the pressure and dangers and troubles they had experienced on this trip and to just enjoy the act of running. It felt free to them and they truly enjoyed it.

At breakfast, Marcus shared a plan he had developed for Nearcus's preparation. During the day, Marcus would train Nearcus and Dioxippus would attend the pankration competition to take notes on the different winners' techniques and weaknesses. After the evening meal, the three would go over Dioxippus's notes and discuss possible strategies that Nearcus might use when he fought.

That morning, Dioxippus was about to leave for the pankration events when Aggelos walked through the courtyard gate. Upon hearing his plans for the day, the tent maker asked if he could accompany the athlete. Dioxippus was honored to have such a mature and well-respected Christian as his companion. The sky was clear, the sun brightly warming the day and Dioxippus felt happy as he and Aggelos walked the streets to the stadium. The young man was sure it was going to be a wonderful day.

He was very wrong!

CHAPTER 25

At the stadium, Aggelos and Dioxippus made their way to a good vantage point near the pankration competition. As the contests began, Dioxippus began to jot down small shapes as reminders on a piece of old cloth he had brought with him. He used a piece of charcoal to mark the linen and this left his finger tips black.

After two hours he had covered one side of the cloth with symbols he used to note any potential weaknesses he saw in the men fighting. It had been Dioxippus's plan to skip the afternoon meal because it would cost money to get food at the games and he had none. However, the big tent maker was hungry and he slapped his stomach with both hands as he spoke to Dioxippus.

"I am famished! Let's see if we can find some food behind the stadium."

Dioxippus kept his eyes on his writing and did not look up as he responded, "I'm fine. I should stay here and keep watching Nearcus's potential opponents." In truth, the young man was very hungry and he would enjoy eating anything that could end the emptiness he felt in his stomach.

"Okay," said the tent maker, "You stay here and I will go buy us some food and bring it back."

Dioxippus looked up from his writing and smiled at Aggelos. "That would be great! Thank you!" Aggelos accepted the gratitude of this boy with a smile, not knowing that the Dioxippus he knew now was nothing like the sullen, bitter, angry young man who had left Chios just days before.

Aggelos was not gone very long when Dioxippus was approached by five youth pankratiasts from Athens and Mycenae. The boys nudged Dioxippus to one side and took his place along the front of the spectator area. Rather than push back, Dioxippus wisely slid to the side and found another vantage point where he could continue his observations. But the ruffians were not satisfied that they had displaced this Christian. They had sought him out to bully him and they were not going to leave him alone until they had done what they came to do to him.

"Look!" the tallest boy said to his friends, "The Christians not only have lying, wicked black hearts, they also have black hands!"

"They are black because he is writing curses against the true believers!" said another of the bullies as he grabbed the linen from Dioxippus's hand. As Dioxippus reached for his notes, the boy quickly passed it to another bully.

This boy examined the cloth and said, "This Christian is so uneducated that he cannot even write! He has to scribble pictures and nonsense to make believe he can write! That is what all Christians do—they make believe they know something when really all of them are just stupid, ignorant troublemakers! I know, because my coach told me."

"My father said the same thing," contributed another of the ruffians.

Inside of Dioxippus there was a battle raging between his old self and his new life in Christ. His old self wanted to pounce on the biggest boy and quickly beat him senseless, knowing that once he had dispatched the biggest the others would back away and leave him alone. But his new, Christian self wanted him to "turn the other cheek" and not fight the boys. Dioxippus stood there, all his muscles tense and his fists clinched as he tried to defeat his old yearnings and to be a good representative of Christ.

The biggest bully saw Dioxippus's hands and shouted to the others, "Look! The little boy from the puny island in the middle of nowhere wants to fight us!"

"Tell us Nearcus the wonder boy of Chios, how is your stupid god going to save you from the beating we are about to give you?" said the bully directly in front of Dioxippus.

"They think I am Nearcus and want to hurt me so I cannot compete against their pagan champion," thought Dioxippus. He started to open his mouth to correct their mistake, but then he stopped when he realized that by beating him they would think they had accomplished their goal and they would not try to beat Nearcus. Dioxippus clinched his jaw shut and stood there stiff with anger and determination not to let them know they should go seek the real Nearcus.

The bully with the stolen linen cloth, threw the notes in Dioxippus's face and shouted, "Take your curses. You're going to need them!"

Suddenly, Dioxippus felt a fist crash against his left temple. When the cloth had temporarily distracted Dioxippus, one of the bullies had slipped to his side. From this unseen position the bully had smashed the side of Dioxippus's head, and when he did it caused instantaneous damage to Dioxippus's vision. First there were tiny flashes that looked like miniature lightning strikes that filled the darkening field of his vision. Next, the little lightening bolts started to swirl in a dizzying pool of light against black. Dioxippus felt his knees start to wobble, and then his vision went totally dark.

When Dioxippus hit the ground he was totally unconscious. The bullies laughed at how hard the Christian had fallen. Then the biggest one kicked Dioxippus's still body in the chest. The other bullies laughed and started to kick the Christian as hard and as fast as they could.

The beating was savage and no adults in the area stepped in to stop the bullies. The adults pretended they were watching the pankration bouts and could not see what the mean boys were doing. After a few minutes of the kicking and punching of the defenseless Dioxippus, one man did step forward and place his hand on one of the bully's shoulder. He was about to tell the boy to stop when another adult said, "Don't stop them. They are just giving that troublemaker Christian what he deserves."

Upon hearing this, the first man withdrew and the boys continued to beat and kick Dioxippus, but now the adults in the crowd stopped watching the pankration bouts and formed a circle around the bullies to watch them beat a Christian. It was not long before some of the men in the crowd reacted to an especially hard blow with a laugh and then another in the crowd urged the boys on by shouting, "That's it! Kick him in the face now!" Then others in the mob cried out similar exhortations and this goaded the ruffians to continue even when some of them knew they should stop because the Christian was being permanently hurt.

Aggelos wondered why the crowd had stopped watching the athletic events and spectators were pushing around one spot near the front of the observation area. As he got closer he heard shouts of "Kick that Christian harder, boys!" and "Stomp on his ankle! Break it! Then he won't be able to fight the champion!" and "Really give it to Nearcus—show him how we do it in the city!" The tent maker dropped the food he had bought and pushed his way into the mob. His size meant that he easily moved aside those blocking his path. When he reached the bullies, a rage—a righteous rage—overcame Aggelos. He saw the unconscious Dioxippus bleeding from his mouth, nose, ears and from his arms and legs where his bones had been broken and pierced the skin. With every kick, the young Christian's body bounced and flopped around and suffered even more damage. The sight sickened the tent maker and the sounds of the mob's shouts to inflict more pain on a defenseless young boy further enraged him.

With one long sweep of his massive left arm, Aggelos sent two of the bullies flying back into the crowd. The other three were concentrating on Dioxippus and did not notice their companions being smacked backwards. Next Aggelos grabbed the boy in front of him and in one swift and easy motion lifted him high over his head and threw him back into the mob, the bully landing three men deep in front of Aggelos. The swiftness of the tent maker's actions stunned the mob so much that it went silent and no one moved to stop the burly Christian. With the silence, the remaining two bullies stopped their kicking of Dioxippus and looked up. When they saw the angry large man with the great scowl on his face lunging for them, the two boys backed away and scrambled to get behind the adults at the front of the mob.

Before the mob could react, Aggelos scooped up the broken body of Dioxippus, the boy's blood dripping from his wounds and his limbs dangling like broken branches in a high wind and his linen notes pasted to his neck by the flow of his blood. The tent maker pushed his way through the crowd to the nearest escape route he could see. He broke through the thinnest part of the mob onto the pankration competition field and started to run with the young Christian cradled in his arms. He had gone just ten yards before a man in the crowd angrily shouted, "That's a Christian too! Get him!" Upon hearing that, the mob lurched forward in an attempt to catch Aggelos. But in doing so, those in the front of the mob did not move quickly enough and were pushed to the ground by the surging pack behind them. This tripped the next row of the frenzied mob and a great pile of bodies that were crying and shouting curses momentarily stopped the crowd's surge. This gave Aggelos the chance to sprint across the competition area and reach the middle before the mob could start forward again.

Along the far side of the pankration field was a troop of Roman soldiers charged with preserving order at the games. Upon seeing a large man carrying a bleeding boy running across the playing field the soldiers grabbed their shields and moved forward to capture this man who was disrupting the games. The Roman leader was mounted on a large horse and swiftly rode ahead of his troops. As he neared Aggelos the Roman saw the mob starting to chase the Christian. Instead of stopping at Aggelos, the officer continued his gallop right to the front of the angry mob. Upon seeing the charging horse, those in front of the mob tried to stop and turn around. None of them wanted to be arrested by the Romans. As they pushed back to retreat, the entire mob became a tangled mess of those in the back trying to go forward and those in the front trying to go back. The mounted officer turned his horse to run parallel of the mob's front and he patrolled there in a back and forth motion shouting for the crowd to back away and to disburse.

Aggelos kept running towards the advancing Roman soldiers. The pankratiasts engaged in bouts on the field stopped fighting and stood around watching the odd scene. The soldiers ran up to Aggelos and a few took him into custody while the majority kept going forward to reach their officer and help turn back the mob.

As soon as he was safely in the custody of the Roman soldiers, Aggelos quickly, but carefully set Dioxippus on the ground. He examined the young Christian's injuries. Dioxippus was unconscious and barely breathing, a bone in his right forearm was broken and slightly protruding from the skin and bleeding, his right ear was nearly severed from the side of his head, his face was a bloody mess with teeth missing and his jaw dislocated, and great swelling was rapidly occurring, a right shin bone was broken and the splintered end stuck out of the skin nearly three inches, and, most disturbing to Aggelos, there was a large knob that had formed on the side of the young Christian's temple and blood was oozing from his ears. If Aggelos did not see the shallow rising and falling of Dioxippus's chest, he would have been certain that the boy was dead.

The Roman soldiers did think Dioxippus was dead. All of these veterans had seen many die in battle and one look at Dioxippus and they knew the boy was either dead or would soon be dead. The eldest soldier looked in the distance and saw the mob was stopped by his compatriots and order was being restored. He knew that the best thing to do was to clear the field of this boy and the tent maker so the games could resume.

"Grab that body and drag it off the playing field," he said to his fellow soldiers.

Aggelos put his hands up to keep them away from Dioxippus and then he slipped his arms under the young Christian. The tent maker looked at the senior soldier and gave him a questioning look asking where he should take the boy. The soldier pointed to the opposite side of the field and then started in that direction. Aggelos and the other soldiers followed him.

It was not long after the pankration competition resumed that the crowd lost interest in the Christian beating and were cheering for their favorite athlete. The officer returned with his men to their post and they resumed a stand-by status to await any further disturbances. After dismounting, the officer removed his armored helmet and unfastened the sword belt from around his waist. He set these on a nearby table and then approached Aggelos who was kneeling by the body of Dioxippus.

"Tell me what all the commotion was about," the officer ordered the tent maker.

Aggelos looked up into the face of the Roman and replied, "A group of hooligans was sent to attack this lad in order to give the pankration champion an advantage on the last day of the games."

"Oh, so this is Nearcus, the Christian boy who thinks his god can defeat Apollo and Poseidon," the officer said as he knelt down to inspect the condition of Dioxippus. "How did the mob get so excited and involved?"

"They goaded the hooligans to keep beating the boy until they killed him."

"Well, from the look of him, they did a good job of it," the officer mumbled as he continued to examine the unconscious boy. "I don't think this lad will be fighting anybody ever again."

"They beat him because he was a Christian and whoever put them up to it must really fear the Lord or why else would they try to cheat to win the match?"

The Roman nodded in agreement with the tent maker.

Aggelos continued, "But they could not stop the great Jehovah. The match will still take place as scheduled."

The officer looked at Dioxippus and then at Aggelos before he said, "I don't think even he can heal this boy in three days, if ever."

Aggelos ignored the Roman's comment and asked, "Can I take him to a physician now?"

"If you think it can do him any good, go ahead and leave. I have no reason to keep you."

The massive tent maker gently lifted the young athlete who was near death into his strong arms. Aggelos whispered a prayer as he carried Dioxippus through the streets of Corinth. He asked that the Lord have mercy on this broken body and the spirit of this baby Christian.

It was mid-afternoon when Aggelos reached the one physician he knew to be a devout Christian. Banging on the doctor's door with his foot, Aggelos waited for someone to answer. Soon he had Dioxippus stretched out on his back upon the examining table in the doctor's great room. The physician listened for the young man's heart beat and heard only a faint, intermittent rattle of a muscle trying its best to overcome a great shock to its system. The doctor knew that he could set the arm and leg and stop the bleeding, and he could repair most of the damage to the face, but he was very worried about the deep comma Dioxippus was in. When he checked the injured athlete's eyes they were rolled back into the tops of his sockets and Dioxippus's breathing was extremely shallow and labored.

"Brother healer," an anxious and sad tent maker pleaded with the doctor, "will he live? Can you help him to recover?"

The doctor turned to face Aggelos and said, "His condition is well beyond my skills to help him get well. He truly is in God's hands and not mine."

Upon hearing this and without getting permission from the physician, Aggelos turned to the attending slave who was the property of the doctor and ordered him to run to Garifallia's house. He wanted Nearcus and Marcus to come quickly so they could say goodbye to their friend before he died.

CHAPTER 26

When Marcus and Nearcus arrived, Garifallia was accompanying them. The three rushed into the great room and gathered around Dioxippus. Aggelos was holding the baby Christian's hand while the doctor was sewing Dioxippus's ear back onto his scalp. The physician had already pushed the broken arm and leg bones back into the limbs and straightened the bones as best he could and applied splints to hold them in place. He had sewn the gashes together and bandaged them which had stopped the bleeding. He had also cleaned the blood from Dioxippus's face, reset his jaw bone and bandaged the worst cuts. Upon seeing his friend, Nearcus stepped back in horror. He was in shock over the terrible condition of his team mate who only hours before was a specimen of fitness and good health. Now poor Dioxippus lay before Nearcus in a motionless lump of bruises, cuts, swelling and mangled flesh.

Garifallia was the first to recover from the shock of seeing such damage to a young man and she said, "Brother healer, you have done well. I can see your skilled work has already tended to many serious injuries."

"God was with us. His unconscious state permitted me to do what had to be done without causing him any additional pain," the doctor responded as he cut the thin line of lamb's gut he had used to repair the ear.

Marcus could not say anything at first. After a few moments he finally pulled Aggelos to the side and asked what had happened. The tent maker told him how the bullies had waited until Aggelos had left Dioxippus alone and then attacked him.

"I blame myself for ever leaving him alone. I should have known that there would be an attempt to guarantee a victory by those who would lose money and power if Nearcus won. I should have known and been there to protect the boy," Aggelos said to Marcus.

Nearcus went over to his friend's side and with tears streaming down his twelve-year old face, he took the hand of Dioxippus. He held the hand, and through his watery eyes he noticed that there were no marks on his friend's knuckles. This told Nearcus that Dioxippus had taken the beating without fighting back. Nearcus raised the hand to his cheek and softly whispered to his friend, "Oh Dioxippus, you must come back to us." Then Nearcus continued with a prayer, "Jesus be with my friend. You gave him a peace he had never known in his short life and now I pray that you will be with him and give him even greater peace. Oh Dear Lord, I ask for healing for this your faithful servant."

Garifallia was standing nearby and heard Nearcus's prayer and said, "Amen."

Nearcus heard her and turned to ask her questions that were burning inside of him, "Why did Jesus allow this to happen? Why would anyone do this to Dioxippus? What had he done to deserve this?"

What Aggelos said in response to Nearcus's questions made the young pankratiast's knees shake, "He took the beating for you, Nearcus. The bullies were sent to injure the one who was fighting for God at the end of the games. They thought he was you."

Nearcus felt faint. His friend had been beaten in his place. This could be him lying on the table near death. He was confused and angry and afraid all at once.

"Why did they have to beat him so severely? Couldn't they just break a leg and that would ensure him—I mean I—couldn't fight the champion?" Nearcus wanted to know.

"We live in a dark and sinful world," the tent maker shared with everyone there. "The crowd kept after the bullies to keep punishing Dioxippus because he was a Christian and in their spiritual darkness they fear the light of Christ. To the mob, Dioxippus represented Jesus and they wanted to kill him to push away the thought of their own guilt before God. It was like nothing I have ever seen. It was pure evil in the middle of the day."

Marcus went to the side of the beaten athlete and kneeled beside the table. He bowed his head and prayed silently. Garifallia followed him and did the same. Nearcus remained standing with his friend's hand pressed to his cheek where he covered it in tears. The physician stepped back and looking at Aggelos, he shook his head to signify that he thought even prayer could not save this new Christian lying on his table. Aggelos just scowled in response and sat in a chair on the opposite side of the room.

Hours past and the sun set and then the stars appeared in the clear night sky. Marcus remained in his worshipful prayer position. Nearcus remained holding Dioxippus's hand as he sat in a chair that a slave had brought to him. Thirty minutes ago Nearcus had fallen asleep, his friend's hand still pressed against his cheek. Nearcus was exhausted from the emotional weight he had been carrying the past two days and sleep came over him without him having any control over it.

Garifallia had risen from her prayer position and left for her house before dark. There she organized the Corinthian churches into a prayer vigil to ask God to spare and heal Dioxippus. By the time Nearcus had been overtaken with sleep, nearly five-hundred Christians throughout Corinth were lifting Dioxippus's future up to God with petitions for a miraculous healing.

These prayers and petitions were sustained throughout the long night. By morning the number of praying Christians was over two-thousand. The beating of

Dioxippus had united a group of churches that was previously having trouble agreeing on most things. Now everyone recognized that Dioxippus had been beaten because he was perceived to be a threat to those who worshiped idols. Dioxippus had been beaten because he was a Christian and because of this, the praying Christians recognized that he had been beaten in their place. In essence, this young man had taken the beating that their neighbors in Corinth and Greece wanted to give each of them. This realization led to a great chorus of requests beseeching Jesus to heal the lad.

At dawn, Nearcus felt the hand he had pressed against his cheek all night twitch. He thought he might be dreaming, so he opened his eyes wide and remained totally still. Then it happened again; Dioxippus's hand definitely twitched! Nearcus stood and looked into Dioxippus's swollen face. The older boy's eyes were still closed, but when Nearcus said in a loud voice, "Dioxippus do you hear me?" the hand he was holding squeezed his fingers.

"Doctor! Come quick! He is awake!" Nearcus shouted across the room to wake the physician sleeping in a chair.

The doctor rushed over to Dioxippus's side and used his forefinger and thumb to open the baby Christian's eyes. In the slits between the great swelling on the top and bottom of the eyes, the physician saw Dioxippus's pupils. This improvement over what he had seen hours before encouraged the doctor.

"Don't try to speak or move, Dioxippus," the doctor directed. "You have a broken jaw and nose. Just try to breathe slowly through your teeth."

Dioxippus's mind was spinning uncontrollably. He was nauseous and dizzy. He heard the stranger's voice but it sounded like the man was shouting to him from under water. Surprisingly, Dioxippus felt no real pain anywhere. He just felt sick and confused. The last thing he remembered was writing down notes on who Nearcus might have to face.

A panic started to rise inside of him as he tried to figure out where he was and why he was here. Then he heard something that sounded sweeter than his mother's voice when he was a little child.

"Dioxippus, it is Marcus. Relax, the Lord is with you."

And Dioxippus did relax. The panic left him instantly and he felt safe and secure. He knew that Marcus was there and he would look after everything.

"Brother, I am here with you, too," Nearcus said with his lips close to Dioxippus's ear. "You were beaten and hurt very badly, but you are awake now and the Lord will heal you."

Dioxippus tried to smile, but he had no real control of his muscles. Just as he realized that he was not able to smile or move his legs or even speak, pain crashed over his entire being like a massive wave in angry surf. His leg was on fire and his arm felt like it had been smashed with a sledge hammer. The pain pulsated up one side of his body and then down the other. It was so intense that Dioxippus wanted to cry out, but he still could not control his muscles. The best he could manage was a low moan. His body experienced a reoccurring uncontrollable shake as the pain waves rolled over him.

The pain was almost unbearable but what happened next really frightened the injured young man. He felt blood pooling in his throat and as the liquid increased it became harder and harder for Dioxippus to draw a breath. He was drowning in his own blood. As he gasped for any air he could draw into his lungs, he made a gurgling noise. This alerted the doctor that his patient was having difficulty breathing. Immediately, the physician grabbed Dioxippus's shoulders and raised him to a sitting position. When he did this, the young man's pain grew beyond what he could bear. Dioxippus went limp; he was unconscious again.

Nearcus saw his friend flop forward and his head roll to one side as the doctor supported him. Nearcus was certain that he had just witnessed the death of his friend. Marcus thought the same thing and when they saw Dioxippus's face turn blue, they were sure of it. But the doctor had not given up yet. He slapped his patient in the back, right in the middle of the shoulders and shook him violently as he did it. His efforts finally were successful and the blood drained from Dioxippus's throat into his stomach. The air passage was clear and the young man started to breathe again, his face color returning to normal.

While still propping up his patient, the doctor directed his attending slave to run to the other room and bring back an inclined board. Once he had the board, the physician eased Dioxippus to a sitting position in order to keep the air way clear. Marcus, Nearcus and Aggelos all looked to the doctor for some indication of Dioxippus's condition.

"He is still alive and that is a miracle in itself," the healer said. "He should be able to breathe in this position and in the next couple of days we should be able to get him to eat some broth. He still needs everyone's prayers, but he has a decent chance of not dying. However, with that head injury, I am not sure if he will be the same again mentally or if he will ever walk straight again, but there is a good chance he will live."

Marcus turned to Nearcus and said only three words, "Praise the Lord."

CHAPTER 27

Later in the morning, as Aggelos, Marcus, Nearcus and the doctor kept watch over Dioxippus, the paedotribae pulled his young athlete to the side of the room for a private chat.

"Nearcus, in three days you are expected to enter the stadium and fight the Isthmian Games champion before the same crowd that did this to Dioxippus. I got you into this by accepting this unfair challenge. If you want to reconsider your choice, I can go speak to the authorities and explain why we must leave Corinth for your safety," Marcus said in all seriousness to his young charge.

Nearcus looked at Marcus and then looked over at his friend who lay broken on the table, barely able to breath and swollen beyond recognition. After a long examination of poor Dioxippus, Nearcus turned to his coach and mentor.

"If I backed out of the match now, after what they have done to Dioxippus, not only would the Lord be insulted, but every one in Greece who despises Christians will think they have won—that their gods are greater than Jesus. And, if I fail to show up for the match, then Dioxippus took this beating for nothing."

"Dioxippus was beaten because they thought he was you. What do you think they will do when they discover their error?" Marcus said to ensure that Nearcus understood the potential danger in his decision. It was no longer about fighting the good fight on the morning of the last day of the games; it was about survival against desperate evil-doers.

Aggelos had overheard the private conversation between Nearcus and his coach. The tent maker rose from his seat and went to them.

"Nearcus, listen to your coach. In spite of what you see here in this room, the Lord is all powerful. He does not need you to be martyred to advance His kingdom. You are but a twelve-year old boy. Your shoulders are not yet strong enough to be asked to bear the entire load of the future of Christianity in Greece. You do not need to end up like Dioxippus for the Lord to prevail," Aggelos said.

"Why did Dioxippus have to end up like this then?" Nearcus asked not with bitterness in his voice but rather a sincere desire to know why Christ had not protected his friend.

"I do not know," the tent maker responded quickly, "I do not know many things, but I do know Jesus and there is no suffering we can ever endure that is greater than what he suffered for us. I do not know what Jesus has planned for Dioxippus's purpose in life, but I do know where this Christian will live and who will care for him as long as he needs or wants help. I should not have left him alone in the crowd and now I know I should not leave him alone ever again. He will come and live with me and I will be his father and guardian until he can make his own path in the world, if that ever occurs."

Both Marcus and Nearcus watched the big, burly Christian's eyes as he made this vow. They saw in them a commitment deeper than anything they had ever seen in any other man. Nearcus watched as Aggelos went back across the room and sat by his new son and held the injured boy's hand. Nearcus knew that what he was watching was a real miracle. Dioxippus had to steal to get money to earn this trip to Corinth. He was not allowed to live in any relative's house at home and his entire village shunned him. Now he has a second chance at life. Now, Dioxippus had a father who loved him and a Lord on whom he could depend. Now

Dioxippus had an extended family of brothers and sisters in Christ who will support him in any trial. He had left Chios a bitter and lost youth, and now he is propped up on a table in a Corinthian doctor's office a new person, born again by the knowledge and faith he has in Jesus Christ. Whether his friend lived through the day or survived for decades to come, Nearcus knew that Dioxippus would never be alone and never feel unloved ever again in his life.

It was the awareness of this miracle in Dioxippus's life that flushed away the doubts Nearcus had allowed to creep into his thinking. He remembered the voice in the orchard and the cleanliness and wholeness he felt when he prayed for Jesus to take away his sins and make him holy. Nearcus again had great faith that the Lord had chosen him to accomplish something special here in Corinth.

"I must fight the champion, Marcus. The Lord will protect me and I will do His will. But whether I win or lose or die out there in the arena, it will be all right as long as I do what I know the Lord wants me to do."

"If that is your wish, young Nearcus, then it is my duty to prepare you. We have only two full days left before the end of the games. Let us withdraw to a safe location, far from the angry crowds, and prepare you properly," Marcus said in a slow but surprisingly confident tone.

The paedotribae went to speak to Aggelos about where they could train in private with good security. The doctor heard the request and joined the conversation.

"I have just the place for you. Outside of the city I own a small farm I lease to a wonderful Christian couple. The farm is far from the main road and there is a grove of trees that blocks the view of the yard from passer-bys. I am sure my tenants will be overjoyed to help you prepare to serve the cause of the Lord."

Aggelos volunteered to escort the slave and athlete to the farm, but Marcus could tell that the tent maker really wanted to stay by the side of Dioxippus. The doctor saw this as well and he told Aggelos to remain with the patient and the doctor's slave would guide Marcus and Nearcus. The trio would leave right after the mid-day meal.

Upon arriving at the farm, Marcus and Nearcus saw that the doctor had been right. It was the perfect training facility and the renters were more than gracious in hosting the men. Marcus did not waste any time in starting the last-minute training. He had Nearcus repeatedly carry heavy logs rapidly back and forth over a ten yard course. Once the new Christian was totally exhausted, Marcus removed his tunic and had the boy wrestle him non-stop for one hour.

"Fatigue will make your mind slow and it is your mind and not your body that will win in the arena" Marcus said over and over. Nearcus was exhausted and he did find it hard to think of his next hold or maneuver when his mind was occupied by the desire to just rest. But the exhaustion had one good effect on the boy; it kept his mind off of the condition of Dioxippus.

After the evening meal, Marcus gave his student a deep rub down and while he massaged the boy's aching muscles he quizzed him on how to defeat different types of opponents. Nearcus was tired, but after eating he was sufficiently strong to think clearly about how to counter various attacks and how to create openings for him to successfully attack his opponent. Marcus was pleased with the abilities of Nearcus to focus and plan. But whenever there was a lull in the conversation, both the slave and the athlete thought about Dioxippus. Was their friend and brother in Christ still alive? Was he suffering terribly? If he lives, will he ever be able to walk again or to take care of himself?

Nearcus had these same questions in his mind as he lay down in the barn loft to sleep that night. But his tough training had made him so tired that it was not long before the twelve-year old fell asleep.

Nearcus was still asleep just before dawn when Marcus shook his leg to awaken the athlete.

"This is our last hard training day. We must use every second of it to hone your skills and mind to a sharp edge. Get up and let's get started," the paedotribae said.

Marcus did push Nearcus very hard that day. It was the hardest he had ever required Nearcus to work. The boy never opened his mouth to complain; he nodded whenever his coach told him to do something and then he did it to the best of his ability without questioning why he should do it. At the end of this hard day, Marcus felt the best use of the night after the evening meal should be centered on spiritual preparation. The coach and the student sat around a small fire located in the yard area just in front of the house but behind the grove of trees. Marcus shared with the younger Christian about the power of God and the value of faith. And the two prayed together that Nearcus would honor God by his best efforts. And they prayed that Dioxippus would live and heal sufficiently so he could enjoy his new family and life. Nearcus was so tired that he had trouble staying awake as they sat there for a couple of hours and discussed Jesus and prayed. When Marcus told him to go to bed, the youth was so exhausted that he immediately drifted off to a deep sleep.

The next morning the sun was up before Nearcus opened his eyes. Marcus had not awakened the young competitor before dawn this morning. In fact, Nearcus barely had time to make it to the house before breakfast was served. Marcus met him at the table and smiled at the athlete who thought he had failed to show on time for training.

"Did you sleep well, young Nearcus?" his coach asked him.

"Sorry I am late, Marcus, but I will work extra hard all day to make up for it," the boy said in great sincerity.

Marcus reacted in a way that seemed unusual to Nearcus. There seemed to be a happy spirit in his coach that had replaced the foreboding concern that had been there for the past days.

"There is no heavy training today," Marcus said. "Tomorrow morning you must enter the arena in peak form and not tired from over-training. Just light exercises and an easy run to keep your body limber are on today's schedule. "

Then the paedotribae shared why he was so happy.

"And we shall review the weaknesses of your opponent to develop your attack plan." Then Marcus pulled a sheet of blood-stained linen with charcoal scribbles on it from under the table. He continued, "I just happen to have some very good notes here on how to beat your opponent!"

"Where did you get that?" Nearcus said excitedly as he reached for the linen.

"Dioxippus made these notes and this morning Aggelos brought them to us! Dioxippus explained what each of his figures mean and I have a clear picture of how best to prepare you today."

"Dioxippus can talk now? He can explain things now!" Nearcus shouted joyously as he jumped to his feet.

"Yes! Aggelos said that Dioxippus was awake and talking and starting to heal! He is still in bad shape but he is not going to die!"

The only words that Nearcus could think of to express his great joy were, "Praise the Lord!"

"Praise the Lord indeed!" Marcus answered.

Robert Bartron

CHAPTER 28

In the late afternoon Nearcus and Marcus had a visitor on the farm. Iro arrived with news of the Isthmian Games pankration results. Garifallia had sent her slave to advise the paedotribae and his student who Nearcus would fight the next morning. When Iro said the opponent would be Adrastos from Athens, Marcus placed Dioxippus's notes onto the table and hurriedly searched them for what the injured boy had seen about Adrastos's style and any weaknesses. Marcus found the section on Adrastos and when he read it, the slave's eyes grew narrow and a frown formed on his entire face.

"I was afraid he would win the championship," Marcus said as he shook his head.

Iro asked the coach, "Is he that good?"

"He is the best. Dioxippus noted only one weakness in Adrastos. And even that is only a guess. The Athenian is so much better than all of the opponents Dioxippus watched him defeat, that Adrastos never had to fight for more than fifteen minutes. No one has ever seen him fight a long bout, so it could be possible that his endurance is weak. It has never been tested sufficiently for anyone to know how he fights after a couple of hours in the arena."

Nearcus joined the conversation, "Then I must make him exhausted before I make my attack to gain a disabling hold."

"That is much easier planned than done, young Nearcus. How will you stay away from his great strength for that long? You can not run around without engaging him. The

230

crowd will think you are a coward and more importantly they will think God is weak."

Nearcus was thinking of a plan, but he needed more information to develop a good strategy. He asked his coach, "How big is Adrastos? Is he fast on his feet or with his hands?"

"I have never seen him in person so I do not know," Marcus answered.

"Dioxippus has seen him fight. Let's go talk to him," Nearcus said. More than just information about his opponent, Nearcus wanted to visit his friend to see how he was recovering.

Marcus desired to see Dioxippus as well. He had trained Nearcus in every way possible and there was nothing left to do but discuss possible strategies. There was no further need to stay at the farm. If they left within the hour, Iro could guide them back to the doctor's and then to Garifallia's house where they would spend the last night before the important fight.

"Iro, Nearcus is right. We should visit Dioxippus to learn more. Please guide us to the doctor's house and from there to your mistress's home."

"Dioxippus is no longer at the doctor's house. Aggelos had him moved to his house so he could care for him and protect him from any who might want to do Dioxippus more harm," Iro answered.

"Then take us to Aggelos please," said Nearcus as Marcus gathered up their gear.

Aggelos lived in a building right on Lechaion Road, one of the busiest streets in the city. This road was the main thoroughfare between Corinth and the city of Lechaion which was the main port on the isthmus serving the Gulf of Corinth. The tent maker's building was two stories with his workshop on the ground level and his living quarters above on the second floor. Although Aggelos had a large sign that said "Tent Maker" hanging just above the main door on a rod that jutted from the front of his establishment, nearly half of his business came to him because of a small sign posted on the door. It read, "Sails made and repaired." Aggelos had been in business sewing canvas into tents and sails for over thirty years, and he normally had a staff of two assistant workers employed permanently in his shop. When Aggelos had a large order to fill quickly he would hire additional craftsmen as temporary help. However, every product that left his shop was made to the high personal standards of Aggelos—no exceptions! If Aggelos inspected a piece of sewing done by another and found a flaw in it, his famous scowl would come upon his face and he would throw the work back at the craftsman and say, "Do it again and this time do it right." Because of his high standards and great personal integrity, Aggelos had a reputation throughout Greece as one of the very best tent and sail makers.

Merchants from as far away as Persia would order his quality, custom-made tents or sails on one trip to Greece and then pick-up the finished pieces on their next journey to Corinth. These traveling merchants had found that it was better to buy the best from Aggelos because their tents lasted much longer and the travelers would never be forced to camp on their route in a tent that had ripped at the seams and allowed rain to soak them.

Aggelos also had many ship owners who would only put to sea with sails from the Christian's shop. Unlike other sail makers, a customer could never get an image of Poseidon or another god stitched into the canvas but that was a small detail to sacrifice in order to buy the best sails available. One ship owner had his sails made by Aggelos and then went to another shop to have the image of Apollo sewn onto the new sail. When Aggelos heard of this, he refused to make any sails for that owner ever again. When word of this spread along the waterfronts on both sides of the isthmus, no ship owner ever again altered a sail made by Aggelos. All knew he was a devout Christian and his word was his bond and that Aggelos would never, ever allow his work to be used to praise idols. This stance had lost him business when the city fathers had come to him a dozen years ago and asked that he make all the flags flown in the city and at the stadium for the Isthmian Games. Aggelos refused the contract because the flags would honor their gods.

When Nearcus and Marcus entered Aggelos's shop they could tell that the tent maker was very successful by the many orders for goods being processed. And the large wooden cross he had hanging on the back wall of the shop showed he was a Christian who was unafraid to worship God and His only Son. The two hired craftsmen were present and hard at work stitching together two large pieces of heavy canvas. They stopped their work momentarily when they saw Iro and the two strangers enter the shop. Iro smiled at them and nodded towards the wooden stairs located against the right wall. Both craftsmen nodded and then went back to their task.

Iro turned to Marcus and Nearcus and said, "It is permissible for us to go up to Aggelos's quarters. Don't ever try to go up these stairs without getting permission first. Those two men always keep heavy clubs hidden beneath the canvas they are working on. More than one intruder has tried to sneak up to where Aggelos lives to try and catch him unawares. But they have all left here severely beaten."

Nearcus stated what he was thinking, "That doesn't seem very Christian."

"Oh, those men are not Christians," Iro said as they climbed the stairs, "but they would die to defend Aggelos, they love him that much."

Upon entering the tent maker's living quarters, the trio found Aggelos kneeling beside a bed that had been moved to the main room. In the bed Dioxippus was sitting upright, large pillows sewn from canvas and stuffed with straw supported the boy's back. Dioxippus's chin was resting on his chest. Aggelos did not stir when the guests entered the room. Finally, Iro cleared her throat to get the large man's attention.

Aggelos remained in his kneeling position and then he said loud enough for the trio to hear, "Amen."

The tent maker rose to his feet and turned to greet his visitors. Before he could say anything he noticed the concerned and frightened looks on Marcus's and Nearcus's faces. The two were focused on Dioxippus who was not moving.

"He is resting now. It is better when he sleeps because the pain is nearly too much to bear when he is awake," Aggelos said to remove their doubts about whether Dioxippus was alive or dead.

In a quiet voice Marcus spoke, "We came to see how our friend was doing and to learn more about Nearcus's opponent tomorrow. Can you tell us about Dioxippus's healing?"

"It is a miracle of God that this young man is still alive. In just the past two days he has gone from totally unresponsive to where he can now take soft bread with his broth—and he is eating four times a day!" Aggelos said with a mixture of pride and joy.

"Praise God," Marcus responded. "He looks a little better. The swelling in his face seems to have gone down a little."

"Yes, it has. He can see out of his left eye and hear out of his left ear, but I am afraid he will never have use of his right eye and ear again. I was surprised that he only lost two teeth, so chewing hard food won't be a problem for him later! I figure he will limp because now one leg will probably be shorter than the other when the bones heal, but I honestly think he will be able to walk again."

Nearcus had one question that was torturing him to the point where he just had to blurt it out, "But is his brain working?"

Aggelos smiled at the bluntness and concern Nearcus showed with his question. The tent maker thought him a forthright lad who was without guile or deceit. He thought, "Here is a boy who is totally honest and cannot keep from asking what is important."

"Nearcus, your friend's brain is working just fine in most things. He knows who he is and who I am and he can remember most of his past. But many things are still foggy in his memory. I think with time, most of what he has trouble remembering will eventually come back to him. But even if it doesn't, he is still the same friend you had three days ago. In fact, the first thing he did yesterday when he could form words was to tell me to give you his notes and he made me learn how to interpret his scribbles! Whenever he regains consciousness, the first thing he asks is if you have fought yet and how did it go. He always starts with, 'Is Nearcus well? Was he hurt?' When I tell you you have yet to fight he asks me again if I gave you his notes."

Nearcus stared at Dioxippus as Aggelos shared this information with him. His friend had taken a beating nearly unto death for him. He lay there in pain, and his first thoughts are always of Nearcus. The twelve-year old did not understand the feeling he was having, but he felt it deep, deep down inside of him. Here was an example of God's love laying on the bed right in front of him. Jesus said that there was no greater love than to lay down your life for another. Dioxippus, the abandoned, bitter ruffian of Chios had become a Christian and when tested by all that was evil he kept the faith and laid down his life for his friend.

Nearcus felt a power start to rise up inside of him. He felt the power of the Most Holy God girding him with the necessary courage and love for his friend to do what had to be done to make certain that Dioxippus had not sacrificed his body and future in vain. Nearcus felt the Holy Spirit come over him and suddenly his arms and legs and neck seemed to burn with a heat the boy did not understand.

Nearcus only knew that seeing Dioxippus and thinking about what he had done caused his muscles to feel empowered with a super strength he had never known before.

Nearcus knew way down deep inside that he was ready to face Adrastos. He did not need to know anything further about his opponent's techniques or weaknesses or how big he might be. Nearcus knew the Lord was with him and he knew he would beat the pagan pankratiast tomorrow. He just knew it. He had been given the gift of faith to believe what the Holy Spirit witnessed to his spirit and now Nearcus was anxious for the morning to come. He did not want vengeance on those who had done this to his friend. He only wanted his Lord to be glorified before the thousands who were going to gather to watch a boy be brutalized by a large, fearfully skilled man.

CHAPTER 29

Aggelos suggested that Marcus send word to the games senior official that Nearcus was ready to fight the champion tomorrow morning. Word had been floating around all of Corinth that Nearcus had left the city because he felt that God could not defeat Apollo and Poseidon and the other Greek and Roman gods. Of course, this rumor was spread by the officials because they knew the truth. The officials had ordered the elimination of Nearcus as a capable opponent and they thought that the ruffians and the mob had done their job by nearly killing the boy. It was going to be a great shock to these officials when Nearcus showed for the grand finale of the Games. It would cause these men to fear that perhaps the boy's Christian god might truly be more powerful than anyone imagined. And Aggelos thought it appropriate that these officials felt fear of the truth.

Aggelos told Marcus that one of his non-Christian craftsmen should deliver this shocking message and that Marcus should not go. If Marcus went, he said, then there was a chance that another "spontaneous mob" might descend upon him in order to beat to death another Christian. Aggelos knew the kind of evil the people of his city were capable of exercising. Marcus wanted to deliver the message himself, but he gave into Aggelos's insistence and they sent one of the tough and loyal workmen to deliver the startling message to the games officials.

Knowing that the games officials might use the cover of the night to seek out Nearcus, Aggelos convinced Marcus that it was safer for the coach and his athlete to remain in his apartment than back at Garifallia's house. Even though she was a wonderful hostess, her household consisted of women and one old man; it was hardly very strong protection. If anyone came to do harm to Nearcus tonight, Aggelos assured Marcus, they would have to fight their way across a workshop, up a flight of stairs and through four strong men. Marcus agreed and sent Iro back to Garifallia with the news in time for her to arrive well before sundown.

Across the city, in a fine house with a reflection pool and shade trees in the large courtyard surrounding the front entrance, the champion pankratiast was enjoying his glorious win. As the guest of a rich Athenian merchant who attended every Isthmian Games and rented the best home in the neighborhood while the games were on, Adrastos reclined on a turquoise marble bench shaped like a dolphin. In one hand he held a full goblet of expensive wine and in the other was the roast leg of a young lamb. On his head, tilted to one side, was the champion's wreath of woven pine boughs.

Surrounding Adrastos was a group of influential men from Corinth and Athens, the major cities of all Greece. These men were the idle rich of the ruling class. Each year they attended in great style whatever games were being held — the Olympics, Isthmian, Nemean, or Pythian. It did not matter to them which of the games; it only mattered that for two weeks each year they would have something different to keep their interest. None of these elderly men were athletic, so they used the victories of the athletes they supported to raise their standing in the group. The ones sitting with Adrastos this evening were his biggest fans and supporters. In their eyes, Adrastos's victory that day also had been a victory for them and now they used their wealth to show him their appreciation in winning. Adrastos had access to the best wine and food and entertainment available in Greece and the champion was making sure he partook in all that was offered.

When one of the elders saw Adrastos gulp down an entire goblet of wine without stopping for a breath, he said, "Champion Adrastos, isn't that your sixth goblet of wine? Hadn't you better limit yourself until tomorrow night? After all, you do have one more fight left!"

All there laughed very loudly. Adrastos answered by raising his right arm and forming a very large muscle with his bicep and said, "I will not need this tomorrow to defeat a little boy!"

All the men laughed even harder and louder. The room was filled with giddy feelings. Another elder added in a very sarcastic tone, "But aren't you afraid of his great and mighty god?"

The man who said it and all there laughed even louder and harder than before. Adrastos nearly choked on his new glass of wine as he tried to drink it quickly while he was still laughing. His coughing made everyone laugh even more!

For the rest of the evening and into the early morning, Adrastos and his well-wishers celebrated his championship and berated, belittled and blasphemed God. Finally, just a couple of hours before the dawn, Adrastos had consumed so much wine that he passed out and slept what was left of the night on the dolphin bench.

Nearcus spent a much different night before the biggest bout of his entire life. He and Marcus sat in the corner of Aggelos's great room around a single candle. They meditated and prayed for courage and power and faithfulness to God and his Christ, Jesus. For two hours after a simple evening meal, the pair quietly drew strength and confidence from their Lord and His Holy Spirit. Then Marcus directed Nearcus to try and get some sleep before the big challenge he faced tomorrow. Nearcus was so confident in the Lord being with him, that he easily fell asleep soon after he lay down. Marcus watched his student drift off to a peaceful rest and smiled at the innocence and honest faith in young Nearcus.

However for Marcus, he spent the rest of the night laying awake and staring into the darkness while he worried about Nearcus's safety and spirit if the fight did not go well. Marcus worried because there was the very real possibility that Nearcus could die in the fight. The boy was outmatched by nearly one hundred pounds and his opponent was more than twice Nearcus's age with over twice the experience. In addition, Adrastos was a very competitive and good pankratiast. Marcus knew that Adrastos would do whatever was necessary to win, even if it meant killing his opponent.

Aggelos spent the night remembering the faces of the men in the mob that had beat Dioxippus. He remembered the evil, sadistic frenzy they had shown. Grown men urging young hoodlums to beat to death an unconscious, helpless boy was something he would long remember and each time he did remember a shudder would run down his back. Then a prayer would come to his mind, "God these lost souls need your love. Save them all. Use me to help you save them." But immediately following this silent prayer, Aggelos would put another request to his God, "And Lord if you cannot save them, then smite them with your Holy judgment and terror!" Aggelos knew that the ignorance and hate that had shown itself in the mob's action against Dioxippus could reappear in a flash if Nearcus started to win against their champion. This worried the tent maker. He planned on leaving his employees behind to protect Dioxippus from any further harm, but he knew that Marcus and he would not be sufficient help to save the twelve-year old should the mob rush him while he was competing in the arena. So, like Marcus, the tent maker did not get much sleep.

Eventually morning did come to Corinth. In fact, it was a gloriously beautiful spring day; not a cloud in the blue sky, the temperature mild and only the smallest hint of a breeze.

Nearcus rose with the sun and stood before the window in Aggelos's apartment to greet the day. He was eager to engage the enemy of his Savior. He had faith that his Jesus would not let him suffer more than he could bear. He was mentally, physically and spiritually ready to do battle on the pankration field this morning.

Marcus prepared the boy a light breakfast of boiled oats and strips of cold lamb tenderloin left over from last night's meal. Then Nearcus was given exactly one large glass of water with two tablespoons of wine mixed in it for purification purposes. Nearcus was directed to drink the water very slowly. An hour after he finished eating, Nearcus, Marcus and Aggelos slipped out the side door of the tent maker's business and swiftly walked the back streets to the stadium. Their plan was to arrive well before the main crowds gathered for the last pankration match and the games closing ceremonies. However, they were surprised by the large crowds pushing to gain entrance and get good seats hours before the event was to start. Marcus and Aggelos were concerned by this turn of events.

They became even more tense when they overhead the conversations of many of the spectators pushing to get in the stadium. Most of the men were saying they were looking forward to seeing the Christian god humbled by the great champion, Adrastos. The spectators were vying for the best seats to see a skilled, large man beat a young boy into submission. They hoped that Adrastos would force Nearcus to admit that Apollo and Poseidon were the most powerful gods in existence. Many said they wanted to see the Christian boy tortured by their champion before Adrastos dispatched Nearcus. With every passing group, Aggelos and Marcus heard harsher and harsher comments. The slave and the tent maker were becoming very frightened for Nearcus. But when they looked at the boy, his face was calm and his eyes sparkled with the confidence of the innocent.

Nearcus completely ignored what the crowd was saying and calmly moved ahead to reach the athletes' dressing area.

The preparation area underneath the north section of the stadium was deserted this morning. For the past days it had been crowded with the many athletes preparing for their events. Now there was just Marcus and Nearcus in the middle of the large room while Aggelos stood guard just inside the entrance. The bout was not scheduled to start for another two hours, so Marcus directed Nearcus to lie down on one of the many empty benches and rest. He told Nearcus that he did not want the youth to start stretching or warming up until one hour before the fight. Nearcus picked a bench and did as he was directed. Marcus looked at Aggelos and both men shrugged their shoulders at the complete lack of apprehension or nerves being shown by Nearcus. The two men were so nervous that if a loud noise suddenly was heard both would probably faint and fall down.

The minutes passed very slowly for the slave and the tent maker. The tension they felt drained the energy from their bodies. With each passing minute, the two became more and more exhausted. However, Nearcus remained reclined on the bench, his left arm resting across the bridge of his nose and blocking the light from his eyes. At one point during the waiting, Nearcus actually fell asleep for a quarter hour. He marveled at how relaxed he was now. He had never felt this ready and confident and relaxed before any bout — even a practice bout at the training camp!

An hour before the bout was to begin Marcus went to Nearcus and told the athlete to begin his preparation. He was to stretch his muscles and then do some light running in place for fifteen minutes. It was to be another forty-five minutes before Marcus applied the oil to Nearcus's body and then the boy would don his robe and the pair would walk to the middle of the arena.

While Nearcus was doing his warm-up drills four men appeared at the door of the preparation area. They were dressed in long robes and had tiny books dangling from the long hair on each side of their foreheads. Three of the men each wore a small, flat cap that just covered the crown of their skulls. The fourth man who was leading the group wore a tall, formal hat with great embroidery all over it. All four men had long, white beards and wore very sour looks on their faces.

Aggelos recognized the men as a delegation from the main Jewish synagogue in the city. The man in the lead was the chief rabbi, a very traditional and conservative cleric. The tent maker stepped outside of the doorway to greet the men and said, "Greetings Rabbi. Why have you come?"

"We come to protest this whole event. It is pure idiocy for a boy to be thrown to an accomplished and brutal man. But since you appear to be going through with it, we want to make sure that you use only the name of your god and that you do not use the name of Jehovah at anytime during this sorted affair."

"This we cannot do. We too worship the great Jehovah and his only son, Jesus of Nazareth," Aggelos answered.

"You can not worship Jehovah! You are not members of his chosen people! If you allow it to be announced that this boy is fighting in the name of Jehovah that will be blasphemy! You can choose to permit his loss to bring disgrace upon your own sect, but do not dishonor God's only chosen people!"

Nearcus had stopped his exercising and moved close enough to the entrance to hear what the chief rabbi had said. Upon hearing the rabbi nearly scream his insistence that the name of Jehovah not be used, the youth spoke up, "But I was chosen by God to do this!"

"Were you born a Jew?" the rabbi snapped back immediately and then when Nearcus shook his head, the rabbi continued, "Then you are not one of God's chosen."

"I heard God's voice say I was chosen even before I came to Corinth."

Upon hearing Nearcus say this, all four Jews stepped back and three covered their ears while the rabbi shouted, "Blasphemer! May God's judgment be upon you!" Then all four turned and hurried away, each visibly very upset.

Nearcus, who had never met a Jew before in his life, turned to Aggelos and asked, "What do they mean that I cannot be chosen? I really did hear God's voice in my orchard!"

Aggelos could see that Nearcus was beginning to think that perhaps he had not been chosen and if he believed this, then all of his confidence would ebb away. Aggelos became mad at these religious men who worried so much about appearances and wondered why God had allowed them to upset his warrior just before the battle. Then a realization hit Aggelos. It was not God who had sent the rabbi; it was Satan who was doing all he could to ensure that Nearcus would not be successful in defending the Lord's name.

"They are not speaking for God, young Nearcus," the tent maker said, "They are worried about their own position in the community. They do not care about what God wants or can do. They only care about how things affect them."

Nearcus nodded, but he had a confused look on his face. He had begun to doubt what he had believed with all his heart just minutes before.

Aggelos drew closer to Nearcus and looked the youth directly in the eye and continued, "I believe you were chosen by God to be his warrior this morning. I believe you were chosen to show that God can use someone younger and weaker than a mighty champion to do His will. I believe that God will give you the victory because to lose would bring dishonor to His Son's name. I believe that you will be victorious because God is with you and that Jesus will be shown to be the one and only true Son of God. I believe this with all my heart, Nearcus, but it only matters what you believe."

Nearcus saw in the big man's expressive eyes that the tent maker was telling him the truth. The doubt that had started to creep into his heart was once again banished. He said, "I have the faith. I am ready to fight for it."

CHAPTER 30

Marcus had begun to think that Adrastos must be using another preparation area. It was already time to start applying the oil to Nearcus's body and the champion had yet to arrive. However, this thought vanished from the slave when Adrastos stumbled through the door, bleary-eyed with an enormously pained expression on his face and gasping for breath. The champion was dressed in his tunic and he carried his wreath in one hand and a robe in the other. Seeing the benches available, Adrastos shuffled to the nearest one and collapsed onto it. He then shook his head a couple of times like he was trying to clear his mind after just awakening. The truth was that twenty minutes earlier the big man had been asleep on the turquoise dolphin bench. He had gotten so drunk last night that he awoke with just barely enough time to run to the stadium before the event was scheduled to start. The champion's head hurt like he had been hit across the back of his neck with a large board. His mouth was very dry and it tasted like he had been sucking on lemons for breakfast. However, even the thought of food made Adrastos want to vomit. His stomach was churning and all he really wanted to do was find a corner where he could lie down and sleep until his hangover had passed. But he was confident that even in his weakened condition he would quickly dispatch this inexperienced boy and then he could sleep for days. "Or," he thought to himself, "maybe I will go out and celebrate this next victory tonight and sleep later!"

Adrastos sat on the bench holding his hurting head in his hands as he kept his eyes closed in an attempt to stop the room from spinning. His celebrating had left him dizzy and dehydrated and weak—which was good for Nearcus. But the champion's condition also had put him in an especially foul and ugly mood. Adrastos was angry that he had to get up this morning to beat a boy in an unfair contest. He was anxious to get the bout done so he could return to savoring his championship.

Aggelos turned and signaled to Marcus that the official party was arriving to escort the competitors to the arena.

"Nearcus, it is time. Let us have one more quick prayer before we go," the slave whispered to his athlete. They both bowed their heads and closed their eyes. Marcus asked Jesus to send a legion of angels to protect Nearcus this morning. Nearcus asked Jesus to help him keep his focus and do his best. Nearcus closed by saying, "Whatever is your will, dear Jesus, give me the courage and strength to endure it."

The chief official led a party of five representatives from the games ruling committee. He looked at Nearcus and saw a young boy who had yet to mature into his adult build. He saw Nearcus fully oiled and sweating from his pre-contest exercises, standing there barefoot and clothed only in a simple robe fully ready to do battle. The chief official looked over at Adrastos and saw a man feeling the effects of a significant drunk the night before. The champion was unshaven, still dressed in his tunic and shaking his head to clear his thoughts. Adrastos was not ready to enter the arena and he was obviously not taking this celebrated match very seriously.

The chief official turned to face Marcus and said, "Follow these men. Take your boy to the center of the pankration area." The official waited until Marcus, Nearcus and Aggelos left the room before he spoke to Adrastos.

The chief official was angry and it showed in his mannerisms and voice. "You do not look the champion, Adrastos! You look like a sailor who is sick from drinking too much wine! Pull yourself together, man! Do you realize who is sitting out in the reviewing box to watch you defend the honor of Apollo and Poseidon? The Roman governor and a delegation from the city council of Athens are there! They expect to see a champion punish the Christian. They did not come to see you stumble around with an embarrassing hangover! Now hurry to change your clothes and prepare yourself. I can stall the start for a few minutes but not much more."

Adrastos did not feel like receiving a lecture from anyone this morning, and especially not from some pin-headed puny administrator! His bad mood was evidenced when he responded.

"Don't delay anything on my account. And don't tell me how to fight! I know why you set this little charade up in the first place. You need all the people to come back for the closing day festivities to spend their money to buy food, drink and souvenirs. I bet the stands are totally full right now! Every Greek will pay to see a Christian beaten and tortured! So you create this whole fake drama by having me face a boy—you could not even arrange for me to face a grown man! What are you afraid of? Did you think that no one would come if they thought the Christian might actually win? You embarrass and humiliate me by forcing me to do this. But I know my role and I will do it well. I can win drunk or sober—it will not matter with this competition. You have made sure of that."

Before the chief official could say anything in reply, Adrastos was overcome by nausea. He turned is head and vomited what wine was still sitting in his stomach.

"You disgust me," the official said as he turned and strode out of the room.

Between his wretches and coughs, Adrastos called after the official, "I disgust you? You disgust *me*!"

As Nearcus drew closer to the opening under the stadium stands where he was to enter the arena, he could hear the sounds of the crowd that had gathered this morning. When he first emerged from the opening no one noticed his arrival. Nearcus looked around him and he was surrounded by 40,000 people who were talking to each other and laughing and eating. It was a more intense experience than the games opening ceremonies. All here this morning have come for one purpose—to see him fight. No other events or athletes to see, only Nearcus against Adrastos. The energy of anticipation that this mass of people seemed to generate filled the large stadium. Nearcus thought he could almost feel the excitement race across his bare skin that was only temporarily covered by his robe. The twelve-year old was stunned by what he saw and felt. He stopped his advance onto the field to take in all that surrounded him.

Marcus nodded to Aggelos who moved to a position near the boundary of the competition field where he could rush to the aid of the boy if it became necessary. Marcus then gently nudged Nearcus forward to get the athlete to resume his entrance. The slave said in a quiet voice, "Nearcus, look now, because you will forget all of these people and the surroundings once the bout starts. Let's go, son, let's go."

Nearcus and his paedotribae started forward to the center of the field. Soon many in the crowd noticed the two making their way to the starting point. Many pointed at the pair and immediately the entire stadium was filled with jeers and loud cries of hate all directed at Nearcus. The hostility and anger being directed at this boy startled both Marcus and Aggelos. Nearcus felt his stomach tighten and a flush of heat race through his body. He had not expected such a negative welcome. He thought some might shout nasty things, but he did think the entire 40,000 would vent such rage at him personally.

The Roman officers and soldiers stationed around the stadium to keep order became alarmed at the crowd's outbursts. They had expected an easy day of festivities with many happy people celebrating the end of the games and now they were faced with a crowd on the verge of becoming a mob. The Roman governor of the Greek Isthmus also noted the fierce attitude of the crowd and he motioned for the commander of the guard to approach him. The governor whispered his orders directly into the ear of his commander. The senior Roman military officer then quickly slipped away to direct his troops. The governor had ordered that all troops be ready to disperse the crowd on a moment's notice should anything unexpected happen. The commander put all his forces on high alert in positions where they could rapidly respond to whatever might occur this morning, and then he mounted his horse and waited.

The jeers of the crowd immediately turned to wild cheers when Adrastos appeared on the field. He strode confidently out to the center of the competition area with his newly won pine wreath sitting squarely on his head. Adrastos looked so fit, alert and in total command of the situation as he waved to the excited crowd that Marcus had trouble believing it was the same man he had seen sitting with his head in his hands just minutes before. But it was the same man because Adrastos truly did understand the importance of this morning's contest and he possessed the unique ability always to draw on his best talents when the situation demanded. That was how he had become the champion.

Crowd directors who stood in front of each stadium seating section waved their hands to signal the spectators to be seated and quiet. Once the cheering had nearly stopped, the formal announcer of the games walked to the front of the reviewing box, stopping directly in front of the governor's chair. He raised both his arms above his shoulders and held his palms upward. Upon seeing this, the crowd quieted completely. The announcer began his speech and paused at the end of each sentence. During this pause, the crowd directors repeated the line so everyone in the stadium heard the speech in its entirety.

"Greeks and Romans!" the announcer started his speech. "Today we have gathered for two important purposes. Today we celebrate two great events. At the close of this year's games this afternoon we will honor all the athletes who spent the last days striving to achieve the great wreath of victory. For all who competed should be celebrated! Win or lose, each participant brought honor to their cities, villages and islands. But that is what we do this afternoon."

At this point in his speech the announcer turned and nodded to the Roman and Greek dignitaries who sat in the reviewing boxes. Then he continued, "But this morning we have all assembled to pay homage to the great gods of our fathers and to, once and for all time, prove that there are no greater gods in the entire world than Apollo and Poseidon!"

He confidently paused for a very long time at the end of this line while the crowd gave a sustained cheer. Then the official continued, "We need to do this because our glorious games were soiled as they began—they were soiled by the blasphemy and dishonor heaped upon the true and righteous god in whose honor these games are dedicated. A competitor refused to swear by the Altar of Poseidon to compete fairly and not to seek any illegal advantage. When asked why he would dishonor Poseidon, the competitor said he was a Christian..." The orator pushed the word "Christian" from his lips like it was a curse and then he paused until he heard the angry shouts he expected from the crowd.

When he was satisfied that the crowd had reacted appropriately to the word, he continued, "This Christian said that his was the only true god and said he could prove it this morning! This Christian challenged the Games'

251

champion to a fight, saying that his god was so powerful that our champion would easily be defeated!"

Again, the official paused to permit the crowd to become sufficiently riled at the villain in this dramatic athletic play he was creating. Now that he had the crowd stirred appropriately, he concluded by saying, "So that is the reason we have gathered this morning. We have come to celebrate what will be the glorious victory of Poseidon and Apollo over this Jesus the Christ in a fair fight against evenly matched opponents. There are no gods more powerful than Apollo and Poseidon in Corinth! We are about to prove this once again! Let the bout begin!"

Upon hearing this command, the roar of the crowd was so great that Nearcus and Marcus covered their ears. Adrastos raised his arms and pivoted in a circle so he could wave to all sections of the stadium.

Marcus slipped the robe off of Nearcus's shoulders and walked back to where Aggelos was standing. The slave did not look back at his student. He kept his eyes straight ahead to signify to Nearcus that the slave had absolute confidence in the youth and nothing more needed to be said either verbally or non-verbally.

Nearcus stood there facing the referee holding the staff at the center of the field. Opposite of him stood a man with bloodshot eyes, a heavy beard and hair all over his body. But Nearcus realized that Marcus had been right. As soon as the boy began his approach to the staff, the crowd noise faded from his consciousness. Nearcus's focus was directed at only one thing—how to beat the man in front of him.

CHAPTER 31

The first thing Nearcus wanted to learn was just how quickly Adrastos could move. And he wanted to learn this without getting himself hurt. Marcus and he had discussed various options and techniques on how to do this, but all of them were hypothetical. As Nearcus and Adrastos moved towards each other and the starting staff, the boy noticed the champion was limping slightly, trying to keep his weight off of his left leg. Nearcus thought this gave him a real opening and not a hypothetical one, so as soon as he touched the staff Nearcus jumped to his right and flicked a lightning-fast flipper kick with his left foot. The top of Nearcus's foot landed exactly where he aimed; it hit Adrastos on the left thigh just above the knee. However, the kick did not do the damage Nearcus had intended. It did not land with enough force to cripple the champion because Adrastos had shifted all of his weight to his right leg and swept his left leg backwards so that he missed absorbing all of the force of Nearcus's quick opening move.

Luckily Nearcus had maintained his balance when he flicked the kick from his left knee, because Adrastos continued his turn to his left and extended his right arm with his hand in a fist. Because he had kept his balance, Nearcus was able to hunch his shoulders and duck his head just as Adrastos's heavy fist came whirling past. Right then it became immediately obvious to Nearcus why Adrastos was the Isthmian Games champion. The more experienced pankratiast had been faking when he limped as he approached the staff. He wanted to draw the quick attack to his left leg. Adrastos had used this technique many times before with inexperienced opponents and it had always resulted in a very quick victory. His opponents had all over-committed to their attack which meant they were off balance and could not avoid his powerful blow to the back of the head. When the opponents were stunned and on the ground, it had been an easy task to get them in a choke hold that forced them to submit. Adrastos knew if Nearcus took his bait and fell into the same trap as so many of his other opponents had, then he would have a very easy victory and he could end very quickly what was, in his mind, a farce.

When Nearcus was able to duck his head and hunch his shoulders, Adrastos's massive blow bounced off the shoulder blades and skipped over the head of the young pankratiast. The blow was still powerful enough to cause Nearcus to place his hand on the ground to keep him from being knocked over. But it was with a speed the likes of which Adrastos had never seen in any opponent that enabled Nearcus to scamper several yards away and turn to face the older athlete before Adrastos could leap on him. The two now faced each other, both in a crouch, arms extended half-way and their left foot slightly ahead of the right. They stayed in this classic pankration pose as they moved in a circle to their right, keeping about five yards between themselves.

Nearcus knew he had just escaped from certain defeat and he knew that Adrastos was only pretending to be in very bad shape after being up nearly all night at a party. The twelve-year old very quickly realized that Adrastos truly was the best in Greece. Only the wonderful training given by Marcus and Nearcus's gifted athletic speed had been the difference between an immediate defeat and a chance to continue. But even knowing this, Nearcus was not intimidated by the older fighter. Nearcus had the very unique talent of total concentration on his objective. He could prevent other thoughts and emotions from clouding his vision of the immediate goal that was set before him. Nearcus was too busy looking for a way to win than to take time to dwell on the possibility that his opponent might be better than him. It was a rare talent, and it was what made Nearcus so special on the pankration field.

Adrastos was extremely surprised when Nearcus had slipped his blow and escaped a maneuver that had always been successful when fighting inexperienced opponents. He was also impressed by the speed of this youth he had to fight today. He thought, "This is going to be a little harder than I imagined. But he is too small to last very long once I get a grip on him. I'll just rush him head-on and get a hold and then it will be over."

Adrastos slightly shortened the radius of his circle as he moved to his right. Without Nearcus noticing, the champion closed the distance between the two a little each time they completed a circle. After just three revolutions moving around the center of the field, Adrastos felt he was close enough to charge Nearcus and successfully clamp one of his massive, vice-like hands to some part of the boy's body. If he could get Nearcus in his grasp then this would neutralize the youth's great speed, and then Adrastos could use his much greater size and strength to overpower the smaller competitor.

Adrastos lunged at Nearcus. The oil covering Nearcus's body made it terribly difficult for Adrastos to get a good hold on the fast moving smaller boy. Adrastos's hands slipped off Nearcus's upper arms and elbows. However, Adrastos was able to clamp his large hand around Nearcus's left wrist and keep the boy from getting away. The hold was not a good one and Adrastos felt his fingers start to slip as he struggled to pull the squirming young man closer. Adrastos knew all he had to do was hold on just a few seconds longer and he would have Nearcus close enough to grasp him with another hand and secure a tight arm lock. Then something happened that stunned the experienced champion. Nearcus stopped trying to pull away. The boy changed directions and pushed into Adrastos and as he did so, he dropped to his left knee and swept his right leg from right to left in front of him. In a flash, Adrastos's feet were taken from under him and he let go of Nearcus's wrist as he used both hands to catch his fall to the ground. Once again, the speed and balance and intelligence of the young pankratiast from Chios had evaporated the advantage the champion had established.

Adrastos scrambled to his feet before Nearcus could get around behind him to apply a choke hold. The champion stood still in the middle of the field and for the first time closely examined his opponent. He thought, "Who is this boy? Where did he get such speed? It is like I am trying to fight a spirit. He is here and then he is gone again before I can clutch him." Adrastos had, for the first time in many years, begun to doubt if he could defeat his opponent. His confidence in winning was waning. Yet he did not become the champion of Greece by giving up when things did not go as expected. Adrastos shook his head as if to clear a cobweb that had landed on his nose and ears. Any ill effects he may have been suffering from his carousing and drinking the night before were leaving him in very rapid order. This had become a real fight, and the champion was determined not to lose.

Nearcus was not sure what to do next and that bothered him very much. He did not want to let Adrastos close him again because such a fight would favor the bigger man. He could try to extend the match by staying on the defensive, but if he failed just once to escape Adrastos's attacks, then the bout would be over. Nearcus was convinced he had to find a way to go on the offensive without getting too close to his opponent. He wished he could stop the match long enough to go to Marcus and ask his coach what could work in this situation. That not being possible, Nearcus continued to circle with Adrastos while he stalled the fight in the hope some opportunity would present itself.

A few minutes later, Nearcus had to react defensively once again. Using a deliberate and controlled approach, Adrastos moved straight towards the youth. Nearcus gave ground initially, then he suddenly stopped, stepped to his left and attempted to give a quick flip kick to Adrastos's face as he slid by. The champion did not move his head. He let Nearcus's foot slam into his nose and then the champion reached up and grabbed the back of Nearcus's calf with both of his hands. Adrastos had Nearcus's leg pressed against his nose, so he ran forward to pull the boy's other foot from the ground. This maneuver put Nearcus in what appeared to be a totally helpless position. Adrastos was about the throw the airborne youth to the ground when once again Nearcus did something that shocked the champion. While Adrastos started to lift him by his right calf, Nearcus leaped off the ground and raised his left leg until its ankle interlocked with the right ankle Adrastos was holding. Nearcus squeezed his legs together with all of the strength he could muster in this precarious position, suspended horizontally six feet off the ground.

The unexpected leg lock Adrastos suddenly felt around his neck and face caused the experienced fighter to temporarily panic. In all of his years of competing, no opponent had ever been able to get Adrastos in a choke hold. When he felt Nearcus's legs tighten around his neck and head, Adrastos wanted to do nothing but escape from what he was sure eventually would lead to the application of a successful choke hold. He had choked many opponents into limp masses of clumped over muscles and bones very often in his career. He knew how to make an opponent submit and he did not want to feel that kind of pressure ever around his neck. In his panic to break free, Adrastos stopped pressing Nearcus's leg against his own face and, with all of his strength, began to pry it away from him.

Nearcus knew he did not have a good hold on the champion. His left leg was behind Adrastos's neck, but his right calf was on his opponent's face. Somehow he would have to slide it down to Adrastos's neck to have an effective choke hold. So when he felt Adrastos try to throw him off, Nearcus quickly unlocked his ankles and fell to the ground. Once again, using his speed he cleared away from Adrastos before the large man could acquire another hold. The two started their rotation around the center of the field once again.

Nearcus knew he could not expect to win the match if he stayed on the defensive. But the guard stance and moves that Adrastos employed were more sophisticated and effective than anything Nearcus had ever seen. So for the next hour, Adrastos attacked and Nearcus escaped. The crowd jeered every time that Nearcus escaped and many were growing impatient and frustrated with the boy's lack of offense. They had come to see Nearcus get beat upon and humiliated and then to celebrate the afternoon's festivities. If the Christian was going to run away all day, then why did he show up? Many in the stands were thinking that, as expected, their gods were showing Jesus to be a puny deity whose followers did nothing but run and run and run.

On the edge of the large field, near the athletes' entrance, Aggelos and Marcus were both thinking, "Nearcus looks so small out there. He is just a boy and it shows. Adrastos is muscular and fully developed, but Nearcus has yet to grow into manhood. He is a boy fighting a man's fight, which most men would be too frightened to even attempt. Lord help your servant!"

The crowd and his friends saw things differently than Nearcus. Rather than getting discouraged or impatient, what Nearcus saw was giving him hope. Five minutes ago, as Adrastos made another attack and Nearcus once again got in a light kick as he avoided the champion's charge, the twelve-year old saw Adrastos put his hand to his left side, just above the waist. Adrastos quickly dropped his left hand and resumed the classic fighting position, but for just a moment Nearcus had seen him wince in pain and hold his side. The boy from Chios was learning quickly and he thought, "Could it be another trap? Could he be faking an injury to draw me in?"

To find out if it was a trick, Nearcus determined to rapidly close the champion twice during each circle they were making and kick Adrastos directly on the left side. Nearcus kept at this tactic for the next ten minutes. Every few steps the athletes made were interrupted by Nearcus flicking a quick kick to Adrastos's left side. Sometimes the champion was successful in blocking the kick, but more times than not, the kick landed with sufficient force to hurt the older competitor. Again and again, Nearcus would step towards the champion and when Adrastos moved forward to engage, Nearcus would jump to his right and land a quick jab using his left foot to the same spot just above Adrastos's waist.

By the end of the ten minutes, Adrastos was breathing heavily from his mouth and he moved very slowly, his left hand now permanently holding his side. Nearcus could sense that his opponent was tiring very quickly. He figured that either he had been successful in injuring the champion's ribs or kidneys or Adrastos was so winded that his side hurt from excessive exertion. Either way, Nearcus decided he should increase the pace of the fight. He knew that it was approaching the time for him to switch from the defensive to the attack. Nearcus would force the champion to stay moving to defend against his kicks. Once he was sure Adrastos's reactions had slowed sufficiently, Nearcus would attack, attack, attack!

Nearcus tried not to smile as he thought about the hundreds of miles he had run and hours and hours of drills he had completed because Marcus felt the best way to win was to be the one in the best physical condition. Now all those miles and hard work were paying off. Nearcus felt his energy level rise the more sluggish he saw his opponent become.

Adrastos was not sure why his side hurt. The pain had started as an intermittent annoyance a quarter-hour ago. He ignored it for the first few minutes, but now it seemed his side was constantly burning inside his skin. The pain could no longer be ignored and it now caused difficulty with his breathing. He thought, "I must finish this boy now. Another quarter hour and I will not be able to stand."

A champion of the games is not a weakling. And Adrastos was champion because he earned it. He was not ready to be defeated; he was ready to get the victory now and get out of there. He took a deep breath, stopped moving in a counter-clockwise motion and slid to his left. He continued this direction and it forced Nearcus to open the circle very wide as he tried to keep moving to his right while still avoiding the champion. The pair was now fighting in a new area of the arena which they had not previously used.

Suddenly, Nearcus's confidence and plans were lost. As he kept his eyes on Adrastos, Nearcus's right foot stepped in a small hole in the field. His entire body was moving to his right, so when the ground stopped his foot for just that instant, the force against his ankle was enough to snap it. Despite the loud crowd noise, both fighters heard a distinct pop as the boy's joint rolled over his foot. Nearcus fell to the ground and immediately scrambled to get to his feet. Before he was successful, the experienced champion was upon him. Nearcus had made it to his knees before Adrastos reached him but the larger opponent slammed the twelve-year old to the ground as he pounced on him.

When the champion's large body landed on Nearcus, all the air from the boy's lungs was expelled in a rush. His ankle shot bullets of pain up his leg, but it was the inability to breathe with a man nearly twice his own size crushing his lungs that made panic rise in Nearcus's mind. Nearcus did not have thoughts of losing the fight or of letting his Jesus down. His only thought was somehow to get another breath. It started to turn black around the edges of his vision. He felt Adrastos shifting his weight from one side to another as he worked to secure a hold that would force Nearcus to submit.

The boy from Chios began to feel for the first time that he might actually lose this fight. As his vision grew darker and darker one memory grew sharper and sharper. He could clearly hear the voice in the orchard saying to him again, "In Corinth, you will be chosen." Then the voice came to him with more words, "Fight the good fight. Do not falter just because it is hard." Nearcus stopped struggling for air and stopped feeling the pain in his ankle. He stopped thinking about his vision growing darker and he stopped thinking about Adrastos setting a good hold on him. Nearcus ignored everything happening to him and concentrated on the voice he heard. "Fight the good fight. Do not falter…"

The strength seemed to come from some place outside his body. For the rest of his life, Nearcus remembered the surge of strength he felt at that instant. He knew he was helped by the Lord. With what seemed a very easy motion to Nearcus, he freed his left elbow from Adrastos's grip and swiftly — powerfully — slammed it into the tender left side of the champion's torso.

Spasms shook the champion's body as the pain raced from his side to every fiber of his being. The uncontrollable movements of his body bounced him right off of Nearcus. The champion rolled on the ground in total agony with blood now erupting from his mouth and nose. Something had ruptured inside of him and was bleeding so profusely that it was running from his face.

The referee had been standing directly over the two fighters when Nearcus punched Adrastos in the side with his elbow. It was a clean and legal hit by the boy, but the result of that blow frightened this experienced official. He had never seen such damage done by one punch. He stood there watching Adrastos writhe in pain. He watched as twelve-year old Nearcus drew his first full breath in over a minute and then rise to his hands and knees. The boy crawled over to the champion and rolled Adrastos to his stomach. The shaking and frightened Adrastos did not resist. Nearcus climbed on the back of Adrastos and then slid his left forearm under the champion's chin. Before the boy could apply any pressure to his choke hold, Adrastos was able to shout through his pain, "I submit! I submit!"

The referee was not sure what to do. The boy was not supposed to win. Yet it had been a fair fight and here was Adrastos yelling that he submits. The referee knew that if he raised the arm of Nearcus as the victor the crowd would go berserk. There was the real possibility that they could descend upon the field and attack the referee for stopping the contest.

While the shocked official considered what to do next, Nearcus rolled off of Adrastos and managed to struggle to his feet, keeping all of his weight on his left foot. Looking straight at the referee, Nearcus said, "You had better get Adrastos to a physician quickly. I think he is dying."

The boy's honest concern for his vanquished opponent had great effect upon the official. If this twelve-year old boy from a small outlying island does what he knows is right, then surely a grown man who has taken an oath to ensure fairness at the games can do what is right. The official moved next to Nearcus and raised the boy's arm over his head.

CHAPTER 32

The Isthmus of Corinth suffers more earthquakes than anywhere else in Greece or Asia Minor. When Nearcus tripped and Adrastos plunged onto the boy's back the crowd exploded in applause and cheers. This roar was so thunderous it shook the spectator stands and many thought an earthquake was hitting the area. This spontaneous outburst that had all leaping to their feet and wildly yelling and waving their hands in the air was the expression of over an hour of frustration. These pent up feelings were freed by many in the stands by screaming "Now kill the treacherous Christian!" and "Punish the troublemaker!" and "Show him who the real gods are!" The Roman governor sat quietly while he observed the cheering crowd move closer and closer to devolving into a mob. The governor looked down to his left and made eye contact with the security forces commander who was astride his large horse at the edge of the field. While the crowd grew more frenzied and blood-thirsty, the governor gave a slight nod to the commander. The Roman officer nodded in return and then slowly walked his mount onto the field, leading a company of armed soldiers marching in two straight columns.

The ecstatic and blood-thirsty crowd went into immediate shock when Nearcus reversed the situation on Adrastos. With a startled suddenness so dramatic that generations of Greeks would recount the event to their children's children, forty thousand people became totally and absolutely quiet. All saw Adrastos submit, but none, not even the believing Christians in the crowd, could believe what they saw. How could a twelve-year old boy from a small island defeat one of the greatest pankration champions ever to win the pine wreath? The shock of this surprise was so great that all stopped their screaming and stood there with their mouths gaping open and confusion across their faces. When the official raised Nearcus's arm in victory the crowd came out of their shocked stupor and with one great voice yelled, "NO!" Then the entire mass of spectators began a chant of "No! — No! — No!"

Despite their faith in the Lord and their belief in His power to accomplish anything through using anybody, Aggelos and Marcus had been stunned along with everyone else when Nearcus gained the victory. When they recovered from their shock the two Christians literally jumped for joy and hugged each other as they shouted, "Praise God! Praise God!"

They were so overjoyed at the miracle that had just been done in front of them that neither noticed the angry crowd becoming an ugly mob being stirred to violence by their disappointment, anger and confusion. Aggelos and Marcus felt the desire to run to Nearcus and lift him high above their shoulders to celebrate the great victory God had given the boy. They charged out onto the field to congratulate their boy-champion.

The Greek spectators who filled the stands were not about to admit that their gods had been defeated by the hand of this Jesus from Nazareth. Throughout the crowd cries of "It's a trick!" and "Unfair! The boy cheated!" were shouted. When Aggelos and Marcus ran onto the field, many spectators thought the Christians were leading an attack to harm Nearcus. Many left their seats and joined the Christians in their charge to the victor. Seeing some plunge onto the field, most of the crowd followed and very quickly the orderly spectators became a runaway mob.

The Roman commander had dreaded such mob lunacy occurring, but he had served all over the far reaches of the

Empire and he had learned to expect bad behavior from crowds. Even in Greece, the birth place of orderly debate and philosophical thought, men were the same when they became part of a mob. They stopped thinking for themselves and abdicated all reason to the emotions of the basest among them. Small minded, angry hooligans were the first to follow the two Christian men onto the playing field. But those who then followed were the average citizens and merchants who would never think of rampaging if they were not infected with the fever of anger and frustration that ruled the mob. The commander had seen this in Hispania and Germania and Carthage and he was not surprised to find this same weakness here in Greece. However, he knew his soldiers were well-trained and disciplined and would not flinch at the onslaught of thousands of screaming Greeks coming across the field. With just a few commands given by the movement of their commander's drawn sword, the troops turned to form a line of battle that faced the surging mob coming from the south end of the stadium.

The officer wheeled his horse around to assume a position behind this line and when he did so, he saw the crowd in the northern stadium section leave its seats and charge the center of the field. Once again he pointed his sword and his soldiers reacted with calm precision and professionalism. Every other soldier turned around and faced the attack from their rear. With their shields touching their neighboring soldier's, the troops formed a solid line of defense that quickly morphed into a square that the oncoming unarmed Greeks would have terrible trouble and great pain to penetrate. As the square assumed its shape, it moved towards the center of the field. Soon it absorbed Nearcus, Adrastos and the referee. Nearcus knelt down to offer assistance to the foe he had just vanquished, while the official held his long staff across his chest and turned in a tight circle, ready to defend himself from any attacker that might break through the ring of Roman soldiers.

"Breathe slowly and lay quietly," Nearcus said to Adrastos by placing his mouth right next to the champion's ear. Nearcus rolled Adrastos onto his left side and this seemed to help the man breathe better. The bleeding from the champion's mouth and nose soon slowed and Adrastos was able to draw bigger breaths. Although he did not know what he had done, Nearcus saved Adrastos from drowning in his own blood by moving him onto his injured side. When the boy had slammed his elbow into Adrastos's side he had broken a rib that punctured the left lung and also damaged the champion's inflamed kidneys. Blood was pouring into the lung where the rib had burst through. The blood was spilling into the right lung before Nearcus rolled Adrastos. Now with the right lung above the left, the blood could not fill both lungs and the champion could draw air into his good lung.

As Nearcus knelt next to his vanquished opponent and helped to hold the champion in a position where he could breathe the best, the boy looked up and realized for the first time that he was now in a fort whose walls were made of Roman soldiers. Outside these walls were the angry faces of the mob shouting all sorts of wild foolishness, "Look! The Christian is torturing the champion!" and "He is trying to cut out Adrastos's heart to eat it!"

Now, in the middle of this treacherous situation, Nearcus thought about his father and sister. How could Nearcus even begin to describe what he experienced on his trip to Corinth? How could he share the anger and hatred these people directed at him?

The Roman officer, sitting high atop his horse, could see over the heads of the mass of angry Greeks who were pressing against his square of soldiers. As he expected, the officer saw four more columns of troops, one coming from each corner of the arena, driving through the crowd to reach his center stronghold. As the Romans forced their way through the mob, the Greeks began to scatter. It was one thing to feel safe as a member of a wild mob, but it was something entirely different when a soldier was attacking you individually! The normal citizens who had come to the stadium to enjoy a celebration very quickly realized that things had gotten out of control and backed away when confronted by armed soldiers. It only took a few minutes for nearly the entire mob to disburse. Soon, only a few hundred hooligans were left pressing futilely against the Roman center square. Seeing that there was a clear path to the northwest corner of the arena, the mounted officer gave directions for the square to join forces with the column approaching from that direction in order to form a corridor to provide safe passage from the field for Nearcus, Adrastos and the frightened official.

"Help me carry him," Nearcus said to the official as the boy tried to get Adrastos to his feet.

The official turned his back on the two pankratiasts and scurried down the path between the troops that led to safety. Nearcus tried to lift the much larger man by putting the champion's right arm over his own shoulder while they both were kneeling on all fours. The ring of troops protecting them was collapsing as the soldiers redeployed to exit to the northwest. Nearcus jerked his left knee forward and got his good ankle firmly in place. Then he pressed on it in an attempt to raise himself and his defeated foe. He was unsuccessful and they both returned to their hands and knees, Adrastos spitting more blood on the ground as they landed. Nearcus looked around and only saw the backs of the troops closing in on them. He cried out as loudly as he could to be heard over the rant of the mob now squeezing closer and closer, "Please help us! This man could die!"

Two soldiers heard the twelve-year old and while continuing to push against the Greeks trying to break the square they looked over their shoulders at the two pankratiasts on the ground.

"We're a little busy right now. I guess if you cannot save him then he will die," said the younger of the two. The older one chuckled at the comment and they both turned around and once again gave their full attention to fighting the mob.

Adrastos was certain he was about to die on this competition field. He knew he was much too big for a boy with only one good leg to lift and he expected his victor to leave him and chase after the cowardly official who had run for safety. Adrastos prepared to lay down his head and rest, hoping that he would die a peaceful death with little pain.

Nearcus kept the champion's arm around his neck and said aloud what he was thinking, "Lord you have given me a great victory, now give me great strength to save this one who you also died for."

Adrastos heard what the boy said and the words were said with such a simple faith in the power of his god, the champion almost believed the impossible could be achieved. Nearcus repeated his previous attempt to position his left foot under his hips in order to use his one good leg to raise the weight of both men. Once again, Nearcus and Adrastos started to rise but after only a few inches Nearcus could give no more and both fell to the earth.

Adrastos heard the Christian boy from Chios say another prayer out loud, "Lord, you know I cannot leave this man to die on this field, the victim of my blows. Raise us up, dear Lord. Some way, raise us up and carry us to safety."

The soldiers were only a couple of feet away from the two athletes crouching on their hands and knees when Nearcus positioned his left foot for a third try. He pushed with all of his strength and through clinched teeth he exhaled, "Please Lord Jesus! Please!"

The duo again reached a height of just a few inches before Adrastos felt they were beginning to slide back to the grass. Then a sudden, strange power shot through his legs. As Adrastos tried to move his legs he felt a miraculous power surge through his muscles. Both of his legs responded to his mental direction. He was not able to add much force to Nearcus's efforts, but it was just enough for the boy to pull his right knee off the ground and place his right foot next to his left.

Nearcus's right ankle felt like a thousand needles were being repeatedly jammed into it, but once again the boy's ability to ignore pain served him well. He pushed straight up with both his legs and together the two opponents were standing. As quickly as possible the two assisted each other down the corridor of soldiers to the safety of a security detachment compound behind the stadium. Once there, Nearcus carefully set Adrastos on a table he cleared of dishes and left-over food.

"Do you have a physician with your detachment?" Nearcus asked the nearest soldier who casually nodded. "Get him quickly. This man needs treatment immediately."

The soldier shrugged his shoulders, nodded and then slowly walked off.

Adrastos used his right hand to signal Nearcus to come to him. "Why did you not leave me to die out there?"

"I came here today to show that Jesus is the only Son of God, not to kill anyone." Then the boy smiled and added, "It is hard to show that God loves us all if you kill someone."

Adrastos's thought for a few seconds and then through the gurgling blood still in his throat he said, "How can I know this god?"

Before Nearcus could answer, the military physician arrived and pushed him out of the way in order to examine Adrastos. As he was being pushed, Nearcus said to Adrastos, "Ask Aggelos the tent maker on Lechaion Road!"

Those were the last words the twelve-year old would say to a champion who had made it possible for God to be glorified and the Greek idols to be shown to be superstitions.

Adrastos did not realize it until much later, but God had used him to bring glory to his Son.

As the Roman surgeon directed troops to take the champion to his tent, Nearcus watched from a distance. He looked around and for the first time he realized that he knew no one there and he did not know how to contact Marcus or Aggelos or Iro or anyone who could help him.

Although order had been restored in the stadium and preparations for the Isthmian Games closing celebration were underway, Nearcus did not think it was safe for him to go looking for Marcus or to try and find his way back to either Garifallia's or Aggelos's house. So, even though he had just been victorious over the best pankratiast in all of Greece, Nearcus withdrew to keep from being noticed by the troops. He took a towel from the ground that had fallen when the table was cleared and used it to cover himself and then he sat on an old wooden box hurting from his injured ankle and afraid of what could happen next.

CHAPTER 33

Marcus and Aggelos had been caught up in the swarm that tried to reach Nearcus after the boy's victory. Before they could get close to their Christian brother, the mob had pushed them aside and blocked their path. Both were terribly worried that God's tremendous victory over the idols of these pagan Greeks would never be remembered if Nearcus was killed by the outraged mob. Both tried desperately to get close enough to see Nearcus before he left the arena, but they were unsuccessful. In fact, the two Christians had been separated in the mass of thousands surging one direction and then another when the Roman soldiers marched onto the field from four directions.

Once the disturbance had been quelled, Marcus found himself in almost the exact same spot he was during Nearcus's contest. Confusion about what had become of the two opponents was everywhere. Marcus could not find anyone who could tell him what became of Nearcus after he had been victorious or where he might be if he was still alive. Not knowing what else to do, Marcus went back to the preparation room to see if perhaps Nearcus had returned there.

Being much taller than Marcus and nearly all members of the mob, Aggelos was able to see the corridor formed by the troops and he correctly surmised that was the path the Romans would use to remove those at the heart of this disturbance. The tent maker fought his way through the yelling, pushing and panicking mob participants to the northwest corner of the arena. Upon arriving there he stretched his neck to see if he could spot Nearcus in the mass of soldiers and Greeks shoving each other. He thought he caught a quick glimpse of the twelve-year old but before he could move that direction he was carried away by those being herded out of the stadium by the troops that had now massed in this corner.

Convinced that he needed to return to the soldier garrison in the northwest arena corner, Aggelos had to make a wide circle through side streets and thick brush that covered the steep hill just behind the stadium to reach his goal. It took him nearly an hour before he had arrived at a six-foot high wall that enclosed the back of the soldiers' security station. He looked over the fence and thought about climbing it, but he hesitated when he recalled how sensitive the Roman's were to their security. If a stranger breached their safe perimeter, they would attack first and ask questions after.

"Hello the compound!" Aggelos shouted into the troops' area. There was no answer so he shouted again. Still no one answered and Aggelos decided he had to take a chance to find out if Nearcus had made it out of the arena alive or if they had his body if he had not. When he looked both ways to ensure it was clear before he climbed over the wall, Aggelos noticed a slight movement in the shadow of the wall a couple of yards to his right. He looked closer and it appeared to be a person sleeping with his back against the high wall. The tent maker slid to his right a couple of steps to where he was directly over the body on the ground. To his great surprise, it was Nearcus sleeping there! The young athlete was still naked from the competition and covered only with a small towel as he slept soundly.

Aggelos checked once again to ensure no one else was in the area and then he hopped over the wall, landing next to Nearcus. The sound of Aggelos's feet hitting the ground did not stir the emotionally and physically exhausted youth. The tent maker kneeled beside Nearcus and gently put his hand over the boy's mouth. Nearcus awoke with a start and with fear in his eyes. Upon seeing the massive frame of Aggelos hovering over him, Nearcus's fear quickly left him and he felt safe and saved. He wanted to hug the big man for finding him when he was lost and confused. Although Aggelos smiled, he kept looking around the yard to ensure no Romans were approaching.

"Quietly, let us get you home," he said in a whisper to Nearcus.

The pankratiast nodded vigorously and tried to stand, but during the past hour his ankle had swollen to the size of a small, full wineskin. Using the wall for support, Nearcus forced his way up and kept his right knee bent in order to keep his foot off the ground. Aggelos looked down and saw the injury and without saying another word, the large, strong man lifted the boy and set him over the high wall. Then the tent maker easily scaled the wall and picked up the boy and effortlessly carried him through the brush towards the side streets of north Corinth. Before they left the brush, Aggelos set Nearcus down at a spot where the boy could not be seen from the nearest street. The tent maker knew that if anyone saw him carrying Nearcus's oiled, naked body they would immediately recognize him as the Christian who had defeated the games' champion and Apollo and Poseidon. Most of the shops were closed because all wanted to attend the closing festivities for the games, but after a quarter hour, Aggelos was finally able to find a shop open and he purchased a tunic for Nearcus.

Soon, a very large and muscled man was casually walking through the nearly deserted side streets of Corinth carrying a young boy dressed in a tunic three sizes too big. Aggelos took an indirect route to his house to make sure they were not spotted. The tent maker was afraid that many of the pagan temple rulers and their hired hooligans would want to seek revenge on Nearcus for the embarrassment he had caused them.

Once they had reached the house safely, Nearcus was carried to the same room where Dioxippus was recovering. The older boy opened his eyes when Nearcus was set in the chair next to him.

"How long did it take you to win?" Dioxippus asked. He had never doubted that the Lord would give Nearcus the victory and his question reflected this faith.

"A little more than an hour." Nearcus smiled as he shared the news with his Christian friend.

Dioxippus smiled too, and said with enthusiasm, "The Lord be praised!"

"The Lord be praised, indeed!"

It was well past dark when Marcus burst into the room where the two injured athletes were sleeping. He had waited for hours in the preparation room and then decided his best course of action was to find his way back to Aggelos's house. He had gotten lost many times, so a normally twenty minute walk took him over two hours. But now he was here and he had urgent news to share with Aggelos and the injured boys. As he made his way back to the tent maker's, he happened to find himself behind a group of angry men who were cursing Nearcus and his god, Jesus. Marcus walked behind them and listened as the group spoke of plans to seize Nearcus and take him out of the city and kill him. What disturbed the slave even more was that he heard the same wicked plans being discussed by other gangs he came across as he hurried through the dark streets of the city.

This news was what Aggelos feared might be brewing. Without saying a word, the tent maker went downstairs to his shop and began sewing canvas. In less than an hour he returned with a roll of heavy white linen, sewn into a long, narrow sack that had one end open. He showed his work to Nearcus and Marcus and said, "I know a way to get you out of Corinth by sunrise tomorrow."

CHAPTER 34

EPILOGUE

Before the dawn, Marcus and Nearcus were dressed and ready to depart but they did not know how they would be able to escape the city when many were seeking to kill Nearcus. Marcus knew that sailing back to Chios directly was not possible this time of year because the winds were against the route. So the best choice was to travel overland, but they could not make such a long and hard trip with Nearcus unable to walk and Marcus nearly out of money to pay for food and lodging. An even greater concern was how to get out of the city. They would be caught trying to leave the city gates. Nearcus's enemies were sure to have men stationed at each gate to catch him should he try to escape.

It was the sterling reputation of Aggelos among his customers that provided the means to get Nearcus and Marcus free of the dangers in Corinth. A merchant caravan was leaving very early that morning heading to Damascus and points east of there. The merchant, a Persian named Bahadur was a long-time customer of Aggelos's and was scheduled to stop by the tent maker's to load new tents he had ordered on his previous trip to Corinth. Bahadur placed so much faith in the honesty and integrity of Aggelos that when the tent maker said he wanted a favor of the merchant, it was granted before it could be asked. When he did hear what Aggelos proposed, Bahadur insisted that he be allowed to provide transportation for Nearcus and Marcus for free.

He said he would consider it an honor to have such a man as Aggelos in his debt.

Marcus and Nearcus said good-bye to Dioxippus. They prayed for each other and then promised to meet again sometime in the future. The slave and the athlete wanted to say farewell to Garifallia and Iro but there was not time before they departed. Dioxippus promised to do this for them.

Aggelos and Bahadur strode into the room with two of the merchant's men right behind. Bahadur carried two sets of long Persian robes. He handed these to the slave and the boy and said, "You must look like you belong with our party."

In a matter of minutes Bahadur's men carried Nearcus downstairs to the sewing shop. The canvas sack that Aggelos had sewn the night before was lying on one of the work tables and they placed Nearcus next to it.

Aggelos approached Marcus and they shook hands in the Greek fashion without saying anything verbally, but with much being passed between them in their eyes. Aggelos had a scroll in his left hand and he gave it to the slave. Marcus nodded as he accepted the gift, for he knew what was written on it.

Next Aggelos went to Nearcus, looked deeply into his eyes and said, "You truly were chosen of God. His hand is upon your life and will be forever. What he accomplished through you yesterday will advance his church as much as any man ever will. I thank the Lord that I was able to live to see the day that he used a boy to prove to all men that Apollo and Poseidon and all the other idols are just superstition and false worship. I thank the Lord that I was permitted to meet you, young Nearcus." Then the husky, brawny man with the terrifying scowl on his face hugged Nearcus. When the tent maker pulled back, Nearcus saw a tear roll down Aggelos's scarred cheek.

Aggelos and Bahadur's men helped the injured pankratiast into the large canvas sack. The tent maker then sewed the end closed, leaving enough holes to ensure Nearcus could breathe easily. Then Marcus checked the street to ensure it was still deserted except for Bahadur's caravan. Seeing it was all clear the slave nodded to Bahadur who had his men load Nearcus on a large donkey located in the middle of the line of packed animals ready to depart. Once he was securely placed in position on the donkey, other rolls of the new tents were packed around Nearcus. There was nothing to show that a boy was hidden among the tents tightly packed on the animal.

It was well that this precaution was taken. There was a band of men checking every person leaving the city that morning. But Bahadur's caravan with young Nearcus concealed within the load of new tents passed without difficulty through the gates. An hour later, the caravan stopped to rest and Nearcus was pulled from the sack and given food and drink. The load from another donkey was transferred to the one carrying the tents and then Nearcus was able to ride that donkey. Marcus held the donkey's bit in his hand and led the victorious Christian boy to freedom and home.

Bahadur had given his pledge to Aggelos that Nearcus and Marcus would reach Chios safely. The trip home took the caravan several weeks and passed through Thessalonica, Philippi, Troas, and Smyrna. In each of these cities and many more, Marcus used the information on the scroll he had received from Aggelos to find the different Christian church leaders on their route to arrange lodging during caravan stopovers. At each stop, Marcus and Nearcus spent time with Christians who were anxious to hear how God used a twelve-year old boy to do battle against and defeat the champion of the heathen gods. The inspiring story of the Lord's faithfulness strengthened and unified many Christians far beyond just the churches in Corinth.

Bahadur kept his promise to Aggelos and after a long journey around the Aegean Sea, the slave and the boy were home and enjoying the summer of cool breezes and bright skies on Chios, both quite certain that there was no other place on earth quite so beautiful.

In the years that followed, Nearcus worked in his father's mastic orchards and sang as he pruned the prickly branches in the spring. He grew into the kind of man everyone on the island wanted to have as a friend and he and Marcus started the first Christian church on the island. Often after a hard day, Nearcus sat under the mastic tree where he had first heard the voice of his Lord. He never heard the voice speak again, but sitting there alone and thinking about all that happened to him when he was twelve-years old gave him a deep peace and satisfaction that served him well the rest of his life.

Nearcus never fought in another pankration contest. There was no need. Having seen Corinth, Nearcus never wanted to leave his island again.

ABOUT THE AUTHOR

Robert Bartron is a retired Navy pilot and education administrator now living in Sacramento, CA with his wife and two miniature Dachshunds. He has authored many books and screenplays and has taught Adult Sunday School for over twenty years. The Bartron's have two grown sons who have served as officers in the Army and Air Force, both having completed tours in Iraq or Afghanistan. Their daughter is married to a Navy pilot who has served in the Iraqi theater and she has blessed Grandma and Grandpa with a beautiful granddaughter.

74144090R00158

Made in the USA
Lexington, KY
14 December 2017